With Strings Attached

For Andi: When you can't find the light, strike a match.

a.a.vacco

Editors: Catherine Sloan, Ashley Weber, Carla Vacco
Preliminary editors: Katherine Walker, Allyssa Hartley, Amanda Michaud, Tracy Walsh

Part 1:

1

New York City, NY, 1888

Frank faced the fire, the glow of the flames illuminating his figure. He elected to leave the electricity alone for the night. He and his wife made sure that their move to New York City was to include an electrically wired house, unlike the one they left back in Kansas. Both he and Myra were from a small town there. They decided to make the move east about a year after they married. Myra worked as a school teacher and could easily uproot. Frank was a medical supplies salesman. The newest inventions were his to promote and New York City offered more clientele than anywhere in Kansas.

The move made sense, Frank reflected.

It wasn't easy, especially their first few years out east, but once the cash flow picked up, and it did, they became the envy of the neighborhood. Their home, the furnishings, the lifestyle all fit a high standard and Frank was pleased with the way it all panned out. *They truly had it all*, Frank smiled as he inhaled the charred smell from the small, orange blaze in front of him.

Another figure became visible as the fire picked up. Frank started, then with a sigh, "Oh, Myra, Dear, it's you! I didn't see you. How long have you been sitting there?"

The slender silhouette of Myra remained still. She sat next to the brick fireplace clutching Lucy, a childhood doll that she often kept nearby. She took pride in making little outfits for the doll, playing with the coils of hair, and using it as a household decoration when she wasn't fussing with it. Frank saw Lucy as Myra's security blanket. But tonight, Myra wasn't gently caressing the doll's hair or mending a hem on the dress. Tonight, Myra was, well, it appeared she was wringing the doll's neck. Slowly, rhythmically, Myra's hands twisted under the porcelain head. Her posture remained motionless, including her arms. Just her wrists moving back and forth, back and forth. Frank felt a twinge of nausea.

"Myra," he ventured, "Is everything alright?"

Without meeting his eyes, Myra's voice answered in a flat tone, "I want to go home."

He sighed.

"We've been over this, Sweetheart, so many times. I've told you that moving home is backtracking. We can't make the same money we do here. We won't have the connections or the liberties the city affords us."

He paused when the wringing quickened. "Think, Myra. You wanted to leave Kansas just as much as I did."

Maintaining a cold, distant tone that Frank never heard before, she replied, "Yes, but that was then. People can change their minds, Francis."

A chill prickled down Frank's spine as Myra's icy tone left an even more frigid silence. Never once had she used his full name. Even at their wedding, he was Frank, or Frankie. To him, she was Myra Jane or simply Myra. 'Francis' existed only on a birth certificate written thirty-five years ago and forgotten ever since. "Myra, please consider this. We move back. We settle close to where we grew up. We live out our days visiting with family while raising our own. It'll be the same cycle. There's no growth prosperity! No change from when we were kids. It'll just be a closed loop unless our kids move away."

"I just want to go home."

"Why? Why now? We never planned to return."

"I just want to go home, Francis."

Frank felt himself flush. "That's not a good reason for backtracking. We got out, and we aren't moving back. We have everything here. We have all we need to start our own family and our own life. We aren't moving back, Myra. I'm sorry. But we made this choice together and this is how we are going to live it out."

"We all have choices," came the monotonous reply.

With a casual reach behind her back, Myra produced Frank's revolver. He jumped. As soon as he moved, she aimed it at him.

"M...Myra, what—what the hell is wrong with you?" he yelled, his voice and hands shaking.

"I said I want to go home. If that can't happen, which you stated that it won't, then I want to restart."

"You really think restarting works by shooting me?"

Myra shook her head. "No, you can stay and live this life. I'll restart. Wherever I end up, I'll make sure to find my way home. But I can't do it here. Goodbye, Frank."

Before Frank could process what was happening, Myra repositioned the gun. With one fluid movement, she pressed the barrel against her right temple and pulled the trigger. In horror, Frank watched her brains splatter against the adjacent wall. The doll, still gripped by her left hand, fell to the ground, soaked in blood.

2

Millerton, IL, 1984

Elle Carter coasted along the gravel road toward the park. The soft rustle of leaves mixed harmoniously with the warmth of the afternoon sun against her face. It was the last day of summer before her freshman year of high school. She knew this year would be a vast improvement from junior high but also that small towns keep the same people around until high school graduation. Therefore, the classroom dynamics would be predictable. At least there was more after school stuff she could join. She often embraced her inner nerd and hoped to find friends that would, too.

Her shift as a lifeguard at the town's man-made beach didn't start for another fifteen minutes. She stopped at the swing set and snacked on some apple slices. The summers were hot and humid, but the job paid well and it was either that or serve milkshakes at the local diner. The Sock Hop did offer air conditioning but the beach gave her a tan and a free swimsuit each year. *Plus*, she considered, *I already know everyone in this town and the one over. I'd rather sit and watch them swim instead of waiting on them for eight hours a day.*

Elle thought about working at the Marionette Mansion. To an outsider, it was a difficult place to explain. It was, like any run-down, ancient building dedicated to displaying historical dolls, notoriously spooky. Elle decided that even if she didn't believe in ghosts, curses, hexes, witches, or any of the things people claimed made the mansion do the things it did, she wanted no part of it. Plus, her fluorescent skin would make people think she was one of the ghosts if she worked there. At the beach, she could count on a tan. And a free swimsuit.

With a final crunch, she finished her last apple slice, hopped back on the baby blue bike and pedaled toward the guard station. Echoes of laughter and splashes of water sounded before she could even see the shore. She set the bike against the brick building that stood at the entrance of the beach and entered the small guard room on the opposite side. The station led straight onto the sand, but only after a four-foot drop down. There were stairs somewhere, but no one liked the walk to find them. The flimsy excuse for a screen door slammed behind her as her eyes adjusted to the room's dim lighting. A series of worn desks lined each wall of the square shaped enclosure. The cream-colored brick walls trapped the warm air, making the humidity almost palpable. Elle guessed that they kept it this way so that the guards wouldn't hang out in there longer than they needed to. The cement floor maintained a layer of sand at all times. Even if they scrubbed the place clean, there would always be that sandy grit atop the cement. Elle added her bag to the cluttered collection of her coworkers' beach supplies and started to fill out her time card. Since there were always two guards stationed on the water's edge, she wondered which spot she'd take this shift. "A four-foot cement wall encloses the sand area," Elle heard her manager's voice explain.

She emerged from the guard room and turned to see Alex orienting a new guard to the layout of the beach. Elle jumped off the short wall and onto the sand to join them. "Let's see," he gestured to the wall, then the sand area, "the sand area's about twenty-five yards to the water's edge. Then there are the two guard stands. Water to the ropes gradually gets deeper, eh, about five feet or so and after the roped area it drops off pretty quick. You can't touch the bottom by the time you reach those rafts out there. They're anchored down, but that was done years back. Since they haven't drifted away, no one's cared enough to see just how far down they go."

Alex noticed Elle approaching and winked, then turned back to the little blonde with more layout information. "The guard station is at the center of it all. See that space next to it? We keep a third guard there to oversee the sand area. They keep backup watch on the swimmers. We take breaks every hour for fifteen minutes, except at three and six o'clock. Those breaks are half hour ones. There's a diving board to the far right of the swimming area, and if swimmers are over there, we send the guard at the station over to make sure no one's getting too rowdy."

He paused and adjusted his sunglasses. "Mister-in-Charge," Elle's mom always called him. The new girl nodded to Alex's last remark. Elle knew everyone in the town, but this girl's face was unfamiliar.

"Just move here?" Elle asked.

"Yeah, from Phoenix," replied the blonde.

Elle attempted to hide her shock at the low rasp of the girl's voice. She stood just over five feet, Elle estimated, with a petite build. Her light hair and blue eyes completed the Barbie doll appearance, but the voice didn't quite match.

Barbie doll laughed. "It's ok, I get that a lot," she said.

"Apparently, I'm not too subtle," muttered Elle, feeling her cheeks redden.

"I'm Kat. My family just moved here. I'll be starting high school out here this fall."

"You mean tomorrow? I'm Elle, by the way."

Kat smirked, "Yea, smart ass, tomorrow. So, I guess I'll see ya there?"

Elle nodded. She meant to say more, but Alex cut her off.

"Ok, ok, get to work. The noon break is almost up." Alex placed both hands around his mouth and yelled, "Break's over! Swimmers can re-enter the water!" He turned to the girls. "Ellbea, take guard tower one. Kat, you're at guard tower two."

Elle's full name, Eleanor Beatrice Carter, was unacceptable to her. There were few things in the world she truly loathed, and her name was one of them. The silver lining was the array of nicknames; Elle, which most people assumed was her first name based on Elle not telling them otherwise. Ellbea (*El-bee*) to those closest to her, which Elle felt honored the first and middle name without fully disclosing either one.

Kat and Elle headed toward the two guard stands on opposite sides of the shoreline. Alex resumed his cross-armed stance by the guard station. He watched Elle throw her dark hair into a messy knot, add aviators to her ensemble and settle in. Alex knew Elle for quite some time. They lived a few houses from each other. Alex was a few years older than Elle, but they rode the same bus and their parents were friends, so their paths often crossed. When Elle turned twelve, he recruited her to help out as a junior guard at the beach. He had her teach swim lessons and perform odd jobs on the grounds. Once she turned fourteen, he trusted her enough to work as a lifeguard and that's how she spent this summer. He always felt protective of her, even though he knew she'd insist she could take care of herself. They were old friends with a fun dynamic and nothing more. Since their parents were close friends, the pair grew up as close to siblings as they could be without living under the same roof.

Elle felt protective over Alex too, but for different reasons. In 1984 rural Illinois, being anything other than a white, conservative Christian drove prejudices in all sorts of directions. Alex was a Christian, and Elle assumed more conservative than not, but his skin missed the white criteria by a mile. His family moved north from Georgia when he was five. Elle wished for all of their sakes that they kept going a little further. Alex was probably the first and only black guard at the beach, and Elle felt certain that the club owners would find any reason to fire him if he gave them the chance. Fortunately, he didn't. He was a great student, hard worker, and all around good kid. But many in the town overlooked these qualities, mostly people over the age of forty, since the younger generation didn't seem to care. It was the parents who often whispered comments and shot side glances to each other whenever Alex came by. Elle was thankful she was finally old enough to be in the same school as him, in case he needed backup. Elle of course noticed their physical differences, but that was never criteria for her to like someone. Being different from someone was just a fact of life. It never impacted their friendship.

3

The first few weeks of school blurred for Elle. She joined the cross country team with three other kids. As pitiful as the team's size appeared, it had doubled since last fall. The coach was thrilled. Kat started on the volleyball team and made friends with kids in her classes. Everyone else already had their cliques and dirt on one another, but she seemed to find her niche nonetheless. Kat lived about a quarter mile from Elle. The two rode their bikes to class as long as they could, planning to catch the bus once the winter winds of Illinois showed no mercy. The two quickly became close friends.

During one of the final tame days of autumn, the pair rode their bikes home from practice. "Hey, I was thinking," started Kat.

"Never a good sign, but go on," said Elle.

"Screw off. I was thinking, we need winter jobs. We can't lifeguard for like, four more months."

"Yeah, I used to just work in the summers, but now that we're in high school, college funding might be a smart move." Elle reached to adjust her backpack, and continued to steer the bike one-handed.

Kat nodded. "Does the club hire for odd job stuff in the winter? Like, can we lifeguard in the summer and keep the woods and grounds picked up in the winter?

With a laugh, Elle asked, "Do you know much about Illinois winters?" Assuming she didn't, Elle continued, "Look, Phoenix, in about three weeks it'll become ungodly cold and windy. Everything dies off, the ground becomes solid from being so cold, and just when you think it can't get worse, it snows."

"Oh, I'd love to see snow!"

"You'll like it for the first day or so, then it sticks around, freezes, and turns the town a yucky, mucky mess. You'll hate it like the rest of us."

Kat glanced sideways at Elle. "Geez, bitch much? What else do you hate? Kittens? Glitter? The laughter of small children?"

Elle rolled her eyes and downshifted as they coasted toward their neighborhood. "No, no, it's just a harsh, dreary time of year. You'll see. Don't want to get your hopes up and then have the cold reality of winter slap the sunshine off of your face."

"So you figured you'd do it for me? You sweetie!" Kat clapped both hands as she balanced herself and continued to pedal forward.

"Show off," said Elle, as she attempted the same maneuver. That lasted about two seconds before she almost spun out on some loose gravel.

"You'll learn," giggled Kat, as she whizzed past Elle, who had slowed down considerably given the circumstance.

When Elle caught back up to Kat, the two rode without saying much for a few blocks. Then, Kat suggested they stop at The Sock Hop for a milkshake and study time. The restaurant sat on the opposite side of the road from the entrance to their subdivision. If they turned toward the houses, they'd hit Kat's first and then deeper into the neighborhood, Elle's. But milkshakes would sound good for a limited time, so the two veered left and into the gravel parking lot.

The familiar fried food smell greeted them as they pushed through the front door. Kat headed for the counter to order the shakes (chocolate for both, but only hers with whipped cream) and Elle secured the right corner booth near the back of the place. The 1950's style setting included a black and white tile floor, olive-green booths lining the dining area walls, and an ordering counter set up like a bar. The servers wore either poodle skirts or jeans rolled at the ankles. They served while wearing roller skates, a skill Kat and Elle envied, but knew they could never replicate. This limited their job options even further. The menu was simple: hotdogs, burgers, fries, shakes, and pickles. An era-appropriate jukebox stood in the corner opposite of Elle, but it remained silent for the time being. Jack, a senior at their school, greeted them and took Kat's order. Elle spread out her math homework and started solving for '*x*' in one of twenty problems.

"Here," said Kat as she set the foamless shake in front of Elle, along with her change.

"Thanks Kit-Kat," and Elle started slurping down the chocolate frost.

"How's the math? God, I suck at math," Kat said as she slid into the opposite side of the booth.

Elle smiled and shook her head, "Twenty problems and we're still finding '*x*'? You'd think they'd pick other letters to use just to switch things up." Elle later regretted that statement at the start of second quarter when she discovered algebra used all sorts of letters.

"Yeah, yeah, but is it hard?"

To Elle it wasn't. Kat, well, it might as well have been in Mandarin, and she gave up after the fifth problem. Swirling the remainder of her milkshake, Kat said, "So... winter jobs?"

"Yeah?"

"Well if the club isn't offering anything for us, where else can we go?"

"Uh, here? I think the McDonald's just before the highway entrance picks up around winter season, then, not much until you hit the uptown area," said Elle between the final swigs of her shake.

Uptown, or Riverbend, its official name, was actually two towns north of them. It had the grocery store, pharmacy, a few department stores, and some other odds and ends Millerton lacked. It took about fifteen minutes to get there on the highway. Everything else was a five-minute drive around the town, but including the McDonalds, The Sock Hop, Jim's Bait and Tackle shop, and a Walgreens, there wasn't much on their side of the train tracks. The Walgreens served as the local 'last-minute item' grocery store, but beyond bread, milk, and junk food, Uptown was the place to go.

"Wait, what about that old blue and white building a little past the freeway ramp? It's a little hidden, maybe you've seen it...think we'd find work there?"

Elle pulled out the straw and sucked on the end of it. "You mean the Doll House?"

"Is that what it's called?" asked Kat. "I haven't heard of it."

"Well, the real name is Marionette Mansion, but everyone around here calls it the Doll House. It's basically a cursed museum full of old dolls on display."

Kat scoffed. "Yeah, ok, aren't all mansions with dolls supposed to be haunted?"

Elle shook her head, "No, um, it's hard to explain. You pretty much have to go there to get it."

"Try me."

"It's known to be haunted or cursed. Like, you go there and stuff moves. A lot. It's expected. The dolls' heads turn when you walk by, mirrors will shift, doors will creak. All the stuff you camp out all night to see maybe a glimpse of at a supposedly haunted house? It happens there all the time."

Kat stared at her with her mouth open.

Elle pressed on. "People around here don't go there much. Not because it scares them, but because they're so used to it always being creepy that it doesn't have an effect anymore. Only tourists really drop by, or of course, antique enthusiasts. They just keep it open afternoons and evenings anymore."

"Who's 'they'?" Kat completely forgot about her milkshake and her math at this point. The chocolate smear on her left cheek went unnoticed and her crystal blue eyes focused solely on Elle.

"Um, Mr. and Mrs. Valor. It's on their property. Their actual house is past the freeway as well, but a fair distance from the Marionette Mansion. They inherited and own a lot of farmland. I think the thing was built like, ninety-some years ago. The original owner of the museum collected dolls from all over the country and after several generations, the Valor family decided to make it a historical spot instead of tearing it down. My guess is no one wanted to live there anyways."

"Probably a safe guess," murmured Kat. "So, um, can we go see it?"

Elle shrugged. The Doll House was the go-to spot in middle school to try to scare friends, especially around Halloween time. The older kids usually convinced younger kids trying to be cool to come see the house with the moving dolls. By the time everyone passed eighth grade, it lost the thrill factor, even the fun of scaring the younger ones. *But Kat just moved here, so her reaction might be one for the books*, thought Elle.

"Yeah, sure," said Elle, closing her math book. She tipped her glass back and finished off the shake.

Kat's eyes widened. "I didn't mean *now*! It's already dark!"

A familiar glimmer of delight lit Elle's eyes. "So...you're saying you're afraid."

Kat glared at her and her antagonistic glimmer. "No, stop it, Elle! I know you'll try to scare me. Hell, I bet the place isn't even that creepy! You're probably just trying to pull some big ole prank."

Although that thought hadn't yet reached Elle's mind, it took flight as soon as Kat mentioned it. "Ah, yeah you're right. It's all bullcrap. But the mansion is pretty weird. C'mon. It's well-lit. We can ride our bikes over there and then have Alex pick us up after ten minutes or so."

Kat sighed. She turned toward the counter and asked Jack if she could call Alex, hoping he wouldn't be able to pick them up in the next twenty minutes. Unfortunately, not only could Alex pick them up, he told Kat, but he could swing by now and bring them there himself, save them the trip. He wanted some fast food, anyways.

"Dammit," muttered Kat under her breath.

"What's up?" Elle finished putting her stuff into her backpack. If they took the bus tomorrow, they could just walk to The Sock Hop after practice and pick up their bikes then. She considered this, having overhead Kat's conversation with Alex.

"Oh, nothing. Alex is about two minutes away."

Kat turned toward the gravel parking lot. A single street light gave a dim glow to the surrounding area, but beyond that, darkness enveloped the lot with outlines of trees and shrubs. The cold season robbed most of the woods' leaves, but the density of the trees remained an 'eek' factor in Kat's mind. "Why wouldn't the damn place be haunted," she vented to herself.

4

Alex arrived and drove them toward the freeway. Within minutes, the trio pulled up the dirt driveway that led to the mansion. Kat immediately realized Elle hadn't been entirely truthful about the place being 'well lit.'

"Ellbea," she moaned, "It's so dark! I can't see my hand in front of my face."

"Sure ya can! So long as the car stays running with the headlights on," said Elle.

Kat scanned the part of the driveway she could see courtesy of the headlights. It consisted of loose, brown dirt. Several tire tracks had left their mark, but certainly not enough to suggest much traffic. She glanced up the drive toward the mansion. The place reminded her of a house on a plantation. A white porch wrapped around the front of the house. Four Corinthian pillars guarded the entrance, two on each side of the centrally-placed front door. The wooden porch needed a new coat of paint, weathered from years of Illinois winters and humid summers. The house itself appeared to be made of wood as well. Some bricks fortified the corners of the home, but they, like the porch and rest of the house, were also painted white. A light blue trim lined the edges of the porch steps, the shutters of the windows, and the awning of the roof. "So, the blue and white mansion it is, indeed," whispered Kat.

Alex stopped the car near the edge of the drive. Kat forgot about pretending to be brave. "Wait, why are you stopping here? Alex? Get us closer, what if we need to run away? *Don't you watch any horror movies?*"

With a grin, Alex replied, "Well if I did base my actions off horror movies, I wouldn't even be here. They always kill the black guy and the frantic white chick first."

"Ok, not even funny!" she cried.

Rubbing her temples, Elle responded with her usual dry tone. "Hey, if it's too much, we can turn back. But the further we pull up the drive, the more backward driving we'll have to do. There's no turn around. It's all one-way or reverse."

"What? What genius decided that was a good idea?" Kat's voice startled both Alex and Elle with its tenacity.

"Geez, take it easy." Elle knew Kat's temper would soon trump her fear, so if she could get Kat pissed enough, Kat would storm into the mansion, no questions asked.

"So some dude in the early 1900's who couldn't design a road went and built a mansion and stuffed it full of cursed dolls. Cut him some slack, he probably passed basic math with flying colors."

That did it. The car door from the back passenger side opened and slammed shut. Kat marched toward the house, up the rickety wooden porch steps, and stopped at the door. "Ok, jackasses, the door's locked. You guys even said yourselves, the place is usually locked. How are we supposed to get in?"

Elle and Alex were at the steps by this point, trying to maintain their composure. Alex was all too familiar with Elle's antics, but never grew tired of them. Both sported smirks and used their hands to hide the lower halves of their faces. Alex turned to Elle. "She doesn't know?"

Elle shook her head. "No, she does not."

Looking perplexed, Kat took the bait. "Know *what*?"

The two locals exchanged glances and Alex said, "Well, it's haunted, cursed, whatever. So, you know, if you're meant to go in, the door will just, like, open."

Grumbling under her breath that this was the dumbest thing she'd ever heard, Kat reached for the handle and gave it a solid shake. Locked. She attempted a shoulder shove to see if the door was ajar. Nothing. With pure annoyance, she turned to the snickering fools behind her and said, "Ok, we just wasted twenty minutes. It's almost nine, and like it or not, we have school tomorrow, so I'd appreciate you quit...,"

A solitary knock on the other side of the wooden door silenced Kat's rant. The other two crossed their arms and waited. Wide-eyed, Kat stared at the door. A single '*click*' broke the silence, followed by a creak as the door swung slowly open. Kat expected Elle and Alex to be just as frightened as she was, but the two just shrugged and said, "Ok, let's go!"

They pushed past her and into the main foyer. Kat, still wrapping her mind around it all, stumbled in after them.

As she glanced around the dark space, she felt a little more at ease. The foyer was redone to accommodate visitors. It was painted bright blue, and a modern counter stood at the front, presumably where greeters sat to give out brochures, take payments, or deliver random mansion trivia. An iron Celtic cross-shaped paperweight resting on the counter caught Kat's eye. The owners maintained the finished wood flooring in that space too. From what Kat could determine, the museum part of the house began after the right and left of the welcome desk. The owners kept the original structure beyond the modern haven.

While Kat eyed her unsettling surroundings, Alex clicked on a flashlight behind her. Kat jumped and then laughed. "Right, because why would there be electricity in here?"

"Well, there is," said Elle, "But it only works when it wants to, so we take on the whole 'be prepared' thing, given what time it is."

Alex headed to the left. He shined the light around the front room that looked like the formal gathering place.

"It's the parlor," Alex told Kat.

"Yea, yea thanks, I got that from the upholstered chairs, hideous dark blue carpet, even uglier pastel pink curtains. Not to mention the floral wallpaper, I mean, what else could it be?" Kat responded, flinging her arms at each piece she critiqued.

"Just making sure you can keep up," smiled Alex.

Elle trailed behind, taking in everything for what felt like the hundredth time. Since she was so set on freaking Kat out, she took added precautions to hide her own nerves. The house didn't really scare her, nothing inside would do anything she hadn't seen before. But she didn't like Millerton at night. The rustling trees, skittering wildlife, and moans of the wind sent her imagination running wild.

Behind them, the front door closed in a fluid motion. Not a slam; no gust of wind. Just a simple *cluh-clunk*, and *click*.

Kat whirled around. "Hey, hey, hey-we're locked in. Are we locked in? Can we get out?"

To her astonishment, both Alex and Elle just laughed. "Rel-*ax*," said Elle. "It's fine. This always happens."

"The Big Guy just wants to ensure the house is safe, that's all," Alex said. His careless tone increased Kat's concern.

"Who the *hell* is 'The Big Guy'?" she yelled.

"Calm down, whoa whoa, easy!" responded Alex, "Everyone knows the dolls are sacred to whatever holds down the fort here. No one leaves with any piece of this house. I guess it wasn't always the case, but too much weird shit happened in the past and well, now that's the rule."

Kat raised her eyebrows. "Alex, you're not making any sense."

"No, no, he is," Elle jumped in, "He's just not telling it right."

They proceeded into an informal-looking room while Elle explained, "Since no one really has a solid explanation for why things happen, we've collected several ideas over the years, and the ones that made the most sense continue to be told."

"Just like the Bible," said Alex.

Kat rolled her eyes, "Seriously?"

"The dolls, for instance," persisted Alex, "which you will see in the next room, are without a doubt, cursed to some degree. They all move, their eyes follow you; it's what they do."

"I know it sounds crazy," continued Elle, "But, we've all seen how this house and these dolls act. And there is definitely something or someone controlling the house. Whatever opened the door is also responsible for taking care of the house."

"Or protecting it," said Alex.

"Right. And locals call that force, 'The Big Guy'. So, whatever happens that isn't related to the dolls themselves? That's him," concluded Elle.

Kat drew in a breath. "You both realize how insane this sounds, don't you?"

Alex passed the couch and rocking chair at the back of the informal room, pushing open two saloon-style doors that led into a narrow hallway. "Why don't you finish the tour, and you tell us?"

Kat found herself holding her breath as she passed through the swinging doors and into the hallway. When she did, darkness flooded her surroundings as Alex flicked off the flashlight, commenting, "No sense losing power completely and having to fumble our way out. We'd be stuck here all night!"

The trio reached the end of the hall and Kat noticed it opened into three different rooms. The doors had been removed from the rooms to allow visitors the ease of stepping in and out. Some rooms even connected through former closets that were long since knocked out. The three rooms accessible from the end of the hall each connected to at least one other room further back. The layout enabled visitors to loop around the displays, exiting the way that they entered. As a result, the house seemed like a series of infinity signs.

A sudden clattering sent Elle and Kat jumping back. Elle giggled and shook her head. "Ok, I lied, some things you'll never get used to."

Kat was less at ease. "Wh-what was that?" she whispered.

Alex clicked the light back on and illuminated the far right of the room. A pile of string and wooden limbs lay cluttered beneath a shelf that it presumably toppled from. A small wooden face peered at them amidst the tangled mess. Kat held her breath as she studied the figure. Then, to her horror, one of the eyes on the painted face winked. *Winked*? But, *oh no*, slowly, as if pulled by an invisible set of hands, the wooden figure slowly rose, until each limb stood as close to anatomically-correct as possible. The strings hung vertically and taut, but how, Kat had no clue. Her heartbeat drummed into her ears. She felt like she would pass out. When Elle grabbed her by the back of the arm, she screamed. Unaffected by Kat's piercing yell, the doll continued to straighten itself, levitating until the feet were no longer touching the floor. Whatever was controlling the doll lifted it back to its original place on the shelf, and dropped it in a seated position with a 'click-clack-clack' sound as the toy resettled.

As horrified as Kat was, she was even more appalled at Alex and Elle's lack of amazement. The two shrugged nonchalantly and kept walking. They continued through that room, and followed it into a sunroom. However, in addition to a large picture window on the exterior wall, whoever designed it lined the remaining walls with mirrors. "Oh, c'mon! This isn't even fair," yelled Kat.

"Mirrors, shadows, haunted dolls, it all adds up!" responded Elle, as she turned to face Kat. Her patented smirk appeared as she saw Alex slinking up behind Kat with the flashlight under his chin, causing his face to glow. The middle school scare tactic had been successfully deployed, and the two later mused how Kat remained friends with them after that night.

The mirrored sunroom contained many dolls. Shelves and hutches lined every available space and dolls representing all eras took up residence along them. *The sight itself is unsettling*, Kat thought. *Hundreds of porcelain, wood, or plastic faces with dark eyes following your every move?*

Plus, the mirrors added to the eeriness of it all. She might have been able to get past the floating marionette and the accommodating front door, but this room caused Kat to fold.

When Elle told Kat that the dolls and house repeatedly did the same thing, losing its scare value with time, she didn't clue Kat into the specifics.

As Kat stepped further into the sunroom, all three hundred and some doll heads turned toward her, acknowledging her presence. Their eyes were wide, and the ones capable of blinking exercised this ability. As Kat turned around to bolt, Alex startled her further with his face-illuminating prank. Kat shoved him aside and sprinted through the mirrored space. The dolls continued to watch her, heads turned from her, and some back to Elle and Alex, then back to Kat. It was too much. Whatever sense of security the other two local idiots possessed, Kat lacked, and quite frankly, didn't crave. She continued her sprint, knocking several dolls over in her wake of panic. She passed the initial marionette, and spotted him just long enough to see that he transitioned from sitting to lying on his side. She stumbled down the dark hallway and toward the saloon style doors. She felt Elle try and grab her shoulder to slow her down, but she shook her hand away and continued running. When she finally reached the front door in the main foyer, she feared it wouldn't let her out. *The Big Guy? Whatever, first thing's first*, she thought.

Kat tried the lock. It clicked open and with an unnecessary shove, Kat tumbled out of the house and onto the porch. She sat a moment, catching her breath. Elle and Alex strolled out, holding their sides, laughing. Kat didn't care. She made it out and vowed never to return.

That vow was short-lived. Later that evening, safe in Elle's decidedly *un*-haunted house, Elle badgered and eventually convinced Kat to return to the Doll House during the day to show her it wasn't as terrifying as her initial encounter. Kat wondered how any sane person could find comfort in the building, regardless of lighting. Still, she reluctantly agreed.

"You'll see," coaxed Elle. "The night time always makes things spookier. Especially in bumpkin-nowhere, Illinois."

Kat started to protest, but then remembered that everyone else in the town found nothing fearful about the mansion. Half-determined to understand this collective mindset, Kat answered with, "I'll give it another shot, but if it's just as awful, never again. I don't want to hear a word about it, any suggestions toward a third visit, nothing!"

"Fine, fine, all that and a bag of chips."

"Good. When do you want to revisit this nonsense?"

Elle grinned. "Well it isn't like we are doing much this weekend. Mandatory Sunday service, and then nothing but grey skies and the crisp autumn air to contend with. Why don't we go then?"

"Consider it a date," said Kat, and before Elle could say anything further, she added, "And Alex isn't invited. You two probably teamed up on me and made it even worse. You're flying solo this go-round. Aside from being with me."

"The dynamic duo it is," Elle concurred with a nod.

The two shook on it. They'd been sitting on Elle's living room floor in sweatpants and hoodies, debating whether a jump start on their English assignments would be worth the time save. Since neither felt overly motivated to dive into Austen's world of wit, they wound up sprawled over the couch with a box of Oreos between the two of them. They didn't move until Kat's mom dropped by to walk her daughter home.

"Until tomorrow, Charlotte Mack."

Kat rolled her eyes. She also despised her full name, and regretted ever telling Elle there was more to it than just "Kat." The name Charlotte Marquette was far too formal and outdated for her liking. Kat felt a shortened version summed her up much better.

"Later, Eleanor."

Unable to suppress a smile, Elle responded with, "Get out."

They hugged and parted ways for the night.

5

New York City, NY: 1888

Frank stood motionless, staring at the macabre scene of his wife's insides strewn before him. Numbness entombed him as he slowly moved to call the police. His initial reaction was to lunge forward and stop the bleeding. The more he stared, though, the more he realized the bleeding was actually the entire left side of his wife's face, marred and disfigured. There wasn't a place to stop the bleeding unless he were to smother her entire head. *But maybe*? *No,* the logical side of his brain kicked in briefly enough to tell him there wasn't more he could do. Instead, with the police on the way, he gathered the doll and started to clean it. "Lucy," he whispered.

This was the name Myra gave the life-like porcelain figure. With great care, he took a damp cloth from their kitchen and started to wipe the blood from the pale face. The dark eyes seemed clean, but he wiped them anyways, as if to erase the vision of their recently witnessed horror. He filled a basin with water and carried it back into the living room. He removed the hand-sewn dress and stockings from the doll and placed them into the cold water. Myra always said blood stains came out with cold water and a day's worth of patience. He hoped she was right, because there was a lot of it. A ruby swirl tainted the water's clarity, and as he squeezed the fabric, more crimson flourishes painted the basin. Frank was so mesmerized by the sight that he jumped when the police banged on the door. His trance-like state continued, as a swarm of officers, then medics, and finally, a health inspector came in and out. In the end, no one found anything more than a distraught, irrational woman unable to cope with her circumstances, and they all left Frank with their sincerest condolences. He was told he could stop by the morgue in the morning if he wished to view her remains. He did not. He just sat for a moment in the silence from the cold shoulder of the remaining night.

Returning to the basin, Frank decided to replace the cherry-colored liquid with fresh water. He found it hard to believe that cold water by itself would remove the stains, but even without his wife there to argue the point, he didn't feel like altering his course of action. The naked doll sat with a vacant stare in Frank's direction. It wasn't a comfortable feeling, causing an icy churn in his gut, but at least the doll survived. It was, in fact, dropped face down once Myra passed.

Returning with the basin once again, Frank began the process of scrubbing the blood splatter off the surrounding walls and surfaces. This time he added bleach to the water. He scrubbed until the sun blazed through the picture window in the east corner of the room. He realized he had been working since eleven o'clock the night prior, once all of the commotion settled. He also realized that he had scrubbed over areas that were already clean, but he kept seeing the splatter, seeing the brains of his wife falling in bloody clumps from her gaping skull, seeing red--

Clah-clunk-CLASH!

The noise interrupted Frank's thoughts. He spun around to survey the room. Nothing looked out of place. Silence resumed, apart from his heart thundering in his chest. He saw no source of the cacophonous clatter. Just as he started to calm himself, with the reassurance of "just the house settling" or "probably a cat digging around some trash outside," he heard a faint *clink*, so soft he almost missed it. If it were any other time, he would've ignored it completely, but at that moment, a cold bead of sweat trickled down his shoulder blade. The hair on the back of his neck prickled like spines on a cactus. Wide eyed, he stood up and turned to face Lucy.

The doll, previously seated against the wooden chair that Myra occupied moments before ending her life, looked to have toppled over and rolled almost a foot from where Frank left her. No obvious chips or cracks were visible on her delicate face or body, which Frank anticipated to find. The *clink*, to Frank's dismay, replicated when he witnessed the doll blink.

"Oh no, no I did *not* sign up for this," muttered Frank. His lack of panic surprised him, but he attributed it to the shock of his evening. He sat the doll upright again and waited. Sure enough, within moments, the naked porcelain figure tipped to its side, rolled over twice, and blinked its black eyes in Frank's direction. This time, Frank panicked.

He sprinted into the kitchen and slammed the door behind him. He started to phone the police, but then realized how ridiculous the whole thing sounded. What would the police be able to do about a self-moving doll? They would assume he'd gone mad. Delusions brought on by stress, no doubt. He had been awake for over twenty-four hours; how could he explain that and the story of what he just saw? And how could he explain the feeling that Myra was in the house?

"No," whispered Frank, "It's not her." He remembered a story an old neighbor had once told him, a tale Frank had previously laughed off as a ghost story meant to scare children. "It's some demon taking over the doll," he muttered "A curse; she took her life and it wasn't hers to take. Maybe whatever was meant to take it later in her life showed up to reclaim her. She wasn't available, so it took the next closest thing." In his sleep-deprived state, this was the best rationale he could muster. He was not convinced of it entirely but it sounded good enough to wrap his mind around for the time being.

He lost track of how long he stayed in the kitchen before he fell asleep. The doll, the suicide, the blood all swirled in his mind, creating a hypnotic effect. In his spinning state, he laid on the floor to peer under the kitchen door. This way, he could keep an eye on the doll, but would have a barrier should the thing somehow become mobile and come for him. Within moments, his weighted eyelids closed and he fell into a deep sleep.

Frank found himself in what looked like one of his family's wheat fields back in Kansas. He stood far enough away to where he could only see grains of wheat bowing in the wind. The late afternoon sun created an orange and gold glow as Frank surveyed the horizon. He spotted the wooden table owned by Myra's family. He recognized it immediately because growing up, Myra's father often told the story of how his father's father built it as a teenager, and it still held up, even to this day. Frank approached the family table and sat in a chair provided with it. As he did this, another chair appeared across from him, and in it sat Lucy. The doll's size increased to where she was almost...*life-sized*, realized Frank.

She sat with her hands clasped, but her face remained expressionless. The two stared at one another for what felt to Frank like hours. Finally, Lucy in a soft but clear tone, said, "I just wanted to go home."

The familiar phrase pierced through him like a bolt of electricity. Frank woke up drenched in sweat. "I just want to go home", echoed in his mind. He peeled off his shirt and tossed it in a ball onto the floor. The late afternoon sun fell through the slats of the kitchen window, and it took Frank a moment to recall why he was on his kitchen floor. He wondered what else Lucy would have said if he hadn't awoken so suddenly. Then, all of the memories from the past day and a half flooded his thoughts. He slowly sat up and started to sob.

Afterwards, Frank pulled himself up onto shaky legs using the table for support. He rubbed his eyes, and cautiously opened the kitchen door. To his relief, the doll sat in its original place where he had set it when he first started to scour the walls and furnishings. Still, naked, and lifeless, the doll did not even blink. Frank stared at it for several minutes, and finally chalked up the prior instance as a result of combined shock and sleep deprivation. He picked up the doll and examined it from head to toe. With clarity, he recalled of how Myra acquired the doll.

It was May of 1885, and they had been married for about a year. Together, they decided to make the move to New York City. It was a big change for both of them, but Frank knew it would be harder for Myra since she had a close bond with her two sisters. Myra's family was a tight-knit group. Whenever she spent time with them, she always seemed to be at her best. She laughed more, lit the room with smiles, and never ran out of things to talk about. But she had told him it would be good for both of them to branch out. She needed more than just her hometown to hang her hat on, and he couldn't agree more. Did he pressure her? He didn't think that he had. At the time, it felt like a mutual decision.

They packed as many of their belongings as they could fit into a few suitcases. The day they planned to take the train east, Myra's younger sister Rosalyn, or "Rosie," gave her the doll. It was a toy they shared as children, and one that they both admired. They fought over it growing up, and when they reached the age where they liked each other more than their toys, they took turns dressing the doll and trading off who got to keep it in her room. The doll was more than a toy to the girls. It was a bridge they built between them. It kept them connected and giving the doll to Myra was Rosie's way of extending the bridge over the distance the two would soon face.

Frank remembered watching Myra caress the doll's hair on the train ride to New York. Tears fell from her eyes and splashed onto Lucy's face. It took Myra almost a full year to even change Lucy's clothes because the ones originally worn were sewn by Rosie. The doll was more than a piece of decoration, or a sentimental childhood toy. It was the connection between Myra and her family, and Myra's only piece of home in New York.

6

Millerton, IL: 1984

Sunday arrived sooner than Kat hoped. She sat through a Sunday service that dragged on for two hours. Kat initially sat by Elle, but soon realized why none of her other friends did. Elle had this uncanny knack of making everyone else within earshot laugh while she maintained a straight face. Her family probably caught on, figured Kat, but found it worthwhile to ignore her rather than bring it to light. Elle also had a way of amplifying her antics once she knew it either bothered people or gained her an audience. Kat settled for a seat behind Elle. That way Elle couldn't lean forward and whisper anything, attach anything to Kat's back (oh yes, this was done more than once), or subtly move her hair, just enough to cause Kat to whip her head around.

The two met in the back foyer after the service and outlined their afternoon. As the congregation exited the chapel, Elle snagged Mrs. Valor's sleeve to ask something about the mansion. Kat assumed this, but missed the conversation when Alex pulled her aside to inquire about a movie later that night. The two shared the enjoyment of action flicks. *Indiana Jones and the Temple of Doom* just released on VHS, and Alex was the proud owner of a brand new copy.

"Yea, yea, I'd love to come by later!" exclaimed Kat.

She felt like she had waited forever for the stupid film to come out on video. Of course, she could have shelled out a few bucks to see it in the theater, but the drive to Uptown just seemed like an added inconvenience. Fortunately, Alex shared these sentiments.

"Come over around six. We are going to eat a late lunch, sort of a family Sunday thing. But that usually ends around four. We can order a pizza and allow Harrison Ford to mesmerize us."

"You had me at pizza. Make sure it's pepperoni. I'll be there."

"Sure, sure. Hey uh," Alex shifted his weight, "let's keep it just us, ok? Elle isn't that big on action flicks anyways."

Kat started to protest, but then realized their potential situation, so she nodded in agreement. It was rare for the two of them to be alone, and Kat was curious to see how that would pan out. Besides, Elle wasn't big on action flicks. Alex smiled, and moved to join his family who was on their way out. Kat found Elle, and the two girls made their way to their bikes where they had left them outside the church. They hopped on and headed to the Valor house.

As they passed the Marionette Mansion, Kat noticed that with some sunlight and a little more insight to the place, the structure was almost appealing. Instead of following the gravel one-way drive toward the worn front porch, Elle veered right and the pair followed a well-paved, winding road toward the Valor residence. The Valor home, in contrast, was updated and allegedly free of any paranormal antics. Elle pounded on the dark oak door and Mrs. Valor answered with a smile.

"Elle, Darling, good to see you. And Kathy is it?"

"It's Kat," Kat answered, put off by the error.

Mrs. Valor continued to smile, "Sorry, Kat. Of course. Come in, you two. What can I help you with? Here, give me your jackets and kick off your shoes over there."

She pointed to a vacant area in the left corner of the entryway. The girls slid their shoes off and made their way into the main foyer. The Valor home stood as one of the largest homes in the area. The downstairs started as a small entryway, where the girls came in, and opened up into a foyer that served as the convergence point for three hallways. There was a short hall to the right that led to the living room and adjacent formal parlor. A longer hallway in the middle connected to a kitchen and additional dining room. There was also a staircase that stood between the middle hallway and the one on the left. The stairs were made of finished wood and at the top of them, a solid white door guarded a loft and spare bedroom. The short hallway on the left led to the master and two smaller bedrooms.

Mrs. Valor led them through the foyer and turned right toward the living room. A sweet scent of cinnamon and flowers came from a jar of potpourri on a nearby end table. Elle heard classical music playing from one of the adjacent hallways, fading as they walked down the short hall. They stopped in the living room, and Kat and Elle took a seat on the dark leather sofa. Mrs. Valor sat across from them on a peach colored recliner.

"We are wondering if you need any help taking care of the mansion this winter," began Elle.

Mrs. Valor considered this. "We usually hire help to maintain the grounds and clean the interior. Great that you girls came by when you did, since the help we usually have won't be returning this season.

We need someone to take care of the usual pick up; vacuuming, dusting, all that fun stuff. You two wouldn't be responsible for any hefty repairs or yard maintenance, but some raking, weeding, and of course, taking out the garbage would help."

Kat nodded. She appeared amenable to the offer. Elle wasn't huge on the outdoor care part, especially in the winter months. She then considered how everything would be decayed and she too nodded affirmatively.

"Pay would be sufficient for your efforts. The mansion is open to the public and since people run out of things to do indoors, winter is one of our busier times. You two also have the option to man the front desk. You'll take tickets, give directions, tell stories, keep visitors entertained. This would be weekends. The cleanup can be after hours, either during the week or once we close up for the night on weekends."

Kat and Elle glanced at each other and shrugged. It would keep them busy. They both had a break from sports. Plus, they'd be making money, which was the selling point to both of them.

"Now Kit," Mrs. Valor continued.

"Kat."

"Yes, yes, Kat. You are aware of the, err, unexplained occurrences that take place in the mansion, right?"

Kat shot Elle a glare. "Yes, Ma'am, Elle introduced me to its phenomena just recently."

"Good, good. Nothing dangerous ever takes place, so we have no reason to fear for the safety of our employees. With that said, you both will need to sign some paperwork and fill out a few forms. Just typical hire-on stuff to make it official. Let's see here," Mrs. Valor paused and bit the bottom of her lip, "pay is going to be $7.00 an hour. You'll have time cards to fill out when you come and go. We used to keep those in our main foyer here to monitor people closer, but that proved to be more of a nuisance than anything. So, you'll find the time cards in the top right drawer of the counter at the main entrance."

"Thank you for the offer, Mrs. Valor. We'll discuss it with our parents tonight. When can we give you an answer by?" asked the ever-so-calculated Elle, even though she knew they'd both end up taking the job.

Kat rolled her eyes and sighed. "Well, I can say I'd be thrilled to work for you, Mrs. Valor. I can start as soon as next weekend. Do we need a key or anything to get into the house?"

Mrs. Valor nodded, "Yes of course. Here."

She reached into her back pocket and pulled out a key ring. Removing a silver key with a red marker on the end of it, she said, "This will get you into the main entrance of the mansion and the shed out back. Everything you need should be in the shed and in the closet at the end of the main hallway. I'll leave a checklist for things to clean and another list for things to do during business hours. It's fairly straight forward, but if you need anything, please give me a call. The phone at the front desk has our number written next to it."

Kat leaned forward and took the key from Mrs. Valor. Mrs. Valor turned her attention to Elle. "Can I expect a reply from you by this Wednesday? Otherwise I'd like to give Kat another set of hands and will need to see who else wants to apply."

"Yes, of course," said Elle, "I can let you know by then. Um, do you mind if we go through the mansion on our way out? I'd like to get a look at what we'd be taking on." She'd seen the place dozens of times, but sizing it up from a maintenance perspective warranted another viewing.

"Oh of course! Well, Kat has the key; you two can head over there now and just give me a ring once you have a decision. Kat, I'll see you Friday evening to go over some things for Saturday morning."

Both girls stood, made their way down the short hall and into the main entry. They slipped back into their shoes and jackets brought to them by Mrs. Valor, who thanked them and directed them toward the mansion as they left.

They arrived at the rickety porch of the mansion and Kat felt a familiar prickle of fear crawl into her chest. Her heart rate picked up and her hands felt clammy. Elle noticed and nudged her with her elbow. "C'mon Kathy, it'll be fine. There's light this time, and you know what to expect. It really doesn't get much spookier than it did the other night, I promise."

Kat wanted to believe her. Also, if that nickname stuck she would never forgive Elle, and advised her of this. Elle smirked and gestured toward the door. Once again, the door clicked without the use of a key and slowly creaked open. Elle's prerogative to terrify

Kat no longer existed, so she took the lead. They entered the main area and located the time cards and checklists. Nothing out of the ordinary in terms of reasonable expectations. Elle still wanted to see the building and grounds to ensure she wasn't getting in over her head. She took the papers from Kat's hands and stuck them back into the top drawer of the counter. She grabbed Kat's forearm and pulled her into the first room on the right. They made their way down the hallway once again. The stringless marionette sat motionless on the shelf in the otherwise vacant room. Kat did not entertain the thought of who placed it back there. As they passed, however, it once again clattered to the floor. Kat jumped a little, but then caught herself. "Right," she whispered, "that is normal for this house."

"Uh huh," replied Elle, unfazed as she studied the floors and windows. The floors would be easy enough with the right mop. The windows had some hand prints, but they weren't too dirty. Most didn't have a screen, she noted. The trick would be the dusting, especially the mirror-lined walls around the sunroom that was packed with too many dolls to see much shelf space.

As Elle calculated the amount of work they'd be doing, Kat continued to try to take in the place. Her intense fear and limited vision on her first walk through clouded her assessment considerably. She missed most of the rooms' arrangements as a result of both. It was easier to evaluate things without being limited to the single beam of a flashlight. The dolls' heads still turned as Kat and Elle passed by. Kat wasn't sure she'd ever get used to that, especially when they blinked.

Elle knew all the exits, so she showed Kat how to get out of the maze of rooms through several back doors. They were hard to see and hidden behind bookshelves cluttered with dolls. Kat decided the worst were the baby dolls because they were the closest to being lifelike. Their makers put in a great deal of time with the detail in their faces, eyes, and moveable limbs. She also felt a general uneasiness as she walked past a brass cabinet with glass doors in one of the back rooms. The encasement displayed three dolls and it stood apart from the other cluttered displays. The doll in the center caught the most attention. It was dressed in what Kat assumed to be a hand knitted dress. It stood for the time being, but according to Elle, changed positions quite a bit. The thing Kat found most disturbing, though, was that it was one of the few dolls with a hand painted face, including the eyes. Even still, those dark eyes seemed to blink and follow her as she walked by. The other two dolls were from a similar era with just as much detail as the one centered. They moved too, but never past the centered doll. They wore different clothing. Vibrant, bright robes and sashes, Kat noticed. They had darker skin tones and thick, dark hair. Aside from the mansion’s general eeriness, Kat felt the most apprehension when she stood near that display. When she asked Elle about it, Elle didn't seem to notice it. "You'll get used to it, Kit-Kat," she kept repeating.

"Yea, yea," grumbled Kat. "If you say so."

The outside felt different. Once Kat stepped beyond the threshold to any door leading outside, the heavy, chilling sensation dissipated. The quarter acre of land that the mansion sat on consisted mostly of grass with a few bushes on the east part of the lot. In the backyard, a white birch tree stood in the back corner. Most of the leaves had already fallen from its branches and gathered in crunchy piles around the base. A stubborn few, though, kept a delicate hold onto the birch, finishing out their color changes.

Elle unlocked the wooden door to the shed. A lone bat screeched and flew out, causing both her and Kat to duck and cover their hair. With a giggle, Elle shook her head and stood to examine the contents inside. She found a rake, a shovel, a lawn mower, a red gasoline tank, and other random yard care items. It was plenty, and surprisingly organized. Elle expected a cluttered, rusty collection of equipment based on the wear on the shed’s outer walls. Kat eyed the damp space and stopped at the far back corner of the shed. There hung a freshly cleaned rifle. Familiar with firearms, Kat took it down and examined it further. It was fully loaded. The end smelled of gunpowder, and Kat told Elle she thought it was fired recently.

Elle shrugged. "Well, we are in the woods. I'm sure Mr. Valor hunts. God knows there are plenty of deer out this way."

"Yea, that's true," agreed Kat. But she wasn't satisfied. She saw that the Valors had a much newer shed of their own, and wondered why they wouldn't keep their gun in there.

The thought left her, though, as they walked back inside and toward the main entrance of the mansion. Just as they were about to exit, Kat felt her heart jump into her throat. A cool, icy sensation set onto the left side of her neck, as if someone's cold hand pressed against her. No other part of her felt it, and when she turned to see what it was, she saw nothing. She tried to call out to Elle, who was a few steps ahead of her, but words weren't coming. After a few dragged out seconds, Elle turned back to see what was holding Kat up. She smirked at Kat's pallor and said, "C'mon, you knew what you were getting into," and moved past the door frame and onto the porch.

Kat rushed after her and they turned for home. As they walked, Kat began to regret her winter job decision, but she hated backing out of commitments. She turned to begging Elle to take the job too. If she was stuck in a haunted hell for three months, she might as well take Elle down with her. Elle just smiled and said, "We will have to see."

7

New York City, NY, 1888

Frank sat in silence, watching the rain pelt the glass of the kitchen window. Four months since he lost Myra and the house maintained a resounding melancholia in her absence. He barely slept, and spent most of his time drowning in a bottle of whiskey in front of the fireplace. When he did leave the house, it was for food or to make an appearance at whichever job site required a quick sale of medical supplies. He could do the work in his sleep, and complete sobriety was not necessary. Unfortunately, he found himself able to catch several hours of sleep only if he took down enough of the whiskey to pass out. Otherwise, he kept close company with his thoughts. The short bursts of sleep Frank managed to get were filled with dreams, and more often than not, he found himself back in Kansas at the table with a life-sized Lucy. No substantial conversations occurred, though, because he woke up frequently.

The actual Lucy doll didn't help the situation, either. He often found the doll anywhere but where he left her. He convinced himself he moved Lucy in his drunken stupors, forgetting about it until the following day. But even more unsettling, Frank kept finding blood stains on the doll. He spent hours the night Myra died scrubbing the doll, but he would randomly discover missed stains. Sometimes there were distinct, dried dark droplets on the face, other times the hem of the dress appeared dipped in crimson. Although it had been months since Myra's death, Frank was still unable to come up with a valid explanation for the odd feeling he got around his wife's doll. He kept coming up with fresh reasons for the otherwise unexplained occurrences. The bloodstains, for instance, were just residual stains that appeared to come off, but once the water dried, resurfaced from insufficient scouring.

One evening, Frank threw back a few more shots of whiskey than his usual intake. With his gaze toward the fireplace, he slowly watched the fiery flourishes blur into an orange ball of light. The glow grew dimmer as Frank's eyelids grew heavier, gradually closing. Soon he was unconscious.

8

Several hours passed. The flames simmered; their warmth replaced by a cool draft. Frank slumped down into the couch, whiskey bottle leaning against his right side in a loose grip. The left hand rested on his chest rising up and down with each deep, audible breath. He stirred when the fire hissed out completely. The damp air chilled his drunken figure, and Frank's eyes fluttered. He wasn't sure if he was dreaming or actually seeing this, but Lucy, initially placed on Myra's chair next to the fireplace, was now resting next to the hand on his chest. The heaviness of his body prevented him from moving. He wanted to run, scream, push the doll to the floor, but he was unable to do anything. The doll sat facing him, staring. The head slowly tilted to the right, mirroring the angle of Frank's head. A slow, cherry-lipped smile crept across the hand-painted face. *The lips are typically pursed,* Frank recalled, *but they're definitely moving now.*

The smile stopped just before it became a full grin. Just a thin smile, nothing more. The dark eyes locked with Frank's. He felt beads of sweat rolling down his back. His legs ached with cramps from trying to move them. Even that traitor of a left hand refused to give him even a tremor to tip the doll off his chest. He focused on the eyes. With his full attention on the doll, Lucy's thin smirk grew. Now it was a full grin, and there were teeth. Frank's heart clamored against his ribcage. Part of him hoped that it would burst out and cause the doll to fall to the ground. The doll's right arm lifted from her side in a slow, steady motion. It stopped when it was just above Frank's hand, and dropped atop his. He felt the smooth porcelain against his clammy skin. It felt like a heavy stone and he was unable to move from under its touch. *But the teeth, when did this doll develop teeth?* Frank frantically processed. They sat moments longer, Frank's inebriated, petrified body in a stare down with a porcelain doll.

To Frank's increasing horror, the pearly white grin widened. The incisors on the doll were notably pointed. *Fangs? Does she actually have fangs?*

Fangs or not, the grin maintained its width that now seemed menacing. Frank's heart began to skip beats, causing his vision to blur. His shirt clung to his back from his profuse sweating. He felt the dampness on his forehead starting to trickle into his eyes, but he couldn't blink. Lucy's frozen gaze persisted. Then, the painted right eye winked at Frank. The quick break in eye contact was enough to return mobility to Frank's body. He flung his left arm away from his chest and launched the doll into the wall. He expected the doll to shatter, but only its arm separated from the rest of the body. Frank leaped to his feet and stood over the doll, fists clenched and ready to fight. He panted and continued pouring sweat that now splashed onto both the floor and Lucy's still form. The doll remained face down. Frank still hovered.

By the time the early morning rays broke through his windows, his heart rate was slowing, close to normal. Frank shivered with the chill of the damp house enveloping him. He was completely sober, and a migraine threatened to emerge. His legs felt like someone bludgeoned them courtesy of the relentless cramping. As shaky as he was, Frank refused to even consider sitting back down, fearing the charade would replay as soon as he dozed off. At last, he gathered his remaining strength and kicked the doll onto its back. No more teeth. No tilted head. Not even a smirk. Lucy's vacant stare and pursed lips appeared as they always did. The only proof of last night's freak show was the detached limb. Frank had no intention of reattaching it. In fact, he fully planned on disposing of the doll once he believed he could walk more than several steps without falling. Trembling, Frank ambled back toward his bedroom, closed his door and locked it. He flopped onto the bed face down, quickly possessed by a deep slumber.

9

Eventually, Frank's shivering broke his stupor. He fumbled to pull the blankets on the bed over him. It was no use; the chill had settled into his bones. He lumbered toward the washroom and filled the tub halfway with water. Then he made his way into the kitchen and started up the stove to boil some water. *One of the first sophisticated stoves available for in-home use*, he recalled, but was too exhausted to relish the thought.

He hoped a hot bath would ebb out the cold. Frank was certain he had a fever at this point. Each of his joints ached, and his muscles felt bruised. As he stood in the kitchen, he gulped down a glass of water to quench his dry mouth. Finally, the water on the stove came to a boil and he carefully took it back and added it to the bath. He peeled off his clothes and sank into the warmth of the tub. Once again, Frank succumbed to another feverish sleep.

He slowly regained consciousness once the water temperature dropped enough for the shivering to return. He dragged himself out of the tub and dried off with a nearby towel. He hurried back to the bedroom and started layering on clothing. Once dressed, Frank sat on the edge of the bed and took in some deep breaths. He was still terrified of returning to the living room where Lucy presumably remained. He needed to figure out how to dispose of the porcelain gargoyle.

But did the doll pose a real threat? Frank mulled this thought over. He was incredibly drunk during the ordeal, and once he sobered up, the doll returned to its lifeless state. *Regardless*, Frank decided, *it must go.*

Even if his intoxicated brain did enjoy bringing the doll to life, it was now too frightening to deal with, real or not. With a final exhale, he stood up and made his way to the living room. He found Lucy's arm still on the floor where it landed, but the doll was back in a seated position on Myra's chair. Several droplets of dried blood pooled under both eyes. Methodically removing a handkerchief from his back pocket, Frank wiped the maroon crusts from the doll, picked up the arm, and made his way toward the backyard.

It wasn't much of a yard, mostly a concrete garden with an iron fire pit and a solitary red oak tree in its early stages of growth. Frank smiled as he recalled Myra picking it out at the nursery just down the road. She hoped to watch it grow into a full-sized tree over the course of their lives. She told him she could fit both hands around the trunk and over the years she would use that to measure how big it grew. When she couldn't wrap both arms around it, then it would be done growing. Frank never argued the logic; it made sense to her and it made her happy, so why disagree? The tree stood surrounded by a lone patch of grass. The remainder of the small grounds were covered with cement. The fire pit was piled with logs, but it was usually too rainy or cold to enjoy an outdoor fire just yet. Tonight, however, Frank had plans to do just that. Not considering its porcelain structure, he lifted the top log and replaced it with Lucy. He then anchored the log atop the doll and lit a match. The rain had stopped hours before, but the damp wood hissed into an ascending trail of smoke when the match kissed it. Frank sighed and went for the canister of kerosene he kept just inside the back door. After retrieving it, he proceeded to saturate the wood with fuel. Lucy's dress and hair soaked up the kerosene as well, until the entire pit was flammable. Frank took two steps backward and lit the match. He carefully leaned forward. He flicked the lit match into the pit and jumped back. With a whoosh, flames engulfed the structure. Fortunately for the cement foundation, the fire remained in one place. Frank sat and watched the fiery battle within the metal basin. Black smoke poured up toward the sky and he wondered if the fire department would drop by. He stared at the blazing enchantment for a few minutes, then went back inside, glancing out the kitchen window periodically to monitor the flames. Finally, as the fire settled, all he could see was a large pile of ashes and embers. He didn't bother going back out to dig and see what was left of the doll. He doubted anything would be left of it after the amount of heat the fire concocted. Turning from the window, Frank poured himself a glass of whiskey, and sat down. He stared into the backyard and watched the rain start to peck at the window once again.

Frank dozed off with his head down on the kitchen table, empty glass in his right hand and an almost empty bottle to his left. His face smashed against the hard, oak tabletop, but this wasn't what woke him. He coughed a few times, but couldn't clear his throat. The room felt warmer than he expected, and even after blinking several times, his eyes felt dry and the room remained hazy. Suddenly, Frank noticed a familiar glow coming from the living room, accompanied by more haze. *No, not haze, smoke. Smoke?*

He hadn't even lit the fireplace. Before he had time to think about how this had happened, he heard a loud crash where the staircase stood near the front entrance. He believed the banister or something from upstairs likely caved and fell. A strong gust of fiery smog blasted Frank onto the floor just as he attempted to stand. He sat, mystified, staring as the flames swallowed the living room. A few licked the kitchen door frame. Frank frantically scooted toward the door leading out to the yard. He tried yelling for help, but ended up in a coughing fit. He prayed the fire department saw the smoke this time, and wondered if he could even make it out the back door. Still gasping for air, Frank flipped himself onto his stomach and started dragging himself across the floor by his elbows. The exertion caused him to breathe heavier, and the coughing increased. Frank's vision started to darken. He was only an arm's reach away from the door, but even that seemed too far. Every reach took maximum effort. The coughing turned into a raspy wheeze. Frank used the last of his strength to lean up against the back door and try to catch his breath. He grasped for the knob and turned it as hard as he could. *Locked.*

A wave of defeat washed over him. He watched the raging orange beast burst through the kitchen door and devour the table and cabinets. Frank saw the fierce glow dimming as his eyes grew heavier and heavier. Soon, he slipped unconscious, and the final curtain closed on his world. Outside, a gust of wind scattered the ash pile in the fire pit. Propped against the metal basin facing the yard, out of view from the kitchen, sat a slightly singed, but perfectly intact porcelain figure with a crimson painted smirk across its pale face.

Then, darkness.

10

Millerton, IL, 1984

Kat pulled up to Alex's house later that evening. The sky was almost dark, and she felt the temperature drop noticeably. She laid her bike against the side of the garage and pushed her way through the screen door that Alex had left unlocked for her. Alex's mom greeted her with a warm hug and a table full of food. Kat was trying to figure out how to politely decline when Alex popped in from the other room. Laughing, he said, "Mom, let her breathe! C'mon in Kat. We can decide food later. But as far as soda goes...,"

"Coke, please."

Alex nodded, opened the fridge, and produced two glass bottles. He slid one across the counter toward Kat.

His mother smiled. "So glad you're here, Kat! It's been a little while. How're you? How's your family? We need to get your parents in on another Euchre night soon!"

A return smile lit Kat's face. She loved that the Kingman family and hers were close. It made starting over again much easier. She agreed to helping set up a game night and thanked Mrs. Kingman for having her over. Alex's mom gave Kat another squeeze and started to clean a stack of dishes. Alex and Kat headed toward the TV room in the back of the house. It was perfect for movies. A tan, worn out couch stretched across the back wall, opposite the TV set. The room stayed dark for optimal viewing, and there were always plenty of blankets and floor space for when the couch became crowded. The room also had a faded maroon recliner in the corner, often reserved for Alex's father. Sometimes, when he wasn't using it, Kat claimed it as her throne and Alex usually fought her for the spot. Between the couch and the recliner stood a short metal coffee table. Alex set out two coasters and they put their bottles down. Kat wrapped herself in one of the blankets and sat on the floor with her back against the couch.

"Behold," professed Alex, as he held a Wal-Mart bag out with one arm, "The reason we are gathered here tonight. Ladies and gentlemen, may I present to you," he reached in and produced an unopened copy of *Indiana Jones and the Temple of Doom*, "Harrison Ford in his latest performance!"

Kat laughed and applauded. Continuing with his presentation, Alex spun dramatically toward the TV set and unveiled the tape by powerfully pulling open the case. The snap made Kat jump and Alex shook his head with a snicker. He put the tape into the VCR and plopped down next to her.

As Alex and Kat embarked on a vicarious journey to find a stolen artifact with Harrison Ford, Elle sat down to dinner with her family a few houses away. Elle's younger brother Scott sat facing her. Age five and full of energy, Elle wondered if anything slowed the kid down. She loved the randomness he brought to the family and didn't mind watching him when their parents were out. This evening, Scott took it upon himself to redecorate the table with the vegetables. He placed the string beans end to end, circling his plate. He then placed a pea every few inches around the beans, and between those spaces, a carrot slice. Elle knew she should probably intervene, but for a five-year-old, it was a fairly advanced pattern, so she left it alone. Elle's mom stood with her back to them, focusing on the stove top while her dad rummaged through the fridge, attempting to locate a beer. "Make it two," Elle heard her mom call to him, and, "You got it, Babe," from her dad.

Judy and Garrett Carter lived in Millerton for the last twenty years. They moved from the suburbs of Chicago after high school, got married, started their family and never looked back. The community knew the couple well, along with Elle and Scott. Garrett worked as a fireman and Judy started out teaching at the local school, but embraced being a full-time mom once Elle came along. They shared a fun, playful dynamic and provided a warm environment to anyone who came through their front door.

"Oh, Scottie, sweetie, what–"

"–an interesting collage you created!" Judy interrupted Garrett. "Tell me what you made!"

Scott grinned. "I put a green circle 'round the plate. Cause we can't draw on the table, but this isn't drawings. This is food! And food goes on tables!"

Elle giggled into her hands. The kid had a point. Garrett, now smiling too, pressed further with, "Well, that's great, Buddy! And you added some carrots for color too?"

"Yea. Plust I don't like them." Scott scrunched up his nose as he said this.

"Fair enough, but you got to give us three bites before we will let you donate the rest to your table art," Garrett answered, bringing his and Judy's beers over and setting them down at the table.

Judy followed, pork chops in one hand and gravy in the other. "So Ellbea, tell us what you were up to all day," she said, as she set the rest of dinner down.

Elle reached for a pork chop. "Oh, nothing crazy."

Garrett took a sip of his beer. "Well, there had to be something, E, we didn't see you after church. You and Kat vanished on us."

"Oh right, um, I got a job for the winter," said Elle. Dousing her plate with gravy, she glanced at her parents, who seemed surprised.

"What? Why the raised eyebrows?"

Judy smiled, "No, Honey, that's wonderful. We just thought you'd take the winter off. But fantastic! Who hired you?"

"Mrs. Valor. Said she needed some help at the mansion. Kat's doing it too."

Judy and Garrett exchanged a quick glance. "Uh huh, and tell me, Elle, you don't think that mansion is better left, well, alone and kept far away from?" Judy's voice quickened as she said this.

"No? Oh c'mon, you guys are scared of the place too, aren't you? You let Scott go there for cripes sake! The whole town knows the house has a beat of its own. This isn't a new thing."

Judy nodded. "No, no it isn't new, but there's a difference between walking through for a half hour versus spending all your free time there. You'll be spending a lot of time on the property. I just don't want things to, you know, escalate."

Elle chewed her food a moment, then said, "Well, I'm confused. Nothing worse happens than the stupid dolls' heads and eyes moving. Sure, occasional footsteps, doors opening and closing, but it isn't anything that we don't know about or haven't seen."

"Elle, don't get upset, I'm not saying you're wrong. I just, I don't know, it seems—"

"Cursed," cut in Garrett with an affirming nod toward his wife.

Judy rolled her eyes. "Yes, Garrett, we all know it's cursed. What I mean is, it's out of anyone's control. No one can promise it won't get worse, no one can make it go away. It's its own entity. And, to be frank, it's creepy."

Elle smiled. "Yea, it is. I guess I just expect it since it really hasn't changed. What about this: if things get worse, or I feel like Kat and I are in danger, we'll stop going?"

With another sip of his beer, Garrett looked to Judy, who took a gulp of hers and paused. Elle was independent and stubborn. If they said no and banned her, she'd probably sneak off and work there anyways. She always had odd forms of rebelling. Judy sighed and leaned back in her chair. "Ok, Ellbea, ok. But, promise me, if it gets weirder than it already is, or if you start having nightmares or stuff seems like it's happening and you're not at the mansion, or if *we* start experiencing weird stuff here, it's over."

"Mom, the dolls like that place too much to follow me home. I think you'd have to steal one to get it to take over your own house."

"Ok, so for the sake of all sanity, don't do that either," added Garrett.

"Yea, no, I won't. I promise. I'll keep work at work." Elle glanced at Scott, who was attempting to saw his pork chop in half with a butter knife.

"Oops, right, guess that's my cue," laughed Garrett as he reached over to help.

Elle finished dinner and went to her room to do her homework. While they cleaned up the kitchen, Judy and Garrett discussed Elle's new employment in more detail. In the end, they concluded that it was out of their hands; both the activities of the house and Elle's decision to work there.

"Think she'd notice if we stuck a cross, salt, and a candle in her purse in case she needs to ward anything off?" asked Judy.

"Pretty sure. Let's give it a week and she how she does. If something seems off, we'll know. And we can press it further, ok?"

Garrett kissed Judy on the forehead and made his way into the living room where Scott was already stationed and playing with his toys. Judy heard the TV flick on and the evening news mumbling in the background. She finished off the rest of her beer and went to join them.

11

New York City, NY, 1887

Myra and Frank walked hand in hand toward the yellow and red canopy tops that covered the county fairgrounds. The loose dirt created a low cloud of dust that trailed behind them as they stepped. Myra's head rested against Frank's arm, while keeping their hands firmly clasped. In her bag, she carried Lucy among the rest of the contents.

"What do you want to see first, Love? The man-eating tiger? The bearded lady? Food?" Frank asked her with a smile.

Myra glanced up at him. "Hm, that's a tricky one. Maybe a trip to the chocolate stand, and then I'd love to see the tiger! Though I find it hard to believe he eats people."

Frank chuckled. "No, of course he doesn't. They just have to say that to get people to want to see him! Or, her."

Myra nodded and they made their way toward a chocolatier, trying his hand at different candy designs. The pair spent the entire afternoon trying new foods, seeing strange sights from allegedly all over the world, and by the end of it, Frank purchased a beautiful sapphire necklace and gently clasped it around Myra's neck. "You're beautiful and you deserve beautiful things," he told her, as he often did.

Myra smiled and pressed her hand over the deep oceanic-colored gem, admiring its striking appearance. She now had a collection of sparkling jewelry from Frank, along with dresses, coats, and of course, shoes. It was his way of making up for his frequent absences due to work. When home, she spent most of her time alone. His constant additions to her wardrobe seemed to be his way of acknowledging this.

Before they left, Myra noticed a booth where a young woman stood, selling porcelain dolls. Knowing how much she appreciated Lucy, Myra was curious to see if there was another worth purchasing. Frank was busy eyeing the conjoined twins and their juggling act. Not wanting to break his focus, Myra took a few steps back and made her way to the doll booth.

"Come, Child," came a sweet, accented voice.

Myra looked up and saw the young woman motioning at her. The woman was small, thin, and adorned in vividly colored shrouds of material draped into a dress. She had large silver earrings and wore many gemstone rings, at least one per finger. She had on purple eyeshadow and ruby red lipstick. Myra walked over and started to introduce herself. "Hello, my name is Myra. Your dolls are lovely."

"Hm, not just dolls, my Dear. No, these each carry their own tune."

"Oh yes! I can see that no two are the same."

"That is for certain," the woman's dark eyes stared at Myra's pale countenance.

"I have one of my own...well not entirely like yours, but a doll that I take great care of. I might possibly get another one, you know, a matching set!" said Myra.

"Ah, yes. These dolls do well with others. I made each one myself, I would know. You want to see how it's done?"

Myra nodded and as an excited smile overtook her face. The woman walked toward the back of the tent, and lifted the corner, taking them behind the scenes of the carnival. Myra stared at all the people moving carts and boxes. She hadn't considered the amount of work behind one of these events. Directly behind the woman's tent were three chairs. An older woman that could easily be related to the one who summoned Myra occupied one already. She had a large, woven basket beside her on the ground. Dressed similarly to the younger woman, but with a much heavier figure, the older woman glanced at Myra and smiled. "I'm Panella, Dear. Have a seat."

Myra gingerly sat across from Panella, who seemed all too comfortable with whatever was about to take place, *like she's anticipating something*, thought Myra.

The other woman, fastening the ties to the tent where they entered, turned around and stood over Myra's shoulder. She bent down and put her lips close to Myra's ear and whispered, "And I'm Renni. Pleasure is ours, Child."

A queasy sensation started to work its way through Myra's stomach. Her heart rate picked up, and she began to look around for a way to escape. But of course she could get away. They hadn't held her hostage, tied her down, even threatened her, for that matter. So why was she nervous? She took Lucy from her bag and sat the doll on her lap, hugging it close to her.

Renni broke her train of thought. "You seemed so captivated by the dolls, Dear. We thought it best you learn more about them."

Myra cocked her head, puzzled. "Well, I mean, yes, I do appreciate the work you've done on them. Anyone can see how personalized you've made each one. But, you don't need to show me how to make them from the start. I get the general idea--,"

Panella reached into the basket and produced two more dolls. Each mirrored the image of her and Renni. "These are the originals, Dear. We started with this, and then created more...marketable styles for others to purchase."

Panella placed both dolls in a seated position on the vacant chair between her and Myra. Both dolls had mocha colored skin, dark eyes, and maroon painted lips. The detail on each was exquisite. Myra hadn't seen anything quite like it. The eyelids were even moveable. When Panella tilted one back, the eyes closed, and opened again once Panella sat it upright. The hairstyles matched the women's. The clothes were hand-sewn, brightly colored layers of fabric that formed dresses. The shoulders rotated the upper limbs, knees bent and extended, and the heads could turn whichever way the women chose to position them.

"They're just lovely!" exclaimed Myra. "Goodness, how much time did you take to get them to look so lifelike?"

With weighted smiles and an exchange of serious expressions, Renni placed her hand on Myra's shoulder and gave it a squeeze. "We do more than construct the dolls," she said.

"We give them life. We bring them to life," continued Panella.

The uneasiness returned. "Bring them to life? You don't mean literally, do you? You can't do that. L-life, the soul, that c-comes from God!" Myra paused to consider this statement and added, "or whomever you believe in."

Renni let out a soft laugh. "Well, God sometimes needs a hand bringing life into the world."

Panella started mumbling a chant in a language unfamiliar to Myra. She knew Latin, French, and German, but it wasn't similar to any of those.

"S-stop, what are you doing?" Myra felt Renni's grip tighten.

"Shh, you'll see, you'll see, Child," whispered Renni. Myra could feel the warmth of her breath as she said this.

Panella paused, opened her eyes, and stared at Myra and Renni. "Look. Here they are."

Myra's eyes widened. She didn't believe what she saw. This was a dream, it had to be a dream! But as her mind screamed for her to wake up, her eyes watched as the two dolls turned their heads toward her, blinked several times, and grinned. Their small chests even moved up and down, as if they were actually breathing. The one closest to Panella spoke first, in a way. It would turn to Panella, and then back to Myra, the lips moved, but Myra heard nothing.

"No, no, no, no!" whimpered Myra. She couldn't stand up. Renni now placed her other hand on the remaining shoulder and held her down. She continued whispering in her enchanting, soft tone. "Yes. Wait. Watch, Dear."

The dolls came to life. That was the only way Myra could describe the situation to herself. They were no longer porcelain dolls. Well, the skin stayed porcelain. Everything stayed the same material, but it was like someone placed a person inside these dolls and that person could now make them move, talk, and see.

The dolls moved their heads, glancing at Renni and Panella as if for permission to do anything further. The two women just smiled as Myra struggled to free herself from Renni's grip.

"You said no one can create a new soul," said Renni. "But we do not create new souls. No, we share our own with what we treasure, and they in turn, become our extension."

"I don't know what you mean," grunted Myra, continuing to thrust her shoulders side to side, still unable to break Renni's hold on her.

The two women only grinned at her. "The dolls speak their own language, and only the one they belong to can hear what they say," said Renni.

"Why would you curse such beautiful dolls?" mumbled Myra.

"Curse? We do not curse things. Magic is not evil unless it produces evil or is intended for evil. We use the energy to create amusement. We don't believe in curses," answered Panella.

"These dolls reflect us," Renni repeated. "Unless there is darkness in our intentions, these dolls remain an imprint of our good energy. And neither was created in darkness."

"In fact," added Panella, "the dolls can share their own energy with others."

As Panella said this, the Renni doll turned its dark eyes toward Myra, and then dropped its gaze to Lucy. The lips began moving and the eyelashes fluttered. Slowly, the head of the Panella doll turned and joined in. Myra felt Lucy start to twitch.

Myra's scream broke the enchantment. In a final attempt to free herself, Myra turned and bit Renni's hand. The woman spat and swore, releasing her grip on Myra's shoulders. Myra jumped up, grabbed her purse, and blindly ran past Panella. She knocked the chair with the gypsy dolls over in her haste, and heard both women yelling in a foreign tongue. Myra did not take the time to figure out what the language was. She just wanted to go home.

Frank grew tired of watching the conjoined twins' juggling act. He went to tell Myra he was set to go, but realized she wasn't anywhere in sight. He backtracked to the jewelry stand, but didn't see her. He scanned the area, and saw two Gypsy women brushing themselves off, and muttering to one another. They were adjusting their tent and presumably closing up shop. He saw dozens of homemade dolls, along with hand sewn dresses and other accessories lining the tent walls. He was about to make an inquiry when Myra ran into him, winded and disheveled. Her golden hair that she usually kept pinned back stuck to both sides of her face. Dust clutched the hem of her dress, and her face was bright red and beaded in sweat. She almost fell into his arms when he reached out to embrace her. Frank felt her shaking and noticed she was not able to articulate much.

"Ok, ok, let's go over here," he said, when she seemed to panic more as they walked toward the tent full of dolls.

Still unable to say much, Frank checked her purse to see if someone tried to rob her. Her money, handkerchief, and Lucy all appeared present and intact. Her clothing was worn the way he last saw her, so if someone had tried to grab her, she must've broke away quickly.

Finally, Myra's breathing slowed enough to where she could speak. "The Gypsy ladies, those two women!" Myra started, pointing back at the doll tent, "They have live dolls! Dolls that move and act like them! But they can't talk, well they can, but just to whoever owns them. And each other. Oh God, it was awful!"

Still unsure what to make of it, Frank nodded along, beginning to smile at the thought of small dolls chasing his frantic wife around a carnival.

"Sweetheart, don't you think it was part of an act? We are at a carnival. The point is to scare, amuse, even confuse in this case."

"Don't make fun of me," she whispered, "I know what I saw."

"Well, Darling, of course you saw it! All magic shows let you see exactly what they intend for you to see!"

Myra paused. She did remember the women talking about magic. Was it all an act? Of course it was all an act, how else could any of it be explained? Myra let a small smirk creep onto her face. Frank answered it with a bigger one. "You see, Love?"

"Yes, yes of course you're right. What else could it have been? Voodoo?"

"Well, no, Gypsies don't practice Voodoo...but, but that's neither here nor there," Frank answered.

Wiping her eyes and face with her handkerchief embroidered *M.J.S*, Myra steadied herself, gave Frank a warm kiss, and said she'd had enough fun for the day. Frank tucked back the loose strands of hair behind her ears. Then, joining hands, the pair turned and left for home.

12

Millerton, IL, 1984

Elle arrived at the mansion a few minutes early. It was yet another crisp autumn Saturday afternoon and the doors opened in about thirty minutes. She figured it best to do a run-through to ensure it was as well-kept as possible. She and Kat had closed up around eight o'clock the night prior, but things always found their way out of place when left unattended. It had been almost a month since they took the job. So far, nothing beyond the expected dolls' heads turning, eye movements, and random sounds had deterred their presence in the building. Elle noted that Kat wasn't as jumpy as when they first started. She still acted uneasy, but nothing compared to her first few visits. Elle managed to freak her out now and again, but the house's tricks were becoming as routine to Kat as they were to the rest of the town. *Still,* thought Elle, *even if we are used to it, we aren't in control of it.*

Her mother was right about that, and she kept it in mind. Elle hoped that whatever they did, they wouldn't alter or influence the mansion's dynamics.

Elle fanned out the information pamphlets across the counter in the main entry, securing them with the iron cross paperweight. She took out the lock box for money collections and laid out waivers that everyone had to sign, along with some pens. Kat walked in just as Elle was about the head back to check on the doll displays.

"We were just here. Do you really think the Big Guy threw a rave party last night?" asked Kat.

"Well, it wouldn't be the first time," Elle answered.

Kat nodded. "True, but that was on Halloween. You can't expect anyone to behave then, dead or alive."

With a thin smile, Elle murmured to Kat that she didn't believe the dolls or forces behind the house's disturbances fit into either category. Kat whispered back that if Elle tried making this any scarier than it already was, she would take one of the dolls and hide it under Elle's bed. Elle shook her head, "Don't you fucking dare."

Kat stopped and raised an eyebrow. "Wait, really?"

Elle looked back at her. "Yea, Dude, it could throw the whole thing off. No one's allowed to take anything out of this place because they don't want whatever controls it to, I don't know, spread. Or react."

Kat laughed. Until now, nothing about this place even got Elle to flinch. "Are you serious?"

Elle crossed her arms. "Fine, if this is something that doesn't freak you out, you take a doll. Put it in your room. I dare you."

"Wait, do you know what will happen? If you're hiding something from me--,"

"No, I just think you're being ridiculous. The only reason this place isn't freaky to anyone is because they know what to expect. You go and pull a stunt trying to get something unexpected and it could be detrimental!"

Kat sighed. "You're really being dramatic, Ellbea. Go eat something."

Now more annoyed, Elle snapped back, "Whatever, Kathy. Make sure everything else is in place. I'm going to make sure the front is set to go."

Elle pushed past Kat and returned to the counter in the entrance. The doors were already unlocked from when the two of them showed up. Elle continued arranging the items on the counter. She heard some footsteps opposite of where she left Kat, and didn't bother looking toward the noise. She did, however, hurry after the clashing sound that followed. Even if the house notoriously came to life, Elle prided herself on attempting to keep it maintained the best she could. The crash came from a small sitting room with pink carpet and formal, floral patterned chairs. The room was more of a break from the larger, cluttered rooms of dolls and other antiques. It served as an antique itself, as Mrs. Valor claimed it was part of the original construct, including the furniture. To display it well, the Valors kept a minimal number of other items on display. Behind the two chairs stood a wood hutch where a single, porcelain doll sat. The doll had dark, short hair and green eyes, with the appearance of a toddler, and the doll's attire suggested it came from the 1920's.

Well, the doll usually sat on top of the hutch. When Elle entered the sitting nook, she found its sole occupant smashed in pieces on the ground. Puzzled, Elle looked around to see what had caused the fall. It was uncommon for the dolls to actually break. Sure, they moved and sometimes fell, but always remained intact. The green-eyed cherub laid at her feet amid a tangle of limbs with its cracked face and punched in nose staring up at her. Elle continued staring back until Kat walked up behind her, startling her back to reality.

"What did you do?" Kat asked.

"No-nothing. The thing just fell. But it shattered. They usually don't shatter."

Kat shook her head. "Well, in my experience, when porcelain hits the floor, it breaks."

"True," agreed Elle, "but there's carpeting in this room. Plush carpeting at that. So it shouldn't have shattered like this."

Kat glanced around the room, looking for a source of the fall. Nothing else appeared to be shifted or even remotely close to where the dolls previously sat. Unable to come up with a sound reason for it, Kat just shrugged and said, "Well, in any event, people are heading up the drive. Go greet them. I'll get the vacuum and we can figure it out later."

Elle headed toward the counter and plastered on a bright, cheery grin to welcome the people trickling in. Kat ducked into the supply closet. When she returned to the little room, she saw the doll was back intact, for the most part. The right arm remained unattached, and the nose still appeared slightly dented. But otherwise, the green-eyed baby doll showed no signs of the prior impact. Slightly shaken, Kat reached down and picked up the doll in one hand and its arm in the other. It was a clean break and would need some glue to reattach it. She sat the doll back on its hutch and angled it so that the missing arm wasn't as obvious. She placed the detached arm in the top drawer of the hutch and left to return the vacuum cleaner.

By closing time, most of the dolls in the mansion had rearranged themselves in some fashion. Elle gave up returning them to their original spots, and Kat took the liberty of sweeping and dusting once the final visitor exited. Kat was near the back of the house, Elle just a few rooms over, when they both heard a low rumble that shook the floor.

"Oh come on," muttered Elle.

The hair on her arms stood at full attention and the back of her neck prickled. The moonlight suddenly became her only light source when the power cut out. Elle heard Kat fumbling and swearing as she shook the hallway light switch up and down. Elle started to make her way toward the echo of profanities. She admitted to herself it was a bit unnerving dealing with the house in full swing without light. Catching Kat by the arm that was still furiously jarring the light switch, she shushed her and said, "We need to make our way to the entrance."

"Ya think?"

"I do--but you seem more focused on restoring the power," Elle said.

Kat glanced around them. The house fell silent. They paused, and then Elle noticed a *click-clack* sound coming from the room two doors down from them. "We may want to check on that," said Elle.

Kat answered with a hesitant nod and Elle released her grip. She then hooked her arm around Kat's. They shuffled toward the noise. The room had a bit more moonlight than the hall. Elle scanned the shapes and shadows of the room. She didn't see anything to be the source of the sound. "Hey, I think that window is open," said Kat, nodding toward a slightly ajar pane of glass on the back wall.

Elle watched as the window blew open, then closed, then open again. Elle didn't recall opening any windows, especially since it was ungodly cold for November. She pulled Kat with her as she walked forward to close it. The moon afforded her enough light to inspect around the windowsill and frame. Nothing appeared broken. The surrounding dolls on the shelves sat motionless with vacant stares. Kat shrugged and headed back to the door, pulling Elle with her.

Click-click-clack-click

Both girls spun, breaking the link between their arms, and faced the window, again swinging open and shut. This time, it was with more force.

"Ah crap," muttered Elle.

"Yea, seriously, I'm so over this shit," said Kat.

"Leave it for tomorrow?" asked Elle.

"But what if it rains tonight? Or snows? Or...I don't know, someone breaks in?"

"I feel that whatever keeps opening the window can close it if someone tries to break in," Elle said with some panic to her tone.

This didn't go unnoticed by Kat, who sighed, shook her head, and marched back into the room to reclose the window. Elle watched her small silhouette start to head back toward the doorway, then stop.

"Kat? What's up?"

Silence. But she was standing in front of Elle. Elle took a few steps in Kat's direction. Before she could reach out to touch Kat's outline, she felt an icy sensation brush against the back of her neck, as if someone's hand grazed her skin. Now Elle stood, frozen and silent, waiting. The cold touch continued to press against Elle's cheek, then over both of her forearms, and finally left bursts of icy spikes in her hands. She had felt this from time to time before, but not to this degree. It was not a pleasant feeling. Elle’s chest felt like a pinball table as her heart banked around her rib cage. She held her breath, hoping to hear something beyond the deafening silence, especially from Kat. It was like one of those nightmares where her whole body felt stuck, even if she tried to run.

Kat experienced the same stuck feeling as Elle. Once she shut the window, Kat had heard the sound of something dragging across the wooden floorboards. It was a faint sound, but she definitely heard it. She paused to try and figure out what it was. She thought she could move if she wanted, but she found herself in a full-blown fright fit. It felt like the first night, only without a flashlight. Her legs ached and wobbled. She couldn't catch her breath because she kept holding it, hoping to identify the sound. Nothing, now, but Elle wasn't moving anymore either. *Maybe she heard it too?*

Kat didn't bother asking. Without warning, a suffocating sense of terror gripped Kat when she felt a hand take hold of her ankle. The smooth, cool hand felt small, but strong enough to dig its nails into her skin and latch on. *Like stone,* thought Kat, *wait, no...porcelain.*

The touch broke her stationary stance and she launched forward, colliding into Elle. They crashed to the floor. Elle's mystery chills ceased, and Kat managed to kick whatever held onto her ankle across the room during the scuffle. The two scrambled to their feet and rejoined arms. Panting, Elle took the lead.

As they shuffled down the hall, Kat heard the dragging noise resume.

She heard a *scrrrrrrrritch,* then a pause, then another *scrrrrrrrritch,* and a pause. Elle picked up the pace, blocking her face with her free hand, hoping not to slam them into a door or a wall. The noise behind them also picked up the pace. The pauses grew shorter between each *scrrrrrritch.* Kat started screaming while Elle did her best to keep calm, but feared the mansion for the first time in years. "Did we really piss it off somehow?" mumbled Elle.

Kat almost took Elle down with her when her knees buckled. She violently clawed at her legs, kicking and cursing. Whatever was following them caught up to Kat and grabbed her ankle again. This time, it didn't stay latched to one spot. It used her pant leg to climb up the side of her leg, causing her knees to give out. Even with Kat's attempts to free herself, the hand continued up, passing the hip, her stomach and then to her shoulder. Finally, it closed around her throat. The rest of Kat's body hit the ground with a thud. She tried to rip away the clenched hand. Elle heard her start to gasp for air, and saw she was pulling at something around her throat. When Kat rolled near a beam of moonlight shining through a nearby window, Elle saw a white, plump hand holding onto the front of her neck. The hand looked like it belonged to a child. *Part of the arm was there too,* Elle noted, which is what they heard dragging as the hand moved over the wood floors. Kat rolled onto her back again. Elle dropped to her knees and grabbed the chubby, porcelain arm as Kat worked to loosen the grip of the fingers. She was losing strength. Elle worried she'd pass out. "*Get off of her*!" shouted Elle.

Elle noticed Kat's eyes starting to close as her breathing became more labored. Both girls continued to fight the dismembered limb, but it was surprisingly strong. Kat's arms dropped and she now took short, shallow breaths. Elle continued to scream and fight the offender, but it felt like a lost cause. She kept screaming and crying for Kat to wake up. As Kat gasped for one, final breath, a deafening rumble shook the room. Elle covered her ears at the roar, and watched as the lights flickered back on. The once powerful hand dropped to the ground, immobile and no longer clenched. The rumbling ceased, and a stillness washed over the house.

Elle turned her attention back to Kat. Gasping between sobs, she shook Kat's shoulders and screamed her name. It took a few moments, but Kat's eyes fluttered open and she coughed between gulps of air. Elle didn't wait. She pulled Kat to her feet and put her arm around Kat's small waist. Kat wrapped her arm around Elle's neck and Elle dragged her down the remainder of the hallway, through the saloon doors and adjoining rooms, then into the entrance area. Shouldering the front door open, Elle lumbered off the porch, only to feel her own legs give out. The two collapsed on the front lawn. Elle could hear Kat's raspy breathing next to her. She turned her head and watched Kat's body shudder, drenched in sweat. Elle propped herself on an elbow and saw the doorway of the house. In it, a dark shadow hovered near the counter. It moved back and forth several times, lingered a moment more, then dissolved. Elle fell back flat on her back until her breathing slowed. Next to her, she could hear Kat's wheezes quieting. Elle would've stayed on the ground a little longer if the sound of footsteps behind her didn't launch her back onto her feet in a single motion. Elle braced herself for another fight, but breathed a sigh of relief when she saw Mr. Valor.

13

Mr. Valor stood facing the two girls, grave faced and pale. He had on a dark trench coat and work boots. His leather gloved hands gripped something shiny across his chest. Elle realized it was the rifle from the shed out back. Several feet behind him was Mrs. Valor in pink slippers, still zipping up her coat and running to join the commotion.

"You two ok? We heard screaming." Mr. Valor's voice was steady and low.

"I--I am, but I don't know about Kat."

Kat rolled onto her stomach and pushed herself into a seated position. She rocked back and forth, still shivering, and tried to say that she was ok, but the words weren't forming. Elle rushed to her side and rubbed Kat's arms to try and stop the shivering. The harsh air began to chill Elle too, with her adrenaline waning. Mr. Valor continued eyeing the girls, then glanced at the house. He didn't flinch when the front door swung shut and they all heard the unmistakable *click* of the lock. His eyes shifted back to the girls. He handed the rifle to Mrs. Valor, took off his coat and wrapped it around Kat. Without much effort, he lifted Kat's small body and made his way back to his home. Mrs. Valor put an arm around Elle and they followed.

Inside the Valor home, the fireplace snapped and popped in the room just past the formal dining room. Mr. Valor placed Kat directly in front of its warmth. Mrs. Valor brought out a teapot and started to boil some water as her husband layered blankets around Kat. Kat's shivering slowed. Mr. Valor sat next to her and started to ask some basic questions about what happened. Still without expression, he studied her as they spoke.

Once the tea was ready, Elle tried to help Mrs. Valor carry it. However, her trembling hands wouldn't keep the tea in the cups. "Here, Dear. Go sit by Kat and Gregory," Mrs. Valor said as she took the tray and followed Elle to rejoin the others.

The charred smell of wood and orange glow from the fireplace filled the room. Elle sat on the other side of Kat and stared into the blaze. The warmth embraced them and Elle felt herself calming down. Mr. Valor maintained his gaze toward both girls with a stern expression. Mrs. Valor passed around the cups and they all sipped their tea in silence for the next twenty minutes or so. Finally, Mr. Valor asked them how they felt.

Kat nodded. She was still freaked out, but physically she warmed up enough to stop shaking. Elle gave a small smile and a head nod as well. She still kept replaying the incident in her mind and tried to rationalize, or at least fully interpret what happened. "Mr. Valor?" asked Elle, "the house's incidents were always, well, predictable and harmless. I mean, right?"

Mr. Valor sucked in his cheeks and glanced at his wife, who looked down at her tea. Back at Elle, he said, "That, for the most part is accurate, Elle. But recently the activity seems more...aggressive. We lost a lot of staff from last season as a result. Once they were gone and the house wasn't occupied full time, the movements and more threatening behavior died down. Victoria and I went and checked the house daily. It seemed to go back to the normal antics."

"Why didn't you tell us this?" Kat sputtered. "I could've been killed and I don't even know by what!" Her hair stuck out in all directions and rage illuminated her blue eyes. Kat twisted around to face Mrs. Valor.

Mrs. Valor leaned back and met the daggers in her accuser's eyes with a thin smile. How so much tenacity fit inside that small of a person, she'd never know. Elle scooted to the side, sensing the fury. *She's justifiably upset*, thought Elle, but it was still terrifying. Mr. Valor remained silent and still.

"Oh, Honey, I--,"

"You what? We've been here for over a month! You've had plenty of time to warn us. What if that killed me? Us? That's on you!"

"Well, actually," Mrs. Valor stared back into her tea, "those waivers you signed removed any liability from us in the event of anything happening to you on the property."

Kat reddened. She remembered reading it, but assumed it was a standard work form. In a low, steady voice, she uttered, "Then effective immediately, I resign."

Elle rolled her eyes. "Of course, we quit. Who in their right mind would return there? No one should go in that house! No one from the public, no workers; waivers or not, you really want people's deaths on your consciences?"

Mrs. Valor waved her hand. "Of course not, and we considered closing it off for good last year. If we thought things were still as active as they were then, we wouldn't have even considered reopening."

"What happened last summer?" asked Elle.

Mrs. Valor popped on a cheerful smile. "Oh, my, well I can't remember exactly. The workers wouldn't give specifics, but I know that something scared them more than it had in years past. Gregory went over there to check the place out and didn't notice anything we hadn't seen before. But the men we hired at the time were a little shaken and slightly banged up. I think they were overreacting a little, to tell you the truth. Probably drinking, too. But they made such a racket and left us empty staffed that same day."

"I thought you said it was more threatening than usual," cut in Kat.

"Well, according to the work group. They were with us for almost a decade, so it was unusual that they were so frightened...," her voice faded.

Kat and Elle exchanged looks. It was a small town. Usually if something happened, within a few days everyone knew about it. They were a little concerned if something really did happen that the Valors were taking great care to hide it.

They sat without saying much a few moments more. Mr. Valor finally stood up and announced that it was late. He offered to drive them home and talk with their parents, should they have any questions. He went on about taking full responsibility, but Elle lost interest. Her mind was back on the mansion again. "We rode our bikes here," she interrupted.

"We can place them in the back of the truck, not to worry," said Mr. Valor.

Elle always expected Mr. Valor to cruise around in some type of luxury sedan, but he took great pride in his silver pick-up truck. They loaded up the bikes and crossed the train tracks toward the girls' homes.

14

Over the next few weeks, the town learned that the Valors locked the doors to the Marionette Mansion for good. Initially, Kat and Elle were branded as the *Girls that Cried Wolf*. Since no one ever experienced anything more than the anticipated characteristics from the home, the locals assumed the teens were craving attention and fabricated their entire experience.

Being familiar and unfazed by the small-town frame of mind, Elle took the liberty to do some research the weeks succeeding that nightmare of an evening. She went to the library in Uptown and started her investigation by looking back on newspaper articles regarding the mansion. Nothing unusual stemmed from the past five years, so she redirected her focus on the maintenance crew hired during the fall of

1983. Elle knew of two companies that serviced the small region. One was local, and all the employees lived in town. If it was this group, they did a phenomenal job keeping whatever happened a secret. The other was a larger company that operated on contract work based in Chicago. They'd send crews to the rural regions on a paid stint of time, usually a season, rotating workers to different locations over all of Illinois. *Uptown has a hotel*, recalled Elle, *and that's likely where anyone out of the area stayed if they weren't there to visit family or friends.*

The company, Monte's Maintenance & More, had a 1-800 number listed when Elle looked them up in the yellow pages. *Worth a shot*, she thought.

The library had a payphone just before reaching the exit doors. Elle dropped two quarters in the slot and glanced at the number she had scribbled on her hand. She punched them into the dial pad and waited for an answer. The automated recording advised her to push '1' *to learn more about services offered*, then '2' *to speak to a team member*.

"Good afternoon and thank you for calling Monte's. This is Jackson, with whom do I have the pleasure of speaking?" Jackson's voice had a thick, northern accent. Elle figured Wisconsin or Minnesota were his likely places of origin. Canada, if he started throwing in 'eh' after his questions.

"Uh, hi. I'm Elle. I'm calling with a couple of follow-up questions about a group of workers you sent to a town in central Illinois last winter."

She heard some papers shuffling on the other end. "Elle, hello, can you tell me how you are connected with this crew and area? We don't give out personal information regarding our employees, unless they work directly for you or your company."

Elle paused. "Well, I work at the same place they worked at last year. There were some complaints filed, and I'm doing a follow-up to see how these complaints were handled. I'm, uh, from human resources. Trying to make sure the same events don't repeat themselves with our new staff."

More shuffling. Elle worried he didn't believe her. Why should he? If she kept muttering um, and uh, there's no way he'd tell her much. Then, "Ms. Elle, please give me your location and the place of hire."

"Millerton, Illinois, at the Marionette Mansion."

The shuffling stopped and she heard Jackson take in a quick breath through his nose. Apparently, this was already a flagged issue.

"Elle, how are you connected with the Marionette Mansion again? Human Resources?"

Elle thought for a moment. She assumed if this was a situation under current investigation, she didn't want her name attached to it. She also knew that they probably had more information about the place than she did. "Well, unofficially, yes. A few of my distant relatives own the property and I just began working there for them. We ran into some trouble with the place and a few other employees, and I'm looking back on past hires to see if there were other similar instances."

"Ok, Elle, and what is your full name?"

"Elizabeth. Elizabeth Jones. I'm from, uh, Chicago and moved here over the, um, summer."

"Ok Ms. Jones. Relax, let me see what I can do to help."

You're a terrible liar, Elle thought to herself.

She heard Jackson suck in his breath, then say, "Alrighty. Here's what I have. Millerton, 1983. Looks like we sent a total of ten employees down there for ninety days, or three months if you're bad at math like me. Five of the guys we sent were with Lawn and Exterior, three were women from our Interior Cleaning department, and two, a guy and a gal, were from Operations, meaning they'd help run the business with answering phones, taking payments, back office type stuff. Sounds like the place was short staffed at the time."

"Wow, you guys do everything, don't you?"

"Well, not really. We mostly maintain properties and clean the interior with a maid service we contract out for. But the woman that hired us seemed desperate to get anyone to help her run the business side, at least with some secretarial type stuff, so we ended up sending two of the company's interns. We said they were from Operations because technically that's what they were training for here at the main hub."

Elle nodded and said, "Ok, so you sent ten people total, and three were cleaning ladies hired from a separate company through you?"

"Correct. We use that group a lot, though, so they're used to working with us. It wasn't anything out of the ordinary."

"Alright, and did any of them file any sort of complaint after their time working at the mansion?"

Jackson paused. "Elle, did your relatives tell you anything about what happened last year?"

"No. Well, they said that the workers felt threatened by the house," she paused, "Two, they said they lost two people."

"Um, Elle, you seem a little young, and I don't want to frighten you, but that is true. We lost two people at that job site."

"Meaning they quit."

"No," Jackson lowered his voice, "Elle, they passed away. The whole thing was investigated inside and out."

"Who—which ones?" Elle's voice started to shake.

"Sadly, the interns. Both of them."

"*How*? How did they die? Didn't anyone see or hear anything?" Elle's voice echoed through the foyer and she felt her cheeks flush. This wasn't anything close to the diluted story the Valors fed to her.

"Shhh, Elle I can hear you, you don't need to yell. Let's see. We received several reports off the record. The story most told is that the interns were closing up the house for the night. The cleaning crew left already, and the one man left taking care of the grounds had just finished mowing the lawn when he heard screaming from the inside of the house. He rushed inside. He had a rifle with him. He saw what looked like the pair fighting. The woman was sitting, strangling the man, who also had his hands around his own neck. The assumption is that he was trying to pry the woman's fingers off his throat. When the guy with the gun saw this, he tried to help pull the woman's hands off, but couldn't, so he fired the rifle to try and scare her. Unfortunately, he shot her in the chest."

"Holy shit."

"Yes. Not pretty. But it doesn't end there. Once the woman fell off the guy she was strangling, the man with the rifle noticed him still trying to rip something away from his throat. The guy with the gun looked behind the struggling man on the ground, down the room a bit, and saw a taut string. The string was attached to one of the marionette dolls, and this doll seemed to be pulling the strings with a fixed menacing grin."

As gruesome as it all was, Elle stifled a laugh at Jackson's delivery of that final comment. "What the...," she managed to say with a giggle.

"Yea, I didn't say I think it's all true but--,"

"No, no, not that, it's just, wow. That's really messed up." Elle regained her composure, suppressing another laugh.

"The man with the rifle ran toward the doll pulling the string and kicked it toward the guy it was choking, giving some slack in the string. The intern loosened the noose around his neck and ran at the lawn care guy, assuming he was the culprit. The lawn guy didn't want to hurt him, I guess, but they struggled and the guy with the rifle ended up shooting the other intern too, because he thought the intern would kill him if he didn't do it first."

"This sounds like a really dark comedy sketch."

"Excuse me?"

Elle fumbled over a few words, then said, "I'm sorry, I mean, the doll strangling the guy with its strings. That just seems so bizarre. And then some other guy comes in just shooting people? What's up with that? If he didn't have the gun at all, those two would still be alive, most likely."

"How do you know?" asked Jackson. "There was still something attacking the male intern, causing them all to panic in the first place."

"Yea, I guess. It's just that the house was never violent before that winter."

Jackson flipped through some more paperwork. "It looks like we've been sending workers to that house every winter for at least five years. The lawn crew...all the same guys. No incidents prior to this one reported. They all do say the house does some weird things. Like, it is haunted and no one else seems to think that's unusual."

"Well, it isn't when things aren't attacking you," said Elle. She thought a moment, then asked, "What happened to the guy doing the lawn work? Where is he?"

"Long term care facility. They tried him for double homicide after everything panned out. But after a full investigation of the property, it was obvious things were active and the story he told was plausible. Mind you, this entire account came from him, since no one else was there. The owners of the property showed up after the second gunshot sounded. The man that pulled the trigger kept claiming he was in a trance when it all happened. They found him to be temporarily insane, and sent him to a mental health facility so nothing like this would happen again."

"But what if it wasn't insanity? What if he was just so freaked out by what happened that he panicked?"

"And shot two people? That's one hell of a panic attack. In any event, he took the plea bargain, and currently undergoes treatment for psychosis."

"What is his name? Can I find him and talk to him?" asked Elle.

"That I cannot tell you," said Jackson. "Since the incident, we aren't allowed to give out personal information regarding anyone in that case unless it is court ordered or released to the family members of the deceased. Company policy."

"Alright," Elle conceded, "Thanks for all of your help. Hopefully the incident won't repeat itself."

"For the sake of everyone that goes to that place, I hope so too."

Elle hung up and jotted a few things down in her notebook. She then went back into the library and thumbed through newspapers that weren't local. Before she only focused on articles about Millerton. She didn't consider looking at incidents in Chicago. The company was in Chicago, and if the Valors paid off the local press, that's where the story might be printed.

The papers weren't as private as Monte's. Jackson couldn't release any personal information, but the article about the event sure did. Elle was certain she found one about Millerton, even though it only referenced an Illinois small town.

Central, IL: 11/5/1983. Two people slain while working at a museum in a rural town just three hours southwest of Chicago, IL. Janice Cadwater, 23, and Marcus Wills, 22, were shot to death by armed gunman Byron Easton, 42. According to police, Easton claims the paranormal workings of the museum led to the strangling of Wills. In his confusion, he attempted to rescue the man and woman being attacked by one of the dolls in the museum, but accidentally shot both of them. Easton claims he was under extreme duress at the time and his actions were unintentional. After

being psychologically evaluated, Easton will be detained in an undisclosed medical facility for treatment.

It was one of the most ridiculous sounding articles Elle had ever read. She made a copy and stuffed it in the notebook. She then packed up her things and headed out.

She went straight to Alex's house. Elle knew Alex believed her and Kat's rendition of their traumatic night, despite popular opinion. "Ellbea forget the townies," he told her a few days after everyone else found out. "They have nothing better to focus on, so they make crap up to stay amused. Besides, they'll forget about the whole thing in like, a week or two."

Elle knew he was right, but she hated being mocked. There was only one person who hated it more than Elle, and that person was snuggled up next to Alex with her head in his lap when Elle burst through the front door.

"Geez, knock much?" said Kat, not bothering to look up.

"Elle, what up home fry?" beamed Alex, arm still resting on Kat's waist.

Elle rolled her eyes. "Alex that'll never catch on. Just stop."

"Oh, it might. You never know. I'm a pretty trendy guy."

"You're not, but it's cute that you try," smiled Kat, sitting up to give him a kiss on the cheek.

Elle didn't mind being a third wheel to them; they still included her in most of the stuff they did together, and Elle never felt unwanted. Unless of course, she showed up at an inopportune moment. If this was one of those times, Elle chose to ignore that it was. She plopped on the couch opposite from Kat and told them what she discovered at the library, including her phone conversation with Jackson. She handed Kat a copy of the news article. Kat unfolded it and she and Alex scanned over the contents.

"Wow, talk about making Easton seem like a lunatic," said Alex.

"If I hadn't seen any of that stuff first hand, though, I'd think what everyone else was thinking," said Kat.

Elle nodded and said, "Right. I guess according to Jackson there was an investigation that verified the house was active, so the story wasn't completely ignored."

With some consideration, Kat asked, "Well, why don't we find this Easton guy?"

"And say what? We don't think you're crazy and this house is cursed, tell us what you know?" said Alex.

"Well, we could rephrase some of it, but that'd be the general gist." Looking at Elle, Kat continued, "I don't suppose they told you where you could find him?"

"No. Confidential. They wouldn't release any personal information. I came across the article by digging through a lot of stuff printed in the winter of 1983. So unless psych joints keep a log of their patients for the public to see...,"

"Or if we call different places, pretending to be family wanting to visit," ventured Alex.

The girls looked at each other. Kat combed back her hair with her fingertips and murmured, "That could work."

"Damn right it could. We just need to plan what to say. Last time I lied on the fly, I stuttered and sounded like an idiot," said Elle.

"Don't beat yourself up, you usually sound like that," smirked Kat.

There were a handful of mental health institutions in the state. Alex suggested they start with the few listed in Chicago, since that's where the company originated. In his best professional tone, Alex gave the same speech over the phone with each location.

"Good afternoon, I'm Al Kingman. I am looking for a patient who may be residing with you, would you be so helpful as to tell me if a Mr. Byron Eastman lives there? No? That's a shame, I'm overdue for a visit but I heard he was moved several times since we last spoke and I can't seem to find out where. Thanks, and you as well."

Elle shook her head after the third call. "Isn't it slightly illegal for these places to give out the names of their patients?"

"Slightly? A little more than that. But it's usually a young secretary that answers and my money is that she is there part time and not up to speed on the proper formalities of the place. At least that is how the last three places seemed to go," said Alex.

Kat chewed on her lip and looked thoughtful. She thumbed through the phone book and said, "What about this place?"

Alex and Elle glanced at the title under her pink, polished nail that read, "Silverman's Advanced State of Mind" and the number to follow. The facility was in one of the cities north of Chicago. "Rockford, Illinois," read Alex. "Sounds like a nice place."

Elle shrugged. "Give it a go," and Alex punched the numbers into the phone.

After finishing up an explanation on how he needed to get in touch with his uncle to yet another young gal, Alex heard her shuffling through some papers. He mused at the lack of respect for patient privacy each front desk girl possessed.

"We have a 'Mr. B. Easton' that has been here since last year, is this who you're looking for, Mr. uh, Kingman?"

"Yes, yes that sounds right. Would you be so kind as to verify his birthdate and a brief description of his appearance?"

"Oh sure!" Alex cringed at how easily that worked. "Um, date of birth is February 3rd, 1939. He's 45. He's about this high...,"

Alex visualized a doe-eyed Barbie doll holding her hand slightly above her head.

"...and he has tan skin and brownish hair."

"That sounds like my Uncle Byron," said Alex. "Thank you so much for all of your help. Tell me, what are your visiting hours?"

The sugary voice proceeded to fill Alex in on hours, route to get to the building, and the color lipstick she chose to wear that day because it matched her mood better than the other tubes of lipstick that she owned. Since Alex had the volume cranked up on the receiver, Elle and Kat listened to the exchange in detail and rolled their eyes in unison at the last comment.

"Ok, ok, wrap it up," groaned Kat.

Alex smirked and hung up the phone. "Ladies," he said, "it looks like we need to take a road trip to Rockford. If the charming lass I just spoke with knows her directions, it should be about a four-hour drive from here."

"This is insane, isn't it?" asked Elle.

"Oh c'mon, you're just as curious as we are, Ellbea!" said Kat.

Elle agreed, but pointed out that they'd need gas, a solid story to even get them into the building, and of course, a good explanation to give their parents to account for their absences.

15

"But, Mom, Alex is a great driver, and we will leave before dark!" pleaded Kat. "Plus, Elle will be there. It isn't like we are staying overnight somewhere alone."

Kat's mom sipped her tea and glanced at her daughter who paced back and forth in front of the TV, enough to distract her from the evening news. "Kit-Kat, the last time you and Elle went off and did something, you managed to close down the town's historical landmark."

"Yea, because that was our fault," muttered Kat.

"No, that isn't what I'm saying. I just mean you two have a knack for getting yourselves into odd forms of trouble. Can't you guys sneak out and go to parties and drink crap beer like all the other teens around here?"

"Well, we could."

Her mom shook her head. "Please, don't. We've had enough excitement for the season."

"But it's just Chicago! We want to see the Shedd, the Art museum, walk around!" whined Kat.

"Love, do you know how cold it'll be just 'walking around' downtown?"

"Fine, we'll stay inside the museums and stores. It'll be so much fun, plus I've never been. And Alex has driven there so many times, so we will be safe...,"

"Enough! Kat, please. I need to think about it. I'll talk to Judy and Camille and see what they think." Diane set her tea on the coffee table and rubbed her eyes. "But right now, you're giving me a migraine."

Kat shrugged and headed to her room. If Alex and Elle could convince their moms that the trip was safe, she knew she'd be able to go too.

As Kat figured, Alex and Elle's moms were able to help Diane give Kat her consent as well. None of the mothers were all too thrilled, however, when their headstrong offspring chose a windy, sleeting January afternoon to venture north.

"Remember to pump the brakes if you start to slide," said Camille as Alex zipped his coat and threw a knit hat over his head.

"Yea, I know, Ma."

"And don't use the wiper fluid if your windshield gets icy. It'll just make it worse."

"Yes, Ma, I know!"

Camille bit her lip, looking thoughtful. "Oh, and if the handles freeze...,"

"Pour water over them?"

"No, no don't do that! Lord knows...,"

Alex laughed, "Yea, I know, Ma, I know. Don't worry, we'll be fine."

Wrapping her son in a warm hug, Camille kissed Alex's forehead. Smiling back, Alex turned and went out to pick up the girls. Their adventure was underway.

Alex honked the horn with a few, quick beeps. Kat sat next to him, wrapped in one of her many colorful, warm scarves. Her mittens gripped her traveler's mug of black tea. Alex preferred the mug of coffee that sat steaming next to him in the cup holder. Elle, still making her hot brew, stuck her head out and yelled to give her 'just one sec,' and proceeded to leisurely collect her purse and coat.

"Get out here! We need to beat the snow!" yelled Kat.

Alex shook his head. "She'll be a few minutes, whether you scream at her or not."

Elle emerged soon thereafter and the trio headed off. The drive up wasn't as bad as they anticipated. The clouds held out on unleashing their blinding fury, but kept a dreary, gray wash across the sky. It took a little over four hours. Alex pulled up to the building and parked the car. The three exchanged glances, and then Elle said, "Well, here's to hoping the same daft young lady on the phone works today so we can get in to see Byron."

Kat sipped the last of her tea. "Regardless, I have to pee, so we're going to at least do that much on this excursion."

Alex smiled. "Relax, ladies, relax. I got this. We just need them to think I'm related to Byron."

Without raising her eyes from her tea, Kat asked, "And is Byron black? Because if he isn't it'll be a tough sell."

"I could be adopted! God, Kat, you're so insensitive!"

Elle covered her mouth. She tried to remain stoic for the sake of seeing if Kat believed Alex's outburst, but it was done so well that she didn't have a chance. Alex broke into a giggle, too, and Kat rolled her eyes. "Seriously," Kat continued, "If it's obvious Alex isn't related, let's say I'm the niece. You two can be close friends of the family, and we go from there. Keep it short. The best lies are short. It's ok to say "I don't know," or just shrug. Got it?"

Alex raised his eyebrow. "I'm a little concerned you're so good at breaking down how to accurately lie."

Kat smirked, gave him a kiss on the cheek, and opened her door. She set her traveler's mug down next to his in the adjacent cup holder, stood, and straightened out her coat. Elle followed, stepping out into the Illinois icy air. The cold pierced through her every layer, ending with a final spike into her bones. She walked over to Kat. A gust of wind hit them and they both shrieked and jumped toward each other. Alex walked around the side of the car. "Wimps," he muttered. The trio turned and walked to the white, rectangular building standing before them.

Kat pushed open the green, metal door that read "ENTRANCE" in black, precise lettering. A wall of stale, warm air met them as they stepped into the main lobby. The fluorescent lighting revealed a cream and maroon tiled floor that led to the salmon pink front desk. Kat noticed that the waiting area to the right had worn out couches and chairs in similar color tones. A TV sat on an end table central to the sitting space. The low whir of a water cooler against the wall merged with the quietly playing TV set. Sounds of typing and papers being shuffled chimed in, bringing Kat's attention back to the desk in front of them. Alex stepped forward and introduced himself as "Al Kingman" again. The doe-eyed angel behind the counter beamed at the familiar name. Her light brown curls framed her dimpled cheeks, set in place by two, small bows.

"Oh, Mr. Kingman!" she squealed, "I'm excited to meet you in person. You say that Byron is your uncle?"

"Uh, well, he is by marriage. So yes, yes." Alex cleared his throat.

The girl pursed her lips and tilted her head to the side. "I-I don't recall Byron having a wife. I thought he was engaged, but that ended shortly after he came to stay with us."

Alex suppressed a smile. "No, Dear, I mean me. My wife is his niece, but she wasn't able to make it so she sent her two closest friends along with me to check in on him."

"Smooth," whispered Kat.

Elle crossed her arms over her chest and kept her focus on the young secretary. She figured if all else failed she'd stare her down until things were so uncomfortable that the dimpled damsel would just let them through out of sheer awkwardness. Her efforts were in vain, as it turned out. Alex's tale seemed valid, so the three signed in and took a seat next to the TV that currently played *The Andy Griffith Show* reruns. Moments later, a tall gentleman wearing an olive-green suit with a light blue tie entered through a side door of the waiting area. He stood with a clipboard in one arm, and motioned the three teens to follow him with the other. He pushed back his salt-and-pepper-colored hair and introduced himself to the group. "Morning, everyone. I'm Doctor Ernest Karcher. I'm the psychiatrist taking care of your...uncle?"

"Yes, my uncle," said Alex with a nod. "By marriage," he added when Dr. Karcher knitted his brow.

Dr. Karcher stared at them a few moments, not seeming convinced. He finally nodded and led them down a hallway lined with closed doors on both sides. "Alright then, well your uncle didn't seem to recognize your name, but that isn't too unusual. If it has been over a year since he has seen you, there is probably a lot he may appear to have forgotten. We have him on some medications that can affect his memory a tad. He becomes a little groggy when he takes them, you see."

Elle glanced up at the doctor. "What happens when you don't drug him up?"

With a soft chuckle, Dr. Karcher replied, "I wouldn't say, 'drugged up,' Miss, but without his court ordered medications, Mr. Easton becomes agitated. He claims it is a conspiracy that we keep him here, tries to escape with quite a bit of force-- "

"Force?" interrupted Kat.

"He has a history of getting a little aggressive with the staff."

The three paused, hoping for Dr. Karcher to further expound on the statement. He smiled when he saw their hesitance and said, "No, no that was when we were still figuring out which medications would best help him feel relaxed and functional. We don't like to give more than required, but in some cases, a combination of several medications is needed to achieve that goal. Come, Mr. Easton just woke up and is in the lounge."

They turned the corner and headed down another corridor of rooms, presumably patient rooms, figured Elle. She kept her notebook out, jotting things down as they walked. Kat kept pace about a half step behind Alex, partially from her short strides, partially because she had a few concerns regarding their safety on this endeavor. Alex appeared as he always did, confident, engaged, and at ease. Beyond the living quarters, Dr. Karcher pushed open a glass door by a metal handle and led them to a man seated near a window with a vacant gaze. The man didn't acknowledge the group's approach.

"Mr. Easton! Good morning." Dr. Karcher raised his voice and enunciated each word with precision, unlike in conversations with Elle, Kat, and Alex. "I have some family and friends here to say hi to you."

Alex stepped forward from the small group and extended his hand. "Hi, Uncle Byron. It's me, Al." Alex waited as an auburn head of hair slowly turned to face him. Alex watched the dark eyes fall on his extended hand, then raise to meet his own. Well, Alex thought Easton's eyes met his. There was such an emptiness in them that he could have been several hours into a movie marathon, awaiting the end just to say he did it. The expressionless face of Mr. Byron Easton finally cracked with minimal movement of his mouth when he stated, "I don't have a nephew named Al."

Alex did his best to appear wounded. He turned aside and whispered loud enough for Dr. Karcher to hear, "Oh god, he doesn't know me. How...?" and drew in a labored sigh.

Dr. Karcher put a hand on Alex's shoulder and murmured, "Why don't I give you guys a few moments to get reacquainted. I'll wait on the other side of the room," he indicated with a nod of his head toward a desk stacked with papers, "I have some work to complete anyways."

Alex agreed. Kat and Elle pulled up a few chairs and the three created a semi-circle around Easton. Easton's expression never changed. His eyelids seemed to stay open with maximal effort, and the rest of his body slumped in his chair. Once Dr. Karcher was out of earshot, Alex tried again. "Mr. Easton, I'm sorry I lied. You're right. You don't have a nephew named Al. My name is Alex. These are my two friends, Kat and Elle."

Elle and Kat smiled at him, but Easton remained stoic. He did nod that he understood. Alex continued, "But if you could call me Al and pretend that we are related, we would like to talk to you about some things that might have happened right before you, uh, came to live here."

"Live here," repeated Easton in a flat tone. "Yes. Live here...Al."

With this, Easton turned his body to face Alex. The transition appeared to exhaust him. "Tell me," said Alex, "how long did you work in Millerton for Mr. and Mrs. Valor?"

"Yea, don't waste time on pleasantries," muttered Kat.

Easton shifted his gaze to Kat, then back to Alex, but said nothing. Alex tried again. "Mr. Easton? Did you work for Gregory Valor last year?"

Easton's stare darkened, but his face stayed without expression. "That name ring a bell?" asked Alex.

Easton closed his eyes. The teens figured he fell asleep, and just before Alex went to nudge his arm, Easton's eyes opened again. Alex sat back and waited. When several more minutes passed without a word from Easton, Elle spoke up. "Why don't Kat and I wait over there? I see a vending machine and could use a soda."

"Soda?" hissed Kat, "We *just* had caffeine in the car!"

Elle shot her a look and Kat realized what she meant. "Course, an extra dose of it never hurt anyone."

The two picked up their coats and headed toward a small cluster of chairs furthest from where Alex and Easton sat. A vending machine hummed nearby. Dr. Karcher, still on the opposite side of the room, continued to work on his paperwork without looking up.

Once the girls left, Alex clasped his hands in his lap, but didn't say anything. He thought Easton had an idea about what he was asking, even if the man seemed like someone who threw back a few too many tequilas. *Or someone half-asleep.*

Alex wondered what on Earth they gave him to keep him this exhausted.

Without a preceding gesture, Easton broke the silence with his slow, monotonous voice. "The Valors."

Alex glanced up from his hands and sat forward, leaning on his elbows. "Yea, the couple that live in Millerton. You remember?"

"Remember." Easton drew in a breath that Alex almost thought could be a chuckle if his energy wasn't so zapped. "Yes. Ten years at their mansion. But no more. Never again."

"What happened the last night you worked there?" Alex noticed Easton started rubbing his left index finger and thumb together, as if he were rubbing a coin between the two. The rhythmic motion was slow, fluid, and continuous.

Easton's eyes refocused somewhere over Alex's shoulder. Alex turned to see what he was staring at, but the girls were still by the vending machine, and Dr. Karcher by his desk. No one else entered the room. Alex turned back to face him, even if he wasn't in Easton's line of sight, and waited.

Then, as if narrating a play, Easton spoke, "He stays in the house more this time. At night it's where he reads. He takes his evening spirits and walks the house. He's there more than before." Easton increased the pace at which he rubbed his two fingers together.

Alex cocked his head to the side. "Who?"

Without pausing, Easton continued, "More each year, he spends his time there. More each year, he paces within."

This wasn't the ramblings of a mad man, was it? thought Alex. *Had they really come all this way for a delusional man to create riddles from his distorted mind?*

"More and more, but the house embraced him, welcomed him, controlled him."

Alex tried again. "You, Mr. Easton? Were you in charge of the house and kept going inside? Getting more attached to it?"

Easton ignored Alex. "He paces, he waits. He fears its loss. Now those who threaten he threatens back. He is prepared in case someone comes. Comes to take what he owns, but knows what also owns him."

Alex sighed and buried his face in his hands. It felt pointless. The medications and whatever Easton suffered turned him into an inventive storyteller, but a nonsensical, rambling one. *He would do well in a Disney movie*, thought Alex.

"The two were inside, keeping it clean. Counting the earnings. The two were new this year. They weren't from around there. They kept making light of true darkness."

"Who?" asked Alex, "Janice and Marcus? The interns last summer?"

Easton again ignored the interjection. "The two were afraid, but had a plan. A plan that benefited them. They'd tell all. Test the mansion and if successful, make a display to their credit. But they didn't know. They didn't listen."

Alex felt a chill run down his spine. "Byron," he whispered, "What-what did you do to them?"

Easton tilted his head slightly, but kept the flat, stoic expression and robotic tone consistent. "He saw them. He heard their scheme. They were to take what wasn't theirs. Take it and see the effects and events unfold."

Easton's voice dropped to a murmur. Alex wasn't sure if it was due to the drug-induced fatigue or if he was about to reveal something he only wanted Alex to hear. "The night...that night. They spoke of it again, walking up the driveway. Loud, thoughtless...stupid. A doll, removed and cameras to catch the effects. They'd make money. But the man wanted to protect. He had to protect. The house owned him as much as he owned it. He'd been there too long."

Alex nodded. "You worked there a little over ten years. Did the house feel like it was yours?"

"Too long. Too, too long. The house had its weapon...used to protect itself."

"The rifle you had when you came inside," mumbled Alex.

"He the weapon, the weapon was part of him. But he couldn't let them finish. They'd ruin the house. Change would not be good. What exists must be protected."

Alex jumped a little when he felt a hand on his shoulder. He glanced up and saw Dr. Karcher standing next to him. "Dissociative fugue," Karcher whispered, "only speaks in third person when he recounts anything about that night. He removes himself from the situation as a method of coping."

Alex feared Dr. Karcher's presence would stop Easton, but Easton didn't seem to notice. The pieces of his third person account went on. "The house used him as the weapon. It tried on its own. Tried to scare them, tried to force them out. But he showed up."

Easton paused and slumped forward. He drew in several deep, labored breaths. His eyes stayed open, but were looking down at Alex and Dr. Karcher's feet. With a final exhalation, Easton's head snapped back up.

"BANG BANG!" he yelled.

From the vending machine area, Kat jumped back and knocked over a chair. Elle spilled the soda in her hand and swore under her breath. Alex reflexively grabbed Dr. Karcher's hand that was still resting on his shoulder.

"The rifle fired. Then again. Smoke circled the room. They wore red. The walls wore red. The man saw red."

Easton's voice no longer drawled with fatigue. Now, his speech was pressured and almost shouting. His stare bore directly into Alex's startled face. "There they were. There they lay. Tangled. Red. And the man ran, ran from all the red. The weapon stayed behind. Examined with the tangled parts. But none were saved. None survived, except the protection of the house."

Then, as fast as the energetic rant began, Easton blinked, and Alex watched the expressionless mask creep back over his face. His eyes once again stared off and his body slumped back into the chair. Easton said nothing more.

Dr. Karcher slapped Alex on the back and said, "Follow me. It's best we talk outside."

Alex stood. Kat and Elle made their way over to join them. As they headed toward the doors from which they entered, Alex heard a soft, "So long...Al."

He turned toward Easton's slouched figure and replied, "Take care, Uncle Byron."

Dr. Karcher led them to the dining area. They sat around a table in soft, swivel chairs. Dr. Karcher expressed his concerns about Easton. He told them that Easton doesn't say a lot anymore, but when he does, it comes out in fragmented, slow phrases. He said that almost anything related to Millerton would be recounted in third person to avoid Easton reliving or remembering the event with him as the one who fired the gun. Dr. Karcher told the teens that Easton would probably need to live here for the unforeseen future. His medications were strong, and required monitoring. That wasn't all regarding the medications, Dr. Karcher informed them. Since multiple deaths were involved, he had a court order to take them. The only way they could ensure this happened was to keep close watch, and therefore, Easton needed to stay in the facility.

"Besides," added Dr. Karcher, "Without the medications, it is hard to predict what he will do. But from what we have witnessed here, it isn't pleasant or safe."

Kat took a loud slurp from the remainder of her soda and the others turned to her. She smiled, smacked her lips, and said, "So, Shedd Aquarium, anyone?"

16

Alex, Kat, and Elle left Rockford. They decided since the trip only took up a few hours that they could hit one of Chicago's attractions, grab some pizza, and make their way home well before dark. The girls overruled Alex's call to see the Museum of Science and Industry and wound up at the Shedd Aquarium at Kat's insistence. As they drove home at the end of the day, they found themselves discussing Easton's shattered rendition of the double homicide.

"Please keep in mind," started Elle, "we didn't catch the entire conversation between you and your beloved Uncle."

"Yea," added Kat, "So if we missed a few details, we are either exactly on the same page, or like, a chapter off."

With a smirk, Alex answered, "Well, maybe we can all help fill in the gaps. His story wasn't just scattered. It was heavily influenced by antipsychotics. The dude was gorked out of his mind."

"Maybe we should smoke a bunch of pot and have another conversation. Get on his level," said Elle.

Kat rolled her eyes. "Yea, Miss-Ever-So-Calculated, go smoke 'the pot,' and then we'll talk."

"Seriously, focus!" said Alex. After receiving a dual death glare from the girls, he continued, "Drugged or not, the man probably laced a lot of fact into what he did tell us."

"Literally, a verbal puzzle," mused Elle.

"Yes!" exclaimed Alex, "Treat it like a puzzle. We have the objective story...ok we have the newspaper and Human Resources account of what happened. Let's string that together with what Byron said and see what we can make from it."

Kat glanced to her left at Alex driving and asked, "Tell me, did you happen to write down anything that the lunatic said at any point in that exchange?"

Alex shot her a look of pure annoyance. "No, Dearest One, I did not. I don't suppose you did, while you and Elle sat idly by, eavesdropping on the conversation?"

"She did not," interrupted Elle, "But Miss-Ever-So-Calculated happened to jot down a few points of interest."

"Oh c'mon, Ellbea, I wanted to rub it in his face that we did something worthwhile!" whined Kat.

Elle laughed. "You mean that *I* did something worthwhile. You just sat there!"

"My god, you two talk a lot." Alex felt tired, and still had the luxury of driving them back to Millerton. His patience wore thin, and he truly wished to get something out of Easton's seemingly psychotic rant.

"Actually," he heard Elle clarify, "psychotic means a state in which the mind creates scenarios where you hear and see things others cannot. You're in this altered state, either from drugs, illness--,"

He cut her explanation short. "Elle, hate to break it to you, but we don't care. Call it what you will, it wasn't normal. Now, please, what did you jot down?"

Elle sighed and pulled out a notepad. Several pages were littered with sticky notes covered in quotes. Under each sticky note were Elle's thoughts and interpretations. "I wrote, 'everything is in third person,' followed by, 'Ownership of the house,' she said, holding one of the bright yellow sticky notes.

Kat chewed her ring finger and said, "Guess that's a start. So, Karcher said third person was because of this disguised feud state?"

"Dissociative fugue," corrected Elle. "It's when someone's mind actually removes them from a situation they were in and makes them take on another identity. It's like a psychological protection and ironically a mental illness."

Kat looked at Alex. "Is that true?"

"How the hell should I know!" said Alex, "Elle's the walking encyclopedia, not me!"

"Sheesh, calm it, I was just asking," Kat replied, rolling her eyes. "Ok, so say Elle is on the right track with this 'fugue' business. We just accept that as part of the illness?"

"I'd say to keep things simple, we should accept it for now and go off of whatever else we can," said Elle.

Adjusting her shoulder buckle and slouching at an angle to face the two up front better, Elle flipped through her notes. "Right, so that leaves us with 'ownership of the house,' and 'weaponry.'

Alex raised his eyebrows and repeated, "Weaponry?"

"Yea," said Elle, "Easton kept referring to a weapon. He said that the weapon was used to protect the house."

"Ok but who used the weapon?" asked Kat.

"Presumably him," said Elle, "since he shot the interns and keeps removing himself from the incident. So he's stating that the house used him as the weapon, and as a result, he fired the rifle under the house's control?"

Alex nodded, taking it in. "You know, he never exactly said that. But, if we merge the story told by Easton's prior employer, along with the newspaper article and of course, Easton's account of the events, that is what makes the most sense."

Elle laughed. "It almost seems too obvious. Too cut and dry."

Kat sighed with annoyance. "This isn't like some episode of *The Twilight Zone*, Elle. It's based on the facts we know, the facts we gathered, the stuff we endured at the mansion, and now, Easton's own story!"

Elle paused, staring at Kat. "Wait, that's it...," she whispered.

"Hm?" asked Alex.

"What happened to us! That's it!"

Still slightly put off, Kat put her head in her hands and said, "Now what? Me almost getting killed is somehow relevant to this circus?"

"In a way," Elle paused as her mind scrambled to rationalize the thought.

"In a way, what?" coaxed Alex, not quite sure where Elle was headed with this.

"Kat, what were we talking about that day?"

"You know, of all the things I recall from that day, our boring conversations aren't part of it."

"Seriously, you don't remember?"

Kat tilted her head back to face Elle. "No, because we weren't talking about anything important. Just our usual B.S."

"You threatened to take a doll from the house and hide it in my room. Remember now?"

Kat scrunched her nose. "Really? That's your big connection?"

Pushing a strand of hair from her face, Elle continued, "I know it's a leap, but it's the only thing that sounds remotely similar to what Easton said."

"To be fair," cut in Alex, "Easton said a lot of garbled nonsense, so you can make a lot of loose connections with it."

Elle shook her head. "I know, I know, but what he said sounded like the new interns, if I'm not mistaken, wanted to basically stage a reaction from the house. Take something and see if the house would retaliate, and catch it on camera."

"The Valors have a strict 'no camera' policy," said Kat, "I doubt they'd allow staff to have film or recorders of any kind."

"Yea, hence why they would have to plan ahead," replied Elle.

Alex shifted his weight and asked, "Ok so what would be the big issue with that? So a couple of kids film some weird stuff that moves in a house."

"Still working on that," said Elle, "But what I can guess is that since the mansion is only a local attraction and not well advertised, the media these kids could generate might get the house more attention or, even sold to someone who could renovate it and make it more of a commercial attraction."

"That'd fit, actually," said Kat, "because that'd give the house a reason to want to protect itself."

"So it used Easton as its weapon?" asked Alex. "Sort of the raw end of a deal for him. And since when did this place develop mind control that caused people to absentmindedly kill anyone it feels threatened by? I'm not sure I buy that."

"Buy whatever you want, I'm just trying to connect the few scattered dots that we have." Elle leaned against the window and noticed several snowflakes twirl past the glass.

Kat curled a lock of blonde hair around her finger, noticing the snow as well. "But here's the thing, Elle, we never felt like the house had some 'mind control' or 'force' that made us do things. Sure, it tried to kill me, but we were *us* when it went down. There wasn't anyone or anything there beyond menacing dolls and whatever else that place conjured."

"I mean, The Valors were technically there," said Elle. "But that goes without saying, since they live close by."

Silence again, as the three stared at the dancing little, white, ice crystals swirling around the car as they drove.

"Unless," Elle broke the silence, causing the other two to jump a little. "What if, hear me out, Mr. Valor saw the two interns being attacked, rifle in hand, like he did when Kat and I were under siege?"

"Did he have the rifle then? I can't remember," said Kat.

"Yea, it was tucked under his jacket, but I saw it."

"He keeps it in the shed—the shed at the mansion, for that matter," Kat mused. "So instead of running right over to help us, he grabbed the gun?"

"Must've. But if this sort of thing happened before and it was pretty intense, maybe he thought he would need it."

Alex pulled off the highway and exited onto the unpaved road leading into Millerton. The last gleam of the sunset dipped below the horizon. He was developing an uneasy feeling about where Elle was going with this new notion. "Ellbea, what are you saying?"

"Nothing yet. I just...I wonder if Mr. Valor was there a lot sooner than Easton realized. Maybe he saw something else, or knows more about the incident than he lets on."

"Perhaps," said Alex. "But if he saw Easton with the gun and standing over two bodies with bullet holes, I'm pretty sure even if he was there, the story tells itself."

"Do you think he gave Easton the gun?" asked Kat.

"I really don't know," said Elle, shaking her head again. "What I can say is that the Valors did one hell of a job keeping the whole incident silent on this end of town. No one knew even the slightest detail until we went to work there. Remember Mrs. Valor hinted something happened last year but refused to go into it?"

Kat snorted. "Yea, yea, I remember she made it seem like someone walked into cobwebs and got spooked. The whole double murder thing seemed to slip her mind."

Turning into Elle's driveway, Alex put the car in park and turned to face her. "Do you want to ask Mr. Valor anything? Have a sit down with him and see if he adds anything to the story?"

Elle shook her head and shuddered. "No way, that guy gives me the creeps."

Kat wanted to agree, but part of her knew that Mr. Valor may hold more to the story than they currently knew. "What if we went together? Daytime? And made sure our parents knew where we were going? Let them in on it so that if anything dangerous does come up, they know where to...,"

"Find our corpses? Yea, that'll be a great way to kick off the new year." Elle wouldn't budge on this one.

"But Elle," pressed Kat. "What if there's more going on?"

Elle sighed and unlocked the back door. "Of course there's more going on. We know that. But do you honestly think Mr. Valor will open up to three teenagers in town, two of which almost ended up just like his former employees?"

Kat tried to cut her off, but Elle, tired and hungry, yelled over her, "And lastly, there are only a handful of outcomes that actually went down. Either Easton did kill those interns, whatever the motive. Or, and this is why I doubt Mr. Valor will tell us anything more than 'get out of my house,' the Valors were involved. Whether they were involved just a little or orchestrated it all, they aren't going to publicly share that information!"

A little surprised at Elle's vehemence, Kat kept her reply simple. "Hadn't thought of it that way."

"No, clearly not. That's the benefit of calculated thoughts, Kat, they can keep you out of potential shit storms you may not have otherwise seen coming."

"Ok, ok, guys, it's been a long day." Alex regained control of the conversation. "To ensure we are all still friends tomorrow, let's split, eat, and sleep on it. We'll see each other tomorrow and chat more later, cool?"

Elle nodded, thanked Alex for the ride, and slid out of the car. Alex pulled out of the drive and headed toward Kat's home, then his own.

The following day led to a compromised resolution. They knew they'd never get a story from the Valors, and Easton's version was scattered and drug-induced. So they put together what they knew by filling in the cracks with the story from the paper and Human Resource department. Over several weeks, Kat, Alex and Elle lost interest all together. The Marionette Mansion had closed for good, and over time, everyone in the town forgot it even existed.

Part 2

1

Millerton, IL, 2014

His shuffling gait slowed him down even more this year. He wasn't the invincible man he once was. Even back in his fifties, he felt like he could outperform most cocky punks that were half his age. His steely, dark eyes scanned the yard. Overgrown and without much care over the last two and a half decades, he limped toward the shed to see if he could find a rake to clear some of the autumn debris. The wind swirled a collection of red and brown leaves around his feet, and he heard crunching as he stepped over them. It took him notable effort to even reach the shed. Once there, he leaned against the rickety structure to catch his breath. His heartbeat rose and he felt the muscles in his chest ache at the added activity. "C'mon," he grunted, hitting his fist over his chest. "Beat, dammit!"

After a few moments, he stepped back and unlocked the shed. The large padlock wore several layers of rust. He half-expected it to crumble in his hands when he jammed in the key and twisted it. It took him a couple of tries, but eventually the worn lock clicked and he yanked it off the door. He reached for the handle and pulled the door open. Inside the shed were all the same tools he had kept there over the past years. They were glazed in rust and he could tell the shed had mildew residing in its back corners. He grimaced when his eyes fell upon the aged rifle. This too displayed some rust. It hadn't been fired in ages, but he could still smell the gunpowder and smoke. The aching pressure in his chest amplified at this recollection. "Damn!" he growled, beating his chest again.

With caution, he stepped up into the shed and reached for the rake. As he did, a searing pain shot through his left shoulder and down his arm. He yelled out and swore again, stumbling backward out of the shed and falling six inches off the elevated platform. He glared around him and tried to catch his breath. The pressure in his chest felt like an iron vice clamping him on either side with increasing grip. He coiled into a ball, clawing at his chest. Within moments, he lost consciousness.

He woke up in the hospital several hours later. His wife stood over him, frail and nervous. He saw her turn when a far-off voice said, "Mr. Gregory Valor?" and then the words, "massive heart attack." Moments later, he slipped out of consciousness to the tunes of beeping, typing, and muffled chatter.

2

Pinecrest Park, IL, 2014

Her blue eyes blazed with rage. She just lost her serve and her competitive drive started to override her enjoyment of the sport. The game wasn't fun anymore; it was plain pissing her off.

"C'mon Genie, get your head back in the game!" she heard her assistant coach, Billy, yell from the sideline.

Genie glanced his way and managed a head nod, then refocused on the volleyball court. Billy paced back and forth, praying Genie's temper wouldn't cost them the game. For the most part, Genie was one of the calmest girls he knew. But, every now and then, without much warning, her temper sparked. And when it sparked, Billy knew to give her some space. Still, he felt safer on the sideline and in a position of authority. Sort of. A blur of blonde hair and an emerald jersey whizzed by him as Genie dove for the ball heading into the bleachers. She managed to get it back in play, but another missed hit by her teammate didn't alleviate her fury.

"Time out!" called Billy, and the weary team of high school juniors and seniors dragged their way to the bench. Billy ran down a few plays with them, gave them the inspirational pep talk, and after an enthusiastic, *Go Tigers!* the team retook the court. Genie heard none of it. She was in her zone. She was ready to win, and if she didn't--

"Got it, Genie?" Billy's grip on her shoulder startled her, and she managed a, "Yea, yea, got it."

"Just make sure it goes to the front right. Beth will set Angie up for a hit, and we're golden."

"Assuming she actually hits the fucking ball," mumbled Genie.

"Watch your mouth and get back out there. Let's do this!"

Genie scanned the semi-packed gymnasium for familiar faces. She didn't see her mom, which she expected because her mom taught night classes at the University. Her dad, on the other hand, might have made an appearance if he closed up the bar early enough. Genie smirked when she caught sight of him, waving and giving her the 'kill' signal with his finger moving across his throat. *You got it, Dad,* she thought, and took her place in the middle back row.

She didn't mean to take her father's advice literally. On some subconscious level though, Genie may have known what would happen next. Of course, she told everyone it was purely accidental, and most everyone believed her since Genie was usually so even-keeled. But when the serve sailed her way, she lunged and meant to hit the ball toward Beth, ready to go, front right corner. Instead, Genie managed to punch the pass with the front of her balled-up hands. The angle created an impressive line-drive directly into Angie's stupid, smug face.

Genie's hands flew up to cover her mouth, partially smiling at the crimson flourish that sprayed everyone around Angie, and partially agape with shock. She felt sorry, but not entirely sure she regretted it. The rest of the game played out. The Tigers won by just three points in the last match. Angie went to the ER to get her nose examined, and Genie and her father headed home. In all, it was one of their better games.

***

Dr. Elle Conway, formerly Elle Carter, made her way to her office early for a Tuesday morning. She liked how the usual suburban traffic quelled considerably if she left before seven. Her office was only a ten-minute drive from her house as long as no one elected to wreck their vehicle and stop up the freeway.

Elle's phone lit up. "Alexander Kingman," flashed with a green and red circle below the name.

"Alex! Talk to me," answered Elle with a smile.

"Hey stranger, just living large here. How're you?" responded the familiar tone of her childhood friend.

"Great! Heading to the office now. I don't have patients scheduled for another half hour, but figured I'd get a head start on some paperwork I keep putting off. I'm professional like that."

Alex laughed. "You? Putting off paperwork? Rebellious. I like it. How's Calvin doing?"

Glancing at her wedding ring with a smile, Elle said, "Ah he's doing just fine. Went into the city today to get some stuff finalized. Some days he gets away with working from home, but not today. How about your family? Cassie and Justin doing alright? How's Cara?"

Cara and Alex got married a couple years after graduating high school. Elle knew of Cara from a few shared classes, but had moved north around the time Cara and Alex started dating. She did stay in close touch, and their families often met whenever Elle and Cal visited town. Millerton was about an hour and a half south of Pinecrest Park. The drive was almost a straight shot on the highway and always worth it to Elle.

"How's Kat-attack? And that oaf of a husband she acquired?"

Elle put a hand over her mouth. "Oh c'mon, Walt's not that bad! He's just a little...quirky."

"Code for someone who's weird as hell but we have to pretend to like them anyways."

"Stop it, Alex. Seriously, they're doing fine. Hopefully Kat comes with me next venture back home."

"Still teaching?"

"Yep, and she loves it. She's got creative writing this semester. Seems to be right up her alley." Elle paused, then added, "And her mini-monster, Genie, is doing great too. Doing the whole high school scene, and quite well, I might say. She's on the varsity volleyball team. Guess they're crushing it, from what Kat's told me."

"So glad to hear it," said Alex. "Speaking of school, I was hoping Cass could talk to you about med school. I know you moved to Chicago to study there and knock out your residency program. You're a great resource. Can I have her hit you up with any questions? She's working on the college applications and I can't answer everything she wants to know."

Now Elle laughed. "What, Sheriff of Millerton, protector of the peace, and enforcer of those ridiculously slow town speed limits can't answer something?"

"Hey you were going fifty in a thirty zone. Sort of forced my hand there, Dr. Lead-foot."

"Kat was driving, Officer Dimwit."

"Ah. So she was. Well, regardless, can Cassie call you after work?"

"Of course, Alex, anything you guys need. But hey, pulling into the parking lot, so I better go. Stay safe, have a good one!"

"You too, Ellbea. Much love."

Elle hung up the phone and made her way into her office.

3

Millerton, IL, 2014

Opening his eyes, Gregory Valor saw a collection of IV bags hanging to his left, a black monitor with green numbers and lines flashing across the screen, and a TV hanging in the upper corner, close to a window. Outside he could see it was still dark, but he wasn't sure what time it was. He saw his wife standing and making her way toward him. He glanced down and saw that his arm looked as if someone took a five iron to it. In the center of one of the dark bruises was an IV tube that led to one of the bags. He tried to talk, but his mouth was so dry that all he produced was a wheezy cough. "Vickie," he managed to finally say.

Victoria Valor lifted a Styrofoam cup of water to his lips. "Here, Greg, drink." Her voice was harsh and low; her lifelong smoking habit took its toll on her vocal chords and she spoke with a notable rasp. "You look like hell," she smiled.

Nodding forward to sip the water, Gregory choked initially on the cool splash of liquid. He tried again, this time taking down a few, small gulps. He sighed and turned his head from the cup when Victoria offered more. Keeping her tremor as steady as she could, she set the cup of water on the bed stand. She then sat on the side of the bed and held her husband's hand while he took in some more slow, shaky breaths. It was the first time he had been fully conscious since he entered the hospital. "You've been here almost a week," Victoria told him.

He glanced back at her and nodded. "Had this coming. A long. Time."

"No, shhh, no, you didn't, Love."

"I've waited. For this. Finally. My time."

Victoria watched the once-fierce eyes of her husband slowly fill with tears. This startled her, and she felt a lump start to swell in her throat. Shaking her head, she tried to say something comforting, but he cut her off. "Just my time, Vic, please. Let me...go. I deserved this. Long ago."

She remained silent, and Gregory continued his labored breathing. The monitor started to beep as his heart rate picked up. "You know. You must know." Squeezing his hand, she bowed her head. His trembling voice continued. "Vic. The closet. It's there. Find it."

Then, with another final exhale, Victoria Valor watched a shade of grey wash over her husband's face. The heart monitor shrieked and bells clamored. A swarm of people in scrubs and masks flew into the room. One man ushered her from the room. As she crossed the door frame, Victoria fainted, dropping to the floor.

4

Pinecrest Park, IL, 2014

"Little sister! You made it, thank god. I thought we were doomed!" RJ greeted Elle with his usual, over the top and never fading enthusiasm.

With a smirk backed by more warmth than she let on, Elle greeted RJ with a hug and a dismissive "Yet another day to kick off the week."

She made her way back to her desk and booted up the computer. Quickly glancing over her daily schedule, she estimated when she'd have time to pour some coffee and review some labs between her appointments. Because she'd been at this clinic for more than ten years, she knew the majority of her patients. RJ popped his head into her office. "How's the day lookin,' Princess?"

Elle rolled her eyes, but as the nickname was endearing, she let it slide. "Booked with a lot of the usual suspects."

It was the new patients and ones that didn't follow up too often that Elle was less at ease with. She had a knack for keeping people on point and making appointments last about twenty to twenty-five minutes, at most. But the unpredictable ones could throw off this flow partly because, well, people were unpredictable, but also because Elle had the hardest time telling people when to stop and follow up for further complaints.

Dr. Randal Joseph Barringer was in Elle's graduating class back in the days of medical school and residency, or as Elle usually put it, the worst years of her life. Most people saw their education as a launching point that "ended all too fast" and "they'd return in an instant."

RJ and Elle seemed to be the only two that recalled how hellish their program was. Not that either regretted it-they were well-prepared and highly trained for the real world. But where the program built them up intellectually, it consistently degraded their morale. RJ and Elle always felt the staff cared more about the academic process than any of their students' mental states. This seemed to change slightly once one student was hospitalized for severe anxiety. When she and several others dropped out completely, the staff shifted their focus. Numbers, after all, were key to a successful program. If most of their students found themselves hospitalized, traumatized, or in another profession, the renowned Weber-Pinkerton University would not be so highly regarded.

Elle and RJ, therefore, became quick friends. Their running joke was that the program let them in as a social experiment. Neither RJ nor Elle were nearly as personality type-A as their fellow classmates. Between wine nights prior to multiple exams and study guides that were odd combinations of cartoons and buzzwords, the two developed a mutual bond based on sarcasm, alcohol, and straight-up misery.

"You have Mary Slashborne at seven thirty," reminded RJ.

Elle paused and looked up at him. "And?"

"You don't understand, she's completely off her rocker. Consider this a warning."

"You say this about seventy-five percent of my patients, RJ. How is this one any different?"

"She isn't. Just make sure you have your coffee prior to seeing her. Or don't. Sometimes being mildly sedated works in your favor. She feeds off of any energy source in the room, so if you go in caffeinated you've lost half the battle."

"I'll keep that in mind," smiled Elle as she reached for a K-cup and an empty coffee mug.

"Oh cute, ignore me *and* rub it in my face that you are absolutely not taking my advice. It's hurtful, Ellbea."

Elle kept smiling and brushed past RJ toward the break room. He called after her, "Hey, Bacon in yet?"

Billy, their medical assistant, earned the name Bacon from RJ when Billy managed to come to work with a second degree burn on his arm from frying bacon. Elle, upon hearing the new nickname, mentioned something about Empiricism and the scientific method. The other two took the liberty of mocking her for being a nerd for the rest of the day. Needless to say, the name stuck.

"No, I'd bet he's in the break room, though. He's usually shooting espresso about now. If he could inject it, he probably would."

"Thanks. Well, catch ya after I brave my first appointment of the day." RJ waved and headed to his side of the clinic.

"Ta." Elle set down her mug next to the office Keurig, adjusted her white coat, and made her way toward the closed door of Room 4. The coffee would have to wait.

"Mary, great to see you! I'm Dr. Conway. I see you've previously met with Dr. Barringer. What can I help you with today?"

With a deep breath, Mary deoxygenated the room. Elle believed this to be true because she felt her ability to breathe diminish at that same time.

"Where can I begin? I want you to know that I am severely in need of medical attention. My labs weren't done last visit; I had a lot going on. I care for my own kid and her two little ones, you know? Plus, I just don't have the hours available that the lab offers. I also want to make note that I am dieting and exercising, but for the life of me I cannot lose weight."

Her voice was a few octaves too high for Elle's tolerance. She rattled off thoughts without taking much time to pause in between breaths. Elle became anxious just listening to her in those few moments.

"Seriously," Mary emphasized, "I eat all the right things and do all the proper workouts, but I look like this!" She gestured to her overweight middle section. "I tell you, I think my hormones are out of balance, have you heard of such a thing?"

With eyes wild and wide, she focused her gaze intently on Elle, who at this point made up her mind she not only had 'crazy eyes' but needed redirection or this appointment would go nowhere constructive.

"That's always frustrating," Elle cut in.

"I know! I wake up and eat--,"

Elle made a 'time out' hand signal. "Mary, if you want my help, please, let me talk so I can figure out what we can do for you."

Mary nodded, but not without another brief interjection on more personal bullshit Elle quickly lost the rest of her patience for.

"The thing is, Dr. Conway, oh, you need to know my background. Let me give you a quick history."

Elle felt like her eyes rolled to the back of her head. Whenever a patient uttered "let me give you a quick history," she was certain of two things: it was never quick, and she didn't need to hear the majority it. It wasn't a calloused sentiment. It was just that she and her patients had very different views on what was considered important.

"I was always an anxious child; nervous, but never with an anxiety disorder. I'm not one of *those* people." Elle felt herself clenching her teeth at that statement. Mary pressed on, "But I can't eat certain foods—never could. My little sisters could eat egg whites *and* yolks, but me? No. I had to have low fat diets, and the doctors couldn't figure out why. Well, as I got older, I kept trying to advance my diet and then got into a serious car accident." Mary was almost winded she was talking so fast. The pitch of her voice oscillated between high and shrill, depending which syllables she chose to emphasize.

Elle raised her eyebrows. The tangential nature of this story amused her, but as curious as she was to where it would go, she cared more about Mary's visit that day.

"Well, we didn't actually *hit* something, but we did slam on the brakes. I rammed forward and backward. And ever since then, well, my balance just hasn't been right."

Elle sighed. "The point is, Mary, that we need to work-up the symptoms you are talking about."

Sometime early on, Elle learned to say the right things in a way that comforted people, even when she was ready to strangle them on the spot. She found that the people who required the most coaxing and reassurance were often the ones she dreaded working with. *But,* she often told herself, *if ever an acting career presents itself, I'll be damn good at it.*

A few labs ordered and a short dose of anti-anxiety medications later, Elle was onto her next patient.

Elle passed Billy on the way back to her office. He was stroking his reddish-brown beard that he decided to grow out for some 'No Shave November' nonsense. Billy stood about five and a half feet tall. He was in shape and sported blue eyes with rust-colored hair that matched his beard.

"Just don't catch it on anything," Elle advised him.

"No worries, Chief, I need it somewhat tame for volleyball season anyways."

Elle had no idea why that would matter, but she elected not to press the issue further.

"You coming to any of our games, Doc?"

"Soon enough, I'm sure," said Elle.

She did plan to see Genie that weekend, in fact. She knew Genie was on the varsity team and playing some libero position. "El Libre," as Cal titled her. She was too short for them to stick her anywhere else, but she was damn good. Billy adjusted his dark square-framed glasses. *Such a hipster,* thought Elle.

"Coffee's in the break room, Dr. Conway. One of the drug reps for some new cholesterol lowering agent brought it along with some bagels. If you're hungry, of course."

"Thanks, Bacon. I'll pop in there after my next appointment. Shouldn't take too long."

Billy smiled and nodded. "She's ready when you are. Looks like a knee injury from playing a pick-up game of softball."

"Bacon, the woman's eighty-two years old."

"Yea, I'm guessing it happened somewhere between sliding into first base or tackling the guy she thought was stealing second."

Elle laughed and shook her head. As she went into the room, Billy grinned as he heard, "Well, well, Mrs. Louis, trying to show the Cubs what they're missing, are we?"

Billy idolized Elle's laid-back approach to medicine. Since Elle's approach was casual, Billy noticed people responded better when they felt she was on their side and could talk to her like a college roommate rather than a superior. She treated him this way as well, and he always appreciated it.

RJ suddenly pushed past him. "Oops, sorry there, Bacon. Didn't see you standing directly in my way."

Billy smiled. "Hey, I do what I can."

As Billy worked to room the next patient, RJ adjusted his bow tie. Whenever asked why he insisted on bow ties, the response was always the same: "Why the hell not?"

And they weren't just plain bow ties; they were the most ridiculous looking pieces of attire RJ could find. Elle helped on occasion by scouring stores for the most vibrant and psychedelically-patterned bow tie available. With their powers combined, RJ never went a day without a conversation piece attached to the collar of his shirt.

Today's bow tie was candy orange with tiny, bright lime wedges scattered about. He'd have a matching top hat and cane, too, if such things were widely available and more accepted to don in an internal medicine office.

By noon, each person in the clinic welcomed the hour-long lunch break. "Come with me to grab a sandwich, Ellbea," called RJ from down the hall.

Elle glanced at the clock, her list of pending tasks, and then at the door. She stood up and walked into RJ's office. "Eh, why not. I need a new setting for a few minutes. Billy, you want us to grab you anything?"

"No, thanks, brought some leftovers to reheat. Catch you two on the flip side."

"Damn hipster," muttered RJ with a smirk.

Elle giggled, and offered to drive. The two took off to Lou-Lou's Sub Hut, a local place that never disappointed a hungry customer.

They walked into the small shop. Scents of freshly baked bread and a concoction of seasonings greeted them at the door, along with a chime of each worker who looked up and in unison cheered, "Welcome to Lou-Lou's."

The 1950s décor included black and white tile floor, a black counter that ran the length of the back wall, and an old school jukebox in the far back corner. Cut-outs of Elvis and Marilyn danced alongside it, often accompanied by people taking selfies with the cardboard celebs. It was almost an exact replica of The Sock Hop back in Millerton, Elle recognized the first time she walked in. She figured it was either the same owners, or their kids that decided to take on another location and just change the name. Plus, Lou-Lou's had a focus on subs and The Sock Hop still had its limited menu. Like most sandwich places, they took orders on the right and finalized them at the far left of the counter. Elle and RJ wasted no time obtaining their usual order and grabbing a booth in the opposite corner of the jukebox. *Yep,* thought Elle once again, *just like Millerton.*

"Can't stand crowds of people. The older I get the less I tolerate it," said Elle.

"Mmhm, I hear ya. I won't go to the malls on weekends or evenings for that very reason."

"But, when do you find time to go to the mall?"

"It's called online shopping, Elle, c'mon. Join the times!"

Elle took a bite from her sandwich. "Billy still thinking about medical school?"

"Something like that. I told him to consider all of his options with the way medicine is going these days, you know, the PA or NP route?"

Elle nodded. "A Physician Assistant or Nurse Practitioner...yea, sometimes it can be a pride thing, believe it or not. Though he'd be in school only two more years, since he'll have his bachelor's by the end of this school year. Pay's great. No insurance to worry about, in most cases. Plus--,"

"Yea, I know, he can swap fields if he wants. You're right. But we will see, I guess. Medical school wasn't all that bad. We turned out ok."

"You must be forgetting medical school. That was torture."

"Wasn't all bad," RJ repeated, "We met each other, and the few others we've hung onto over the years." RJ smiled at Elle's pulled face. "Well, regardless of what he chooses, as soon as he gets in, and I'm guessing he will first time out the gate, we're going to need another assistant that can handle both of us."

Elle laughed. "So, really, we are going to need two new medical assistants."

With a sigh, RJ replied, "Yes, most likely. But we will cross that bridge when we come to it. Plus, he's got that new girl he sees quite a bit of. If we don't pay him well, he may jump ship sooner."

Elle must have looked genuinely surprised at this, because RJ said, "What, he didn't tell you? Taboo shit; dating one of the athletes on his team. I think she's eighteen already, at least that is what he claims. Little blonde doll. Looks more like a cheerleader than a volleyball player with all her shiny spunk."

"You've met her? Where?"

"Oh, she picked him up last week from work. The typical 'hi-and-bye' exchange that lasted about ten seconds...Elle what is it? You seem put off by this. My god, the kid is twenty-two! He had to meet someone somehow!"

"You catch the girl's name?"

"Jenny? Jean? Jeanie?"

"Genie—with a G?"

"What? Isn't that what I just said? Anyways, yea that seems right. Course they didn't spell it for me."

"She's seventeen. She's a junior."

"You know her? What's the age limit here? Sixteen or eighteen? Doesn't matter. Billy's a good kid. They're age difference isn't that much. Plus, he seems really happy with her. Elle?"

"Hm? Oh, sorry, yea she's a neighbor of mine. Close, actually. She's Kat and Walt's daughter. *Only* daughter."

"Oooooh, shit. I do *not* envy that boy's predicament when he meets her folks."

"Me neither. And thanks for telling me. Now I have a similar jam."

RJ smiled. "You're too serious, Elle. Enjoy the rest of the sub and let's get back to our island of misfits. Oh, by the way, I read this in the paper this morning. Aren't you from Millerton?"

RJ slid a folded newspaper clipping toward Elle. She frowned when she opened it. It was an obituary.

Gregory Valor (89) and Victoria Valor (87), passed away August 25th and 27th, respectively. They are survived by their three children, Edward (Allison) Valor, Caroline Valor, and Greg (Jennifer) Valor, along with 7 grandchildren, 3 great-grandchildren, and numerous nieces and nephews.

Born in Millerton, Illinois, both enjoyed a small-town lifestyle. They married in 1949. They were known as loving parents and grandparents and will be deeply missed. The town of Millerton will remember also their appreciation for history. They were previous owners of the historical museum, The Marionette Mansion, which remained open until 1984. The property still exists today, under ownership of their son, Edward Valor.

Visitations will be held August 31 at Dietrich & Horner Funeral Home. The funeral will be held at Our Lady of Sorrows chapel in Riverbend, Illinois. The family requests to have donations sent to local animal rescues in lieu of flowers.

With a nod, Elle sipped her iced tea. "I didn't even know they were still alive," she murmured. "Been years since I've heard either of their names."

She folded the obituary back and stuffed it into her purse, then attempted to turn her mind off, or at least mute it for the time being. Unfortunately, silencing the racing thoughts never came easy to her.

RJ seemed to have a better handle on it. Growing up in the southwest, he had learned to pick his battles and where to invest his energy. He knew if it wasn't worth getting worked up over, he could redirect his thoughts to better use. Utah was a great place to be from, he'd often tell people. No plans to move back, but hey, it served as a good base. He was accepted to medical school there and in Illinois. He chose the latter to escape the small-town atmosphere. RJ moved to his own rhythm. Getting a fresh start in a new location kept that rhythm upbeat and alive. Plus, there seemed to be more of an assortment of bow ties to choose from in the Midwest.

The day passed slower than most. RJ found himself with a generous ten-minute gap that he used to make some coffee to power through the day's final stretch. He killed the fluorescent glow of the break room to let the afternoon sunlight take over. It was the basic, quadrilateral-shaped, pastel-walled, tiled-floor break room. After sitting in only an office and a patient room for the last couple of hours, however, it was also a sanctuary. He fired up the Keurig and chose the decaf K-cup. It had some flowery name that meant less caffeinated, but still delicious coffee. Plus, no one really ever chose decaf, so there were plenty of them. RJ found that one third the amount of caffeine gave him enough stamina to finish out the day, but not enough fuel to have him up past midnight.

"I think the Keurig's trying to print," laughed Billy, as the Keurig generated its usual roaring start-up sounds.

RJ grinned. "Elle probably sent her labs to the wrong location again. She never was good with technology."

Once the Keurig's production completed, RJ took his mug from the device and leaned back against the countertop along the wall. "So, Billy, what's new in your world?"

Billy stuck another K-cup into the Keurig. "Same shit, different day, Doc. Life's consumed with studying and volleyball at this point. Just trying to finish out the year and enjoy something about it."

"Yea I remember the pressure before graduating. So pumped and terrified at the same time."

"Pretty much, yea. But Genie and I are doing alright. Having her helps distract me. I think some distraction is good, don't you?"

"Oh absolutely. Elle and I depended on distraction when we went through school. If it wasn't for her, I think I'd have gone completely insane"

"Completely?"

"Yes, Billy, completely. Implying of course, that I'm already partially insane, thank you. Up until now, however, everyone has had the decency not to mention it!"

Elle poked her head in. "RJ, don't kid yourself, we tell you every day. You just don't get the message." She winked and slipped into another patient room.

RJ and Billy laughed. Then Billy said, "But seriously, I really like Genie. I'm not going far after graduation, at least not this year. I think living at home with my dad another year and saving some cash will help. Might take some time before trying to apply for medical school, if that's even what I want."

"Ever consider other venues within the medical field?"

"Yea, that might be what I mull over during my year off. In the meantime, I'll work here if you guys don't get too sick of me."

"Well, we already are, but you're good at what you do, so we can't legally fire you just yet."

"Fuck off...I mean, sorry, Boss."

RJ was laughing too hard to continue giving Billy a hard time. Crying, almost.

"Well in that case, apology retracted and the 'fuck off' stands. Anyways. Genie. She's perfect."

RJ caught his breath and shook his head. "No one's perfect, Kid. And I know you won't believe me until you figure it out for yourself, but everyone's got something. It might take years to find, or just might not be an imperfection in your eyes, but people all have their stuff."

"I don't think Genie does, though. We've been together almost seven months. She doesn't get mad over small stuff, she doesn't argue with me, I don't think I've seen her cry, yet she juggles like, a lot of stuff, Doc."

"Like I said, you might not see it just yet, but it's there. I'm not saying study her to find her flaws, just don't be shocked when something surfaces and be ready to deal with it when it does."

"We talk a lot. I think that's what I like about this one. In the past, most of the girls I dated just wanted dinner and uh, uh, a...sleep over, ya know?"

"At your age, yea, I knew it well."

"But, but not Genie. She's not a prude, but damn I have to work for it. She wouldn't let me kiss her for about a month, just to show she wasn't in this for physical stuff. She really wanted a true relationship. I dunno, that's not too common in high schoolers, or even college chicks. Anyways, we talk a lot. Like about life stuff. I tell her stuff I don't think I'd tell anyone else."

"And she opens up to you, too?"

"Well...that's the weird thing, and I guess why I think she's perfect. She never has anything to complain about. I'm sure she could come up with stuff, but she never does."

"Is she hiding something?"

"Like what? She's seventeen and at school almost all the time. I know; I see her there at practices and games. I've never been to her house, but I've met her mom once or twice, and she's cool. I don't know much about her dad. The girls on the team are afraid of him, but I think that's just their age and tall guys sometimes intimidate kids, ya know?"

"Well, I do know I have to get back to my patients, but consider this, Big Guy, what her friends say about her parents are worth listening to. More so, what her friends say about her will clue you in a little. Don't fish for stuff, that'll get ya in trouble, and to be frank, it's dishonest. But keep your ears open for the right stuff. Or straight up ask her, but the other thing if she doesn't give ya much."

RJ finished his cup of coffee and headed back to his side of the clinic. Billy completely forgot to drink his and brought it back with him since he had some catching up to do.

5

"Hear me out," exclaimed Elle, with a forced enthusiasm Kat immediately saw through. Kat answered with an eyebrow raise and thin smile.

"What if, I created a story where it's an alternate universe. Where animals are in roles of superior beings and the people live subordinately to them? The rulers are the more intelligent animals, let's say dolphins or pigs—yes, pigs. That works literally and symbolically. Then the lower class of animals involve another domain entirely, like reptiles or maybe insects. Essentially, different kingdoms of animals would play different roles in this realm and humans would fall in the lower end of the mammalian class. Like serfs for kangaroos or something ridiculous."

At this point, Kat resituated herself on the barstool with one leg classically tucked under her and the other swinging slightly back and forth to the rhythm of the current song playing, which happened to be Billy Joel's *Uptown Girl*. She glanced at Elle, and while trying to remain supportive, she managed to cut her off with, "Say Orwell, you wouldn't have happened to get this idea from high school English? Or the Family Guy episode we watched last night, would you?"

Elle paused with pursed lips. "Maybe, but this is far more detailed and developed."

"Yes, I can tell, especially with descriptors such as 'something ridiculous' and 'like reptiles or maybe insects.' Look, Elle, I'm not trying to shut you down, but as with everything else you've attempted to creatively outline, I can tell that you don't give two shits about what you're generating.

She had a point and Elle knew it. But Elle was determined to convince Kat she could pass her creative writing course without attending a single lecture. *Admittedly*, thought Elle, *it's one of our pettier arguments*.

"What was the goal with the story anyways?" asked Kat

"Oh, the usual, either construct a screenplay or novel that people would go nuts over. Something so captivating that people couldn't get through the next decade without at least hearing about it."

"And the motives for this?"

"To pass your class and win your undying affection."

"You sell out," snapped Kat.

"Fiiiine, fine," Elle smiled, "Our society worships fame over intelligence, altruism, or success. They use movies, TV shows, and music to generate this fame. If someone isn't glamorized by the media, most people don't give a crap. Aptitude and hard work are overshadowed by popularity and materialism. It seems the majority of people will listen to those whose lives the media chooses to unveil."

"It isn't that I disagree with you, but every smug word you just said drips with pure, unadulterated bullshit."

"I'm just trying to make a difference in the world," replied Elle with her same charming grin.

With a loud groan, Kat set her head slightly harder than she intended to on the bar counter. "Oh my god, you didn't just say that."

"I want to create something that touches the hearts of others."

"Oh my god, you're not listening to me or yourself. Please, stop." Kat sat up and sipped her diet coke.

Walt owned The Study, his proudly named bar that he took over ownership of about ten years back. He picked up Elle's empty water glass and wiped the counter. "You know, Elle," his voice rang through every part of the space, "you could talk to my pal, Ben. I've known the guy for years, and he works in publishing out in California. Big names run their stories through his group and if you crank out something worth a second glance, I can put you in touch with him to see if it goes anywhere."

"Thanks, Walt, I'll consider it."

Walt, always the literalist, often missed the point of their hypothetical, worthless discussions. Elle appreciated, though, that he took her seriously enough to try and help. Walt double checked the name and number in his phone and scrawled off the information onto a napkin. "Here, try not to lose it," he grinned as he handed it to Elle.

"I say, stick with what you know: medicine, humor, and booze...Not necessarily to be mixed," smirked Kat. She slid off the stool and gathered her purse and jacket. She hugged Elle and took off to teach her night class.

There was something about the rain that endorsed a certain degree of nostalgia with each pelting drop. As she drove, Kat's mind drifted to the sunny beach in Florida several years ago. It was the summer before her daughter Genie entered high school. Walt finally felt comfortable enough running the bar to leave it to a coworker to handle for the week. A coworker so insignificant now that Kat only remembered him enough to thank him for their first vacation in quite a while.

Her favorite memories were their sunset walks along the coast down to a pier. The pier was about a mile from their condo, and every evening, Walt hunkered down with a book and a cigar. Genie would grab a soda and her mom's hand, pulling her out the door and down to the beach where they'd walk to the pier and back. Like a scene from a brochure, the two would walk side by side toward the sunset, talking about everything under it.

"Know what my favorite Beatles' song is?" Kat recalled Genie asking.

"I didn't even know you liked the Beatles," said Kat.

"Mom, seriously? They're like, a classic favorite. Guess—guess which one!"

"Uh...*Day Tripper*? *Come Together*? *Help*?"

"Swing and a miss...times three."

"C'mon, Kiddo, there are hundreds of options here."

"Fine; *Golden Slumbers* and *Carry that Weight*."

"Really? Of all the....um, ok, why those two?"

"Pretty sure you sang them to me when you ran out of lullabies. Plus, they sort of go together, so you can't really have one without the other. But, I don't know, the idea of the most beautiful rest, followed by an entourage of happiness seems like the best sleep ever. And it seems to give hope to the boy carrying the weight."

"I don't know if you've accurately dissected the meaning, but, if that's what speaks to ya, Kid, I won't tell ya otherwise."

Genie started humming the tune while the two made their way back to the condo.

The remaining details blurred in Kat's mind, but the sentiment stuck. She felt so connected to Genie on those walks. The two could share anything and it stayed a sacred part of their relationship. All of the money in the world couldn't take that from Kat. She only wished she'd done it sooner.

A crack of thunder snapped Kat back to present day. She glanced at her watch and realized just how late she was. Her car was already parked, but she'd sat there a few too many minutes. She hurried from her car and into the lecture hall. Teaching evening courses threw her off, but it did her students as well, so by the time she showed up, most of the class did too. *Professionalism is overrated*, thought Kat, as she prepared to launch into a tantalizing lecture about creative writing and the overuse of adverbs and bombastic adjectives.

She scanned the familiar auditorium that could seat more than three-hundred, but currently held about thirty to thirty-five half-interested students. The stale smell of the old building always greeted her without fail. The chairs were wooden and some falling apart. Kat once had a student (thankfully a short, skinny one) fall through the chair as the seat gave way. How Kat managed not to laugh during the ordeal she will never know, but the poor girl was embarrassed enough, and Kat didn't want to add more injury to the event. The walls were ivory and a worn, scuffed 1970s cream and tan tiled floor completed the ensemble. Kat stood at the front behind a wooden counter; large enough to conduct some type of science experiment, but small enough to maneuver around and not take up the entire front floor space. Some days, she'd just sit on top of it while she lectured.

"This is literally going to bore me to tears," Kat overheard one of her students whisper in the back row. Normally, this sort of remark would not bother Kat, but the combination of a butchered sentence and the way the girl articulated it struck a nerve.

"Perhaps, then, we should make it interesting," said Kat, eyeing the messy-bunned, Starbucks-toting diva. She was sitting with her legs crossed, leaning forward in an oversized sweater and leggings. Kat wondered if she was still hungover from yesterday. "Please, why don't you introduce yourself to the class?"

The girl broke from her slouched position, brushed a piece of fallen hair from her face, and replied, "McKenzie. I'm McKenzie Brookes."

"And, tell us, Ms. Brookes, what would you prefer to discuss? Or rather, take away from tonight's session?"

McKenzie looked perplexed. "I...um, well, like I just thought we'd do the adverbs thing like you said. I'm cool with that."

"I didn't ask what you were cool with, I asked what you wanted to learn."

McKenzie's voice started to shake as her discomfort increased. "Um...,"

"Because literally boring you to tears would be an impressive level of monotony on my part, and a waste of time for you. I wouldn't want either of us to endure that."

"Look, I'm sorry. I'm going through a lot right now, and little grammatical thingies aren't really on the top of my mind."

"I'm sure," Kat paused. She figured she'd end the girl's misery, as the mere act of calling her out quelled Kat's annoyance. "But tell me this, if you really had the chance to pick what we were going to do tonight, what would it be?"

McKenzie regained her unpolished, don't-give-a-damn demeanor and shrugged one shoulder. "Dunno. Maybe something to write about, a prompt and some time to come up with something and see who wrote it best."

Kat raised her eyebrows. It wasn't a bad suggestion and they'd done plenty of writing exercises, but not timed ones to compete with each other. She knew most of those in attendance wouldn't volunteer their work. Plus, the lecture set the class to end early.

"So, a rapid writing contest? I am ok with that. Tell you what, we get through the 'grammar thingies' and if there is time, we can come up with a prompt and see who writes the best piece under pressure. Deal?

"Whatever."

"I'll take it."

Kat went on about sentence structure and unnecessary words. Her goal was to get them to write quality over quantity. "Anyone can use a thesaurus and put three words in place of one, but at the end of the day, if the house is white and made of brick, that's how your reader will see it. The key is to add more to the picture, not just beef up the words describing it."

Kat sighed. She made that point five times in five different ways. If they still didn't get it, their grades would take the hit for all she cared.

"Alright, a rapid writing contest." She liked the title, so she kept it. "I want to put something ridiculous down, and your job is not only to make sense of it, but to create a story revolving around your logic."

THE KLACKERS BALEEZED TO THE STARS ABOVE

Kat scrawled her nonsense words on the whiteboard, the one update the building allowed in the past ten years. She capped the marker. "Go. You have thirty minutes. Define what this means by telling me a story that revolves around it."

She heard their brains scrambling as she jotted down a few thoughts of her own in case no one came up with anything worth repeating. To her surprise, McKenzie furiously scrawled away with a fixed expression. Her furrowed brow and lips set in a straight line gave Kat hope for this class just yet.

Two stories stuck out in Kat's mind, and she deemed it a tie as a result.

The first came from Kyle, the kid in the front row who everyone else knew "was going places." Kyle's story involved a group of women that met in remote areas to watch the moonrise, even when there wasn't a moonrise to be had. They were called 'klackers' because of their high heels and incessant chatter. He defined the term 'baleezed' as 'toasting happily'. Each time one of the Klackers raised a glass to whatever celestial or astronomical sight they enjoyed, it was referred to as 'baleezing.' The story went on from there.

The other finalist's paper didn't have a name. Students had the option, Kat decided, to place theirs on her desk if they were too shy to read it out loud and she could anonymously do them the honors.

The second paper discussed the term 'klackers' to mean outkasts (spelling included) because they were not as emotionally stable as the rest of society. The Klackers functioned on high anxiety, high temper, and volatile mood swings. One night, unable to contain their emotions, the group gathered in an abandoned farmhouse. They each took turns screaming their sentiments to the skies above, or, 'baleezing.' As the author described the shouts of the Klackers, Kat noted that each one suffered some sort of trauma that seemed to manifest in an ongoing emotional issue. By the end of the story, each character found that the most help they'd received in dealing with their pent-up emotion was releasing it to something else. Their energies were sent into inanimate parts of the farm house, as a way to decrease the suffering from their afflictions. In all, Kat enjoyed it. Would she prefer at least one to become a serial killer and spawn a story from there? Sure. But, this worked just as well. No one, however, would admit to writing it once Kat announced it as one of the winners. After a few minutes of attempting to elicit an author to attach to the piece, Kat shrugged and stated, "Well let's hope that your next assignment reflects this much thought," and left it at that.

6

"Pick up, pick up, pick up," Kat grumbled as she tried to reach Elle the following day.

When Elle answered, Kat jumped right in. "So, the girls' volleyball team has a tournament. End of the year stuff, and this year, Millerton's team is ranked highest, so they're hosting."

"Does Millerton still have a team?"

"Apparently. Anyways, since it's our old stomping ground, I say we chaperone."

Elle contemplated the request. At least, she thought Kat posed it as a request. For all she knew, Kat could just be giving her a heads up that she would be kidnapped and taken to Millerton in a few months. "Could be fun. You plan on staying all weekend?"

"Well, that's the thing. I know we both work Monday and this stupid tournament is over their winter break, so unless they lose, they can be there until Wednesday. We drive there Friday evening."

Elle twisted her hair with her finger and glanced at the calendar hanging on the side of her refrigerator. "I think I can swing Friday through Sunday, but after that, I'll head back."

Kat nodded, "Yea that's what I'm thinking too. Perfect, we'll travel together."

"Think Alex or Cara would step in?" asked Elle.

"Can't hurt to ask," replied Kat. "I'll give Cara a call and see."

Once she hung up with Elle, Kat called Cara and made arrangements for the tournament. Cara would be around, and she was more than happy to step in as chaperone if the tournament was extended out a few extra days. Cassie was on the junior varsity team but wanted to watch the finals since her school was in them. She was in the designated cheering squad, which she didn't mind, but come her senior year,

Cassie intended on playing varsity. Kat planned to meet Cara for dinner on Friday, assuming she and Elle rolled in before nine o'clock that night, and their weekend was set.

Billy left work around five and headed straight for the high school. Practice started at five-thirty, but most of the girls hung out between the end of school and the start of practice, so they often started early. Genie was first on his mind. *First girl I really care about, at least in this way,* he thought.

It drove him nuts.

"If only I could think about her, and then other things, and come back to her, but no, she's like a gnat that buzzes around you and never lands; a lingering, persistent, background noise I can't shut out." He realized he said this out loud, but kept going. "I don't mean it negatively, I don't, I just hate and love that I can't stop thinking about her. Oh god, what if I have OCD? Can OCD include thinking about people? I think about her until I text her or call her? Then the obsessive thought quells a bit? Shit! This is how crazy people start out. Oh, I knew it, I knew she'd drive me mad, but I thought it would be in a good way!" He was yelling at this point, not with anger, but with a little bit of unanticipated panic.

His rant was interrupted by the radio that suddenly caught his attention with an old, familiar tune. *Ah James, you've always had my back. Way to distract.* Chiming in with *Fire and Rain,* he and Mr. James Taylor sang the rest of the ride toward the school.

7

Aubrey McDowell spiked the ball across the net toward Genie, hoping for her to return the volley. Instead, she ended up smashing Genie's side of her face. "Ah karma, what a fickle bitch," Genie heard Angie say.

"What the hell?" screamed Genie.

"Oh gawd, sorry Genzie," came Aubrey's east coast accent that only made its presence when she was caught off guard, talking fast, or scared. This time it was a combination of those three.

"How'dya miss it? Ya knew I was hittin' to ya," said Aubrey.

"Yea, thought I saw something, I dunno. Sorry." Even though Genie wasn't exactly sure how she wound up being the one to apologize, she knew exactly what distracted her.

Billy walked in the side entrance of the gym, still in his navy-blue scrubs with his bag slung over his shoulder. She knew he couldn't see her yet; his sunglasses were still on and it took a solid few seconds for anyone's eyes to adjust once they went from sunlight to gymnasium lighting. Plus, she was clear on the other side from where he entered.

"Genzie, Love, c'mon we ain't got all day. Hit to me!"

Genie served the ball back to Aubrey and they volleyed it a bit until the rest of the team showed up. Most were already there, but they sat lined around gym with books and projects to avoid getting stuck with homework after practice. Not a bad time-management approach; finish homework in between practice and go home to unwind, then do it again four more times until the weekend. "God, I won't miss this," mumbled Genie. "One more year of it...just one."

After practice, Genie took her time getting her stuff together. She figured most of the girls knew she and Billy were seeing each other, but she still kept it under the radar. Dating staff was a huge no-no, even part-timers or assistants. Plus, Billy ran a lot of the practices solo because the head coach's wife just had another baby. Seemed to tie up a lot of his time these days.

The last few girls trickled out of the locker room. Genie gathered her stuff and said her casual goodbyes. She then made her way to Billy, who was sitting on the bleachers back in the gym.

"Hey you."

"Hey yourself. Good work today."

"Yea, thanks. You kicked our asses."

"Had to make up for your lousy game last Saturday."

"Hey, we won, didn't we? Take what ya can get!"

"That I do. Hungry? Thought we could grab dinner before I secretly drop you back home"

"Yea, let's hit a drive-through or something. I just had a crappy salad for lunch. I'm starving."

Billy stood up slowly, glanced around the vacant gym, and then gave her a warm hug. She returned it with a kiss on the cheek.

"Ok, ok, don't go crazy," he said, taking a step back. "We're still in the red zone. If we're caught, I'm fired and, well you're fine. Nothing will happen to you."

"Well, not entirely. I'm sure my parents would find out about us and then we'd have to be extra covert."

"Right, as opposed to the public relationship we have currently," Billy said as he smiled and brushed a strand of hair from Genie's face and gently tucked it behind her ear.

The pair drove off in Billy's car. Genie still took the bus to school if she had to, but usually bummed rides home in exchange for food purchases. Today's repayment would be Burger King, "Because we're classy that way," she told Billy.

"Hey, no argument here."

Their first date was at Subway. It ended there too, but only after a two-hour conversation, three soda refills, and a couple of cookies to-go. Billy remembered how he felt so comfortable around her. Regardless of what he said, she returned the statement with either a smile, a nod, or a giggle. He never felt judged, and as a result, he opened up to her more and more. *The age didn't match the character,* he thought.

Genie had him hooked the minute he started talking to her as a friend instead of an athlete on the team. From then on, he saw her differently. He clumsily asked her out at the end of their fine dining of sandwiches and soda. She never hesitated. "Yep," she said, "I think we've got something here." And Billy was sure that they did.

8

About the time Billy placed an order for a Whopper with bacon and a side of fries, across town, RJ was getting ready for dinner as well. Tuna Surprise, as his son liked to call it. There wasn't much of a surprise to the dish; noodles, tuna, melted cheese and bread crumbs on top. It went with anything, and tonight, anything happened to be salad and mashed potatoes.

"Spencer, come down for dinner! Stuff's gonna burn if I heat it any longer," RJ called.

Spencer pushed away from his desk in the loft and slowly made his way downstairs. He found his dad at the stove stirring the potatoes. The salad and casserole were already out.

"Set the table, would ya, Bud?"

Spencer grumbled some form of a reply and ambled over to grab some plates and silverware.

"Talk to me. How was your day?"

Without looking up, Spencer replied, "Fine, I guess."

"School go ok?"

"Yea. Just doing algebra now in math. Refresher stuff. Biology we are learning about the human gnome project."

"You mean genome project?"

Spencer stifled a laugh. "Yea, but it sounds way funnier to picture a bunch o' gnomes running a government conspiracy plan, ya know?"

RJ chuckled and finished up with the potatoes. "I suppose it does. C'mon and sit down."

Spencer finished putting everything where it needed to be and slid casually into the seat across from his dad. Big brown eyes, average height, athletic build, RJ assessed. "Son, why aren't you doing some sport this fall?"

"Seemed lame. Never been into sports."

"Ok, how is that possible? You lift weights and do your own cardio. Not that many fourteen-year-olds have such a strict regimen that they'd follow without a coach or a game to motivate them."

"Maybe. But I like to be in shape without someone telling me what to do."

RJ scratched his head. "What about track? You like running to stay in shape. Why not do it competitively. I'll bet you'd kick ass."

Spencer raised his eyebrows a little. "Of course I'd kick ass. That's not even a question."

"Ok, Mister Cocky, prove it to me."

"Nah, I'm good. I like doing my own thing."

"Spence, we talked about this. You need to get out there, make some new friends, socialize beyond me and Dr. Conway when she drops by."

"You mean Elle? She said I can call her Elle. We're homies."

"Dr. Elle, then. But, son, think about it, you can't just have two friends that include your dad and his coworker, who also seconds as my evil stepsister."

Laughing, Spencer said, "I'm telling her you said that. But really," he shrugged, "I just haven't found my group yet."

"It's freshman year, Kiddo, and only the first semester. This is how you find your group. You have to invent one. Join stuff. Get out, stay out late, do what you need to."

"Mom would have a fit if she knew you told me to do that."

"Well, until she steps in and takes over, Mom doesn't get a whole lot of say in the matter."

Spencer's mother, Noelle, was in and out of the picture. She usually took him on random weeknights for dinner or a movie. Maybe a full weekend, but this was infrequent. A botched marriage, RJ often called it, with Spencer being the only great part of it. The marriage lasted longer than it should've; hell, according to RJ it shouldn't have happened at all, looking back on things. He would never admit to regretting it, because that would also imply he regretted Spencer. They tied the knot when they were young and stretched it out until about ten years ago. RJ was thirty-five at the time, and Spencer was four. Spencer's mom took the final years of the marriage hard. She drank to cope with RJ's absences, which were a lot due to work, and a little due to her. He had no interest in her after some time. He stayed faithful, but distant. Vodka became her water and eventually, things crumbled into separation and an ugly custody battle. Spencer now lived with RJ and Noelle lived wherever the winds blew her.

"Look, Spence, track season isn't until Spring. Why don't you at least promise me you'll think it over? Do your thing now, and if you're in shape and think you can handle it, try out for the team."

"Don't think you even have to try out, but, hey, whatdya mean if I think I can handle it? Course I can! God Dad, a little faith?"

RJ grinned. "Yea, I have faith you can handle it. It's a question of if you will even try."

"Whatever, let's talk about something else."

"Fair enough. So you like any girls yet?"

"No! Geez. From one hell to another."

But RJ just laughed. Messing with Spencer amused and entertained him thoroughly. He'd been playfully tormenting the kid since he was young, and Spencer secretly enjoyed every minute of it. RJ knew it was only a matter of time until he fought back, but until that day came, RJ chose amusement.

9

Kat pushed her way through the garage door into her house with her shoulder and an exaggerated grunt. The cat, Hubris, rushed to meet her, and halfway to Kat's presence, changed his mind and sauntered over to the food dish in hopes of an early meal.

"Honey, you home?" called Kat.

"In here, Mom," said Genie. Kat followed her daughter's voice into the living room, and found her sprawled on the couch with a tattered copy of *Animal Farm*. Her taproot consisted of that plus a laptop and some loose sheets of paper covered in annotations.

"What are you working on there?"

"Well, they finally got to teaching us Orwell's masterpiece, but I feel like we could've touched on this when I first started high school."

Kat smiled, remembering Elle's attempt to create a unique story and wondered if she'd caught the Orwell reference. She guessed not.

"Well, hit me, what's the assignment?"

"The usual. Write an essay on symbolism and what everything in this book represents, blah blah blah...to be honest, I wish they'd come up with something even slightly more original. I mean, you google *Animal Farm* and the essay practically writes itself."

Kat nodded. "Yea, just plow through it, Kiddo. It'll be more challenging once you get to college, at least it does in my courses." She left Genie to make some tea and transition into evening mode.

Kat's golden hair fell past her shoulders as she undid the hair tie holding it in place. She scanned the kitchen for the kettle and some loose tea leaves. She was still petite in all aspects but personality, and she passed this trait to her daughter. She smiled when she thought about Genie's outgoing demeanor. Kat hoped her temper hadn't seeped too much into Genie's genetic makeup. "Panic, react, assess," Elle once called it.

"Mom, you're doing it again."

"Doing what?" asked Kat, suddenly aware of Genie's presence in her periphery.

"The muttering incoherent phrases under your breath thing. Is something wrong?"

"Hm? Oh, no Love. Just thinking about Dad's bar and talking with your Aunt Elle. Here, have some tea. It's all set."

Genie beamed. "Thanks," and poured herself a mug. "Know what's a fun word?" she asked absently.

Kat raised her eyebrows without looking up. "Tell me."

"Placate. But if you say it too many times, it doesn't even seem like a word anymore. Plaaay-cate. Puh-LAY-cate. Placaaaaate."

"Ok, ok, got it. You learned something new."

Genie flashed a bright grin and took a sip of her tea. Kat envied the fact that nothing seemed to put a damper on that girl's day, even an essay on symbolism.

"Mom, the team is going to go out Friday night. Just bowling and probably a disgusting but much needed fast food run afterwards. Mind if I go?"

"Uh, it'll probably be fine. Who all's going exactly? Billy?" *Billy the team manager who worked as a medical assistant during the week,* Kat thought.

Specifically, he worked at Elle's office, which is how the two crossed paths to begin with. Kat knew Billy before Billy knew Genie, and Kat knew that despite his charisma and charm, she wanted him as far away from Genie as possible. *Fortunately, due to their ages, they can't legally date. Wait, can they? Plus, he's her coach, and, and...*

"Oh for god's sake, enough with the muttering, Mom! Can I go or not?" Genie broke her mom's train of thought. "I don't know about Billy, I really don't know more than the place and time. O'Malley's up on Main and Burbank Avenue? Aubrey sent me the info, so at the very least, she and I will have a competitive game of bowling to kick off the weekend, followed by a celebratory milkshake."

"Don't forget to get fries with that. You know, to dunk in the milkshake?"

"What do you think I am, some kind of barbaric wild beast? Of course I'll be getting fries with that."

Before she could dignify Genie's statement with another quip, the door to the garage opened and they both heard Walt thudding through the side entrance. Kat could picture his distinct ritual of bending forward and untying both shoes, loosening the crossed laces up to the toe, and then gently stepping out of them, only to place them in their rightful place in the shoe cubicle beneath the jackets. A moment later, they heard his muffled steps make their way around the house, securing the locks on all the windows and closing the drapes. The final landing point was always at the head of the table in the kitchen where they both currently stood, and a nonspecific comment about the day's end.

10

"Another Thursday off to a close," boomed Walt's voice. "How was your day, Pumpkin?"

Genie met her dad's gaze. "Same ole, same ole. Just working on some homework now."

Just then, Hubris made his own form of an entrance. He gagged several prolonged moments and produced a grotesque hairball directly on the carpet. Three more feet and the cat would have made it to the kitchen tile, but there was something more magical about the carpet that he felt deserved a piece of his inner self.

"Oh dammit, dammit, *dammit*!" yelled Walt. He slammed his hand so hard on the table that the cat bolted without a second glance. Genie and Kat both straightened and remained mute.

"How the hell did neither of you catch that, huh?" he continued. "The short haired son of Satan gave you half a day to relocate him!" Genie could see the spit flying from his mouth as he fumed. "I swear to whatever's worth swearing to, if you two worked half as hard at taking care of that clawed narcissist as you did begging me to get him in the first place, we wouldn't have as much crap to clean up after." With that, he gestured toward the litter box, slightly visible from the laundry room. "Genie? What about that? Hm? Think in addition to cat vomit you could take some time to clear the products of its other end, too? Or do you have more 'quality time' you need to spend with your mother, who I assume is just as 'busy' as you." Walt used his two fingers on each hand to show the quotations.

Genie stood still, mouth opened. The light switch of moods was not uncommon, but coming up with new ways to quell the reaction long enough to escape without further ramification became more difficult as the years went on. She suppressed a smirk that tried to appear when she thought about how she would be graduating in another year, and would be moving as far away as possible. This quickly ebbed from her mind, however, as she scrambled to think of a way out. Her father's stare remained in her direction, waiting for a reply.

Fortunately, Kat was a few steps ahead of Genie. She produced a bag and some carpet spray and almost too cheerfully handed them to her daughter. "Well, here now, Kiddo, let's get this cleaned up. You know the routine."

As Genie removed the hair ball's presence, Kat redirected Walt. "Honey, why don't you tell me what you feel like eating for dinner."

"Seriously? You haven't started anything yet?"

"Now, come on. You know I have several things in the fridge that I can whip up in twenty minutes."

Walt glared at her, but then dropped his stare. "OK, ok well, do we have any chicken? I did like that Swiss cheese and cream of mushroom soup based chicken stuff you made a few weeks back." Realizing his temper once again took over the house, his tone softened a bit, even though he was still annoyed.

Finished with her task, Genie quickly threw away the contents and made herself scarce. Kat continued to run interference with Walt, sensing his temper was on the decline.

"We absolutely have the makings for that." Kat began fixing the food and Walt sifted through the mail on the table.

"Kat, what the hell is this?"

The second wall of the evening's tidal wave swelled. Kat glanced toward Walt's left hand that gripped what she could only guess involved The Study in some way or another. Although he wasn't the savviest businessman, Walt got by running the bar on his own. However, if things went even a fraction differently than he projected, his immediate response was--

"Ah shit, we didn't renew this year's liquor license! Isn't that the most primitive piece of importance in running a bar? Or keeping it open?? Kat *why* didn't you stay on top of this? Now we are going to face another fine on top of the price to renew the damn thing!"

"Walt...,"

"No! You had one job."

"Actually, I have several."

"*Enough*!" Another unnecessary hand slam on the table for emphasis. "When I say 'get this done by this time' there is usually a reason for it! It's your undermining that makes me think you undermine me; is this true? You think I don't know what I'm doing?"

Kat sighed. "No, Dear, that is never the case."

"Then tell me why on earth you let something so imperative slip through your mind?"

Kat sucked in her breath. As bold as she was, Walt was the one person who could shut down every functioning part of her brain when she needed it most. His anger was so unannounced that she never felt prepared for it, especially because it could take root anywhere. She looked back on the evening and thought of all the reasons why she missed this deadline. The main reason was that Walt read the mail and left it at the bar, with her only hearing about it in passing a few weeks back. "Babe, make sure we renew the liquor license," was his exact, nonchalant statement.

Her blood would boil reliving the dumb things he would lose his cool over, but always after, and by then she was usually too tired to rekindle the argument.

"Oh, wait a minute, Kat, my bad. This is just a warning letter. The payment is due next week. They just wrote 'overdue' in red and then listed the overdue date underneath. We are good."

With a sigh of relief, Kat turned back to making dinner. Riding the train of uncertainty during Walt's emotional rages exhausted her, even if they were short lived. He never physically harmed her or Genie. Kat knew he never would. *But regardless of their timing, the explosions of fury are so unpredictable and irrational that even monthly, or bi-monthly,* thought Kat, *is too frequent.*

Having had enough of Orwell's farm, Genie crept out the back and made her way three doors down where she relied on a much calmer setting to welcome her.

11

"Cal, I swear to you, if you spray me with that," Elle raised a hand to cover her face.

Suddenly doused in cold water, Elle stood in her kitchen, both fuming and freezing. A squeal of pure delight escaped Calvin, as he attempted to run out of dodge before his wife retaliated. The water gun was only five dollars at the grocery store and he couldn't just pick up eggs, milk, and cheese. No, that would be far too boring for Calvin T. Conway.

He could hear his wife's sailor mouth listing off every combination of offensive terms she could spew in one breath. He peered around the corner watching her furiously dry off and calling him a shithead who couldn't string together a litany of consonants if his life depended on it...whatever any of that meant.

"I can hear you laughing, Cal. It's *not* funny!"

"No, no, you're right, but can you keep insulting me? I find your creative side most engaging when I am in your direct line of ire."

Elle smirked, then scowled because she knew Cal saw. "HA! I win, I made you grin!"

Cal scooped her up and spun her around the kitchen. He almost knocked both of them out when he slipped on some of the water.

"Good save."

"I know, your head would've been the first to hit something, I am sure of it."

Before Elle could reply, she heard a soft knock at the back screen door. Genie stood with a bright smile and shining eyes.

"Genie, Sweetheart, good to see you!" Elle beamed.

"Hey Aunt Elle and Uncle Cal, mind if I take over the desk in the living room and get some work done? It's a little chaotic at my house. Mom and Dad are working out some things for the bar."

"Sure, sure, here let me clear it off for you. Cal, can you get her something to drink?" Elle moved toward the desk to declutter the space.

"No, no I'm good, thanks. I just need a quieter setting, that's all," said Genie.

"Stay as long as you'd like," said Cal. "We are about to order some pizza. You eat yet?"

Genie's smile grew. "You guys are awesome. I'll pick at whatever's left over. Thank you."

"Sure thing, Pal. Hey, does your mom know you're here?" asked Cal.

"I'm sure it'll be the first place she looks if she hasn't figured it out already."

"Good point. Ellbea, can you call in for the pizza? I'm going to make some lemonade."

Genie settled into the living room, Elle rearranged the kitchen table, and Cal made some lemonade with a questionable amount of vodka added to the mixture. "If you try some, don't tell your folks," he added, when he caught Genie studying his every move from her spot at the desk.

"Don't worry, Uncle Cal, pretty sure this essay will be hard enough to write sober."

"Well, no arguments here."

Genie set to work while Cal and Elle awaited their cholesterol-raising choice for a meal, facing one another at their kitchen table.

"Don't know how she juggles it all," remarked Cal as he sipped his drink. "I mean, she spends, what, four or five hours after school on homework, somehow manages to hold a job, gets good marks on her school work, and, correct me if I'm wrong, works at a college level since that's a thing for high schoolers to do these days?"

"Yea she's something else, and all with a smile."

As Elle said this, however, she felt a familiar twinge in her chest that often occurred when things weren't always as they seemed. Like the time one of her patients explained how her marriage was better than she could've hoped. But Elle didn't feel the joy; she could see and hear it, but as the woman spoke, Elle felt her chest drop with a faint sadness. She later learned, from a few unexplained bruises and a positive STD test months later, that her instincts were right. Elle hated being right about that stuff. But this was different. She was tired, she needed a drink and some food. Probably just acid reflux from the pasta at lunch, she told herself.

"Where'd I lose ya, Love?"

"Oh, sorry. The day was a bit longer than I could stomach. Just need some food and this drink to make things slow down a tad." Elle raised her glass to Cal with a classic head nod, and took a sip. "Did you happen to get the mail? I'm waiting for my DEA license renewal."

"I think it came yesterday. Hope you paid the fee because that thing was due, like, last week."

"Shit...no. Guess that'll come with some additional change."

Cal rubbed his temples. "Damn. Well, another point to the government for useless fines on hard-working people."

Elle stifled a laugh. Cal's anti-government, conspiracy theory attitude led them into some entertaining exchanges over the years. Once, she recalled, when the government shut down for a day or so, Cal lit a cigar, poured himself two glasses of bourbon, clinked both glasses and downed them instantly. The irony that he worked as a business salesman for a corporation did not escape Elle for an instant.

"It isn't much. Plus, they didn't suspend my prescribing abilities, thank god."

"Yes, lord knows the world needs most people sedated. Valium really should be infused into the water supply along with the fluoride."

The pizza arrived, and several hours later, Kat did as well. Her eyes gave her away. Her drained gaze met Elle's. With a half-smile, she asked if she could have her stowaway back.

"Yea, she's just finishing up her paper."

"Good, good, thanks for letting her invade. You two are the best."

"You ok there, Kat?" called Cal from the kitchen.

"Yea, great, just picking up Genie."

Elle studied her face. "Want a drink?"

Kat pushed past her without another word and beelined for the pitcher of what she assumed was only a hint of some sort of juice mixed with alcohol. Taking a sip, her suspicions were confirmed and the world seemed to pause for a few moments.

"Sit, please. I'm just heading upstairs," said Cal.

Cal knew they'd be up late talking, and wouldn't start until he left. He figured he would buy Elle a few hours of sleep by exiting as soon as possible.

Kat took to the barstool at the counter. She slung one leg under her and stayed silent.

Elle returned to her original spot at the table so she could face Kat and still munch on the pizza.

Cal kissed Elle on the forehead, gave Kat a warm side-hug and headed off. "G'night Uncle Cal," Elle heard Genie say.

"Good night, Love Bug. Crush it tomorrow, and see us soon."

"If it's all the same to you," Kat finally spoke, "I'd rather just drink. I don't have much to say."

Elle nodded, "Works for me."

The two sipped their drinks for the next hour and a half without moving from their spots. For Kat, it was by far the most therapeutic remedy she'd discovered in a long time. The session was interrupted by Genie around two o'clock in the morning, when she finally finished the essay and refused to leave without her mom's company.

"Yea, I need to be up early too," sighed Kat. She set her glass in the sink and wrapped Elle in a tight hug.

Elle kissed the top of her head and gave the usual, "Call if you need anything, any time you hear?"

"You know I will."

The two headed toward the door and Elle watched them make their short walk back home. Elle rubbed her chest again. *Damn heartburn. A Nexium capsule and some sleep will do me good,* she reassured herself.

Elle's insomnia was at an all-time high. No matter the position, something felt uncomfortable or off. *And the room, my god.*

Elle swore she was the only person on earth who could interpret darkness as brightness, and then stay awake from it. The screaming silence deafened her.

"Hun, you still awake? Kat go home?" mumbled Cal, half awake.

"Yea, they're gone. Go back to sleep, sorry I woke you up."

"He needs a lid on that temper of his."

"How'd you--Kat didn't even say--,"

"She didn't have to. Genie neither. Both were smiling, but you can just see their worn out expressions. It's in their eyes."

"I suppose that's the best way to put it. Walt's just so, hit or miss. Figuratively, of course."

"Of course."

"I talked to him earlier and there wasn't an ounce of irritation in his voice. His world was at peace and he couldn't have been happier. But how awful, to always have it in the back of your mind that at any moment, there's a fight waiting to spark without so much as kindling to ignite the flames."

Cal cleared his throat and rolled to face Elle. He kissed her nose and said, "I know, Babe, I know. I've known several people with that temperament. It's almost a maturity thing, the 'react, then analyze' bit."

"You do realize you're assessing the maturity of a grown man, right?"

"People don't always grow up, Ellbea. Most of them just get bigger."

"Nanna said that."

"And she was right. Now, this isn't something we can fix tonight. Best thing is to keep the door open to Genie and of course, Kat. But, she will barge in regardless of a door, so I'm not as concerned about her." After saying it, however, Cal realized he actually was.

Elle feigned a smile, regardless of if Cal saw it or not. They said their goodnights and Cal slipped right back to sleep. Elle continued to drift in and out until her alarm clock announced the ungodly hour of five-thirty.

12

Weeks passed, and soon the Pinecrest High Girls Volleyball team prepared to face their final tournament in Millerton.

Billy picked Genie up Saturday night. Genie was excited for making the state playoffs. She needed a few days away and having Billy with her made it even better.

"Yea, but, we have to be careful. Technically, us dating is illegal."

"I'm seventeen, chill out."

"And I'm a coach."

"Blah, blah blah. So we lay low and don't do anything dumb. Or blatant. It's not rocket science."

Billy grinned as they pulled into Burger King for a late night snack. He was still hesitant, but wanted to be with her. Whatever she could convince him with, he'd probably buy it. "Right. No stupid moves. C'mon, I'm starving."

They grabbed a booth along the wall. The restaurant was empty, but they preferred it that way. They discussed Millerton, the line-up for the game, strategy to kick ass, and of course, which shake was better, chocolate or strawberry.

"Chocolate. End of discussion," said Billy.

"No, I'm sorry, I can't accept that," replied Genie. "Plus, with strawberry, there's technically fruit."

Billy snorted, "Yea, yea, and mine is a plant-based nutrient."

Genie dipped her finger into the whipped cream topping and licked it off. "Admit it, you just don't like the color pink. That's pretty sexist, Billy."

Billy glanced down at the pastel pink t-shirt he'd been wearing all day. "Pretty sure that ain't it, Babe."

Genie shrugged, but continued the nonsensical argument for another five minutes. The conversation then reverted back to the Millerton trip. Genie knew the town fairly well. She travelled there with her mom and Aunt Elle several times a year. Plus, her cousin Cassie and Cassie's little brother Justin lived in the area. They weren't really cousins, but their families were close, so it seemed a fitting title. She was excited to get back. She loved the beach in the summer and exploring the dead, frozen woods during winter. Going with a group of friends, and of course, Billy, would make the trip hold even more potential.

Billy sipped the last of his milkshake. "There's a cursed house there, ya know."

She didn't. She knew the town well, but apparently not well enough. "Oooh, do tell. I love creepy stuff."

Billy smiled and lowered his voice, like he was about to start a scary story around the campfire. "They say, at night, the house comes to life, that the things inside move and walk."

Genie giggled. "Uh huh...so original."

Billy ignored her and continued, "The old lady and old man that own the house stalk the grounds, waiting, hunting for the living to fill their house with more ghastly beings."

"Oh c'mon, Billy, that's not even real."

"But the scariest thing," Billy maintained his low, over-dramatized voice, "is that two people died in that home...no for real...they did, I mean, but how did they die? People suspect...murderrrrr."

"Well how else would a house be haunted? Nobody haunts a house because they died miles away in a peaceful sleep of natural causes," said Genie. "But we should totally check it out. See what all the fuss is about. I'm surprised no one ever mentioned it to me. I should ask Mom--,"

"No, no, don't! *She's a chaperone*. She has to be an adult, a responsible one. If she knows we plan to go sneaking off in some abandoned house in the middle of the night, she'd flip."

"Ah, yea, good point. Fine. I won't mention it."

Genie pulled out her phone and did a quick Google search for 'hauntings in Millerton.' The title "Marionette Mansion" popped up, but she didn't get a lot of information about it. Not that she expected to. She didn't believe much in haunted houses, other than the obvious creepiness that dark, shadowy places tend to generate. *The imagination fills in the gaps*, Genie figured, but now she had a name for the place.

"Looks like the place closed down in the mid-eighties," said Genie. "It was known for its collection of antique dolls that seemingly came to life. But after people started getting hurt, huh, not a lot of detail on that, just 'increased liability.' Then the owners closed the building. I guess it sits on some vacant lot across the freeway opposite of the rest of town."

Genie noticed Billy's look of confusion. "Everything in that town is east of the freeway," she explained. "But the mansion sits just west of it where there isn't much else but woods and, apparently the Valor's home. But then, you hit the exit of the highway, then some train tracks, and a McDonald's. After that, just shops, the school, and a few neighborhoods. Oh, and a really old hospital. It's a small place. Uptown has better restaurants and stores if we wanna venture that way at some point."

Billy nodded. "Got it. Small town with spooky stuff. I think we are staying in that Uptown area. Didn't seem to be a hotel in Millerton."

Genie thought for a moment. "Yep. There's a Holiday Inn in Riverbend, or, well everyone calls it Uptown, but it's just two exits up the freeway. So a quick drive to either spot."

"Your mom can be our tour guide," added Billy. "And Dr. Conway."

Genie laughed, "Aunt Ellbea, yes! I'm so excited she's coming. She lets me get away with a lot more than Mom."

"Kind of the role of an aunt."

They finished up their shakes and made their way home. After parking in front of Genie's house for almost an hour, the two officially called it a night and parted ways.

13

"Elle, get your ass out here," yelled Kat, as she honked the horn with several long blasts.

Calvin poked his head out the front door. "You're wasting your breath. She's a good three minutes away from departure."

Kat huffed, turned off the engine, and marched into the Conway house. If they stood any chance of getting to Millerton for a late dinner, they had to leave. "Like, leave about ten minutes ago," muttered Kat, pushing past Calvin and making her way into the disarray of clothing that littered Elle's room.

Kat leaned against the dresser and folded her arms. She scanned the lavender walls adorned with several framed photographs, all black and white. To Kat's right, over the neatly made bed strewn with clothes hung a shot from Calvin and Elle's wedding with Calvin dipping Elle and leaning in for a kiss. Kat faced the wall with Elle's one-of-many Ansel Adams photographs. Elle saw Kat come in but continued throwing the final items into her neon blue duffle bag. She smiled at Kat's still, tiny stature attempting to appear as intimidating as possible.

"What're you gonna do, drag me out of here?" laughed Elle at last.

Kat rolled her eyes. "You're so prompt with everything in the world, unless it involves me. Why is that?"

"Well someone needs to show you they aren't afraid to piss you off. Consider it a courtesy."

"Screw you." With that, Kat lunged forward, zipped up Elle's duffle bag, threw it over her shoulder and said, "Let's go. Now!"

The women made their way out. Elle kissed Cal, who told them to behave, and they headed south for Millerton. *Genie should already be there*, Kat thought.

Genie and the team took a van down to Millerton just after lunch, giving them enough time for a quick practice after getting settled in the hotel. Kat helped her pack earlier that day, and hoped she'd stay out of any trouble before Kat could get there. She knew she wouldn't see much of Genie, but wanted to keep tabs on her as much as possible. Her daughter had a knack for investigating things without much forethought. "No idea where she gets it from," Elle once told Kat.

The drive to Millerton was a dreary blur of grey clouds fading into darkness with nightfall. Silhouettes of leafless trees lined the freeway once they hit the hour marker south of Pinecrest Park. The four lanes narrowed to two and the smooth pavement became worn with potholes and crumbling pavement. Less houses appeared from view and an increase of dirt fields that would produce corn in another season or two let Elle view the horizon for quite a distance. They crossed over a few frozen creeks and rivers along the way. Soon, they hit the bridge marking 'forty-five more minutes,' just after eight o'clock. Kat smiled when she saw they'd make her goal of 'be there before nine,' and sped up a little bit.

When Kat pulled off the familiar exit and onto the unpaved gravel road leading into town, Elle cracked her window. Before Kat could ask her if she was insane, Elle smiled and said, "Yep. Same pine tree smell mixed with car exhaust."

"Well, if we came during the summer you'd have a whiff of humid air and fresh cut lawn. But that'll have to wait a few months."

Elle agreed and rolled the window back up, shivering a little from the frost that stung her eyes and nose. She noticed the McDonald's still stood like a proud relic. The other relic just a few lights down was The Sock Hop. Elle noticed it looked repainted sometime within the past decade, but otherwise it appeared just like it did back in the eighties.

Hours earlier and several miles north of Kat and Elle's nostalgic exit, the Pinecrest High Girls Volleyball van filled with teenagers and their coaches pulled off the exit toward Riverbend. Most of the girls sat, staring at their phones with their earbuds blasting the latest hits. Genie, however, stared out the frosted window, watching the bare trees whizzing past her. She thought about her visit here a couple of summers ago. She came down with her parents to visit her Uncle Alex and Aunt Cara. Although they weren't truly her aunt and uncle, she called them that anyways. They lived near Aunt Cara's childhood home. Her aunt's parents were still alive and well. She spent a lot of time at their place with her cousins when they weren't at the beach. Aunt Cara and Cara's mom, Grandma Cass, as Genie was told to call her, took care of all of the kids while her uncle worked. Kat seemed to find excuses to get away from the family abode as much as possible, and Walt usually wound up planted in front of Grandma Cass's television set in the back room for the majority of their visit.

Genie felt a smile tug at the corner of her mouth as she recalled Aunt Cara and her mom arguing over dinner once. "C'mon, Cara," she could hear her mom press, "it's the last night here. Let's hit up a nice place in Uptown. Give the kitchen work a night off."

"But-but," her Aunt Cara's nervous stammer echoed in her memory, "My mom-we alwaaaays, always eat dinner with them. She'll be really offended. She's been looking forward to cooking for all of us on your last night here!" Genie pictured her aunt's famous hand wringing in her mind, as she stood her ground against the notorious fighter everyone knew Kat to be.

"Cara, for cripes sake we ate here the last three nights. Give your mother a break. It's not like she can't come with."

"N-no! You don't get it! We planned this! Plus, if we go out, she'll insist on paying for everyone. No, it just won't work."

Genie still wondered why her mom conceded. She asked her Aunt Elle this same question once and Aunt Elle told her that her mom learned long ago to pick her battles, and that it was for the better. Genie sighed and watched her breath cloud the window close to her face.

The van bumped over a speed hump, jolting Genie upright to avoid slamming her head into the window. Billy announced, "Alright, gang, we've arrived!" as they pulled up to the hotel entrance. A sleepy swarm of teens piled out, dragging their overnight bags. With the team still plugged into their electronics and deaf to the outside world, Genie took the opportunity to chat with Billy as they went through the main entrance to check in.

"So what's your room number?" she asked him, trying not to appear overly curious.

Billy shot her a look. "Um, well, you and Aubrey will be in room 211. I'll be at the end of the hall from you guys in 216. Make sure you are back in your rooms by ten-thirty tonight. There will be a security guard stationed in the hall at that time. Write ups if anyone is late or caught sneaking out."

"Yea, yea, you told us last practice. Sheesh, calm down. No one can hear--,"

"Hey," interrupted Aubrey, "I'm rooming with Genie?"

"Rock on," she added when Billy nodded in affirmation. "C'mon, Geenz, race ya there. 211, right Coach?"

Billy nodded again, and made sure to give Genie a "told-ya-so" brow raise. Genie responded by rubbing her nose with her middle finger, smirking, and heading off after Aubrey. Billy sighed, hoping no one else on the team saw the final gesture.

The first night, Billy once again reminded the team of their curfew, but beyond that, they had free reign to do anything they wanted, in town, and in pairs. Genie met with her mom and aunts for a late dinner. Billy stayed close to the hotel with Paul, the head coach. Paul drove separate from the team and met Billy at one of the pubs downtown for a drink and some greasy bar food. He planned to help with practice the following morning, catch the majority of the first game, and then head back north, leaving Billy in charge for the remaining trip.

Genie's date with her mom and aunts extended into a group event. Billy even made a later appearance once he finished eating. Elle took it upon herself to sit between Kat and Cara; the two usually got along fine, but sometimes Cara's quirks crept under Kat's skin. Elle knew if Kat had a drink in her, the ability to filter or stay quiet would lessen significantly. As the majority of girls that joined the family fun for dinner left to head back for the hotel via the hotel's complimentary shuttle, Genie, Billy, and Audrey hung back. Cassie convinced her mom to stay a little longer, and Elle and Kat thanked her for the extra time to order another drink. Cassie was the designated driver. Elle figured it best for Cara to take advantage of her daughter's offer and ordered her another glass of moscato. Kat went with a glass of chardonnay and Elle stuck with sipping some bourbon. The remaining kids continued their overindulgence of unlimited soda refills.

As the women engaged in a slightly tipsy conversation about the latest local drama, Cassie glanced at Genie and asked, "So, since you're here, think you'll visit the Doll House?"

The question caught Genie and Aubrey's attention. Aubrey propped herself forward on her elbows and inquired further about this doll house. "Is it some toy that you townies have?"

Cassie shook her head. Being the youngest and wanting to fit in, she excitedly pressed on. "So, get this. Up until the 1980s, there was this museum of dolls and other antiques. The mansion was built before this place was even a town, and it's filled with things from as early as the 1800s." Cassie dropped her voice and everyone listening crowded closer to hear her. "It is said that the place was known to be haunted. Not because of a rumor, but because the things in the house actually moved around without any help. My dad says there's a dark force there that keeps things alive, but not the way you and I are living. Anyways, the place used to let people come in and experience all the movements of the dolls, noises and sounds, all that crazy stuff. Like, you could walk through the entire downstairs and explore."

Wide eyed, Genie whispered, "So what happened?"

She was curious of course, but also still confused as to how she knew everything about this town except this mystery mansion. Why hadn't Mom and Aunt Elle mentioned it? They had to know about it. They lived here at that time. She recalled talking to Billy about it a few weeks prior, so was this the same house?

Cassie continued in a hushed tone. "Apparently, for whatever reason, someone was murdered...by the dolls in the house!"

The group gasped, then giggled at their reactions. They leaned back in to hear what else Cassie was saying. "The old couple that lived next door died last year. Their house is thought to be haunted too, because they lived close by. Their kids cleared out anything that could spoil, but then left the furniture and stuff covered up. They kept the water on, according to my dad, but everything else is shut down. It's been abandoned ever since. No one but their kids goes to that area. Ever."

Now the group was laughing, but not at Cassie. "God, and we thought we'd have nothing to do this trip," said Aubrey.

Genie nodded. "Thanks for the heads up, Cass, we are definitely checking this out."

Cassie's eyes widened. "What? No, seriously guys, this place is dangerous!"

Her tone alerted the chaperones, and the teens all dropped their heads and sipped their sodas until the gossip picked back up.

Whispering, she said, "You guys can't go there! You really can get hurt."

"Cass, listen, we appreciate the concern, but it's a story, nothing more. Ghost stories are for kids. We just wanna check out the place from the windows. No breaking and entering. It'll make for a great story to tell when we get back home," said Genie.

The two went back and forth a bit longer, then the conversation changed course. The girls started talking about shopping and other ways to fill their time in Millerton. Billy got up to leave. Elle smirked and said, "Later, Bacon."

"Bacon?" Genie leaned forward and grinned.

Billy scowled as Elle smirked at him. "Blame the office. And while we're at it, keep it at the office."

The volleyball tournament took up most of the following day. By that evening, Billy told the girls if they stayed in pairs that they could explore Uptown, as long as at least one of them had a phone. It may have been a bit on the trusting side, but Billy figured it would give him at least the chance to hang out with Genie. Supervised, yes, but still worth it. They had a long day and managed to make it through to play in a match the next day. Elle and Kat took to this small-town expedition as well. They knew the stores and town layout and could keep tabs on whomever was within their line of sight. So, technically they were doing their job. Cara opted to hang out at home. She said her mom was a little bummed about missing out on the night prior, so they were going to watch a movie and bake.

What Kat and Elle didn't take into consideration was Genie's familiarity with the area and her alternate motives to explore a little further south. When her mom and aunt were out of sight, Genie grabbed Aubrey's arm and whispered, "This way!"

She led her to a small wooden building central to the shopping center. The building looked like an old fashioned train station and parked out front was a minibus painted bright red with gold lettering on the side that read, "Riverbend Trolley." Pulling Aubrey like a mother does a reluctant child, Genie led her to the white ticket counter on the outside of the small building. She placed a ten-dollar bill down and said, "Two round trip for Millerton," she paused when she saw Billy walking up behind them, about to inquire what they were doing. "Make it three," she said, pulling a crumpled five out of her front pocket and adding it to the pile.

"Genie, Aubrey--," Billy started.

Before he got anything else out, Genie grabbed the tickets and led Aubrey toward the trolley. As Aubrey walked up the steps, Genie turned and grabbed Billy, pulling him on as well. The three sat in the back and Billy tried again. "Where are we headin,' girls?"

"Millerton," replied Genie.

14

Billy knitted his brow and ran his hand through his beard. "Uh, ok well, I said stay within a few blocks of the shops and the hotel. Pretty sure that was the only rule I left you guys with."

"Well, that and staying in pairs," murmured Aubrey, still trying to piece together their adventure as well.

Meanwhile, Genie produced her phone and started texting. It buzzed a few times back, and she locked it with a satisfied smirk. "Relax, you two. It'll be fine. We're not going far and we'll be back before it gets too dark or too late. Plus, Mom and Aunt Elle are still in Uptown."

Several miles from the trolley's location, in her room surrounded by thick pink and white stripes, Cassie sat on her hand-made quilted bedspread, re-reading her text messages and thinking, *What did I just agree to?*

Her hands shook a bit. But Genie was one of the 'cool kids,' and stuff like this never happened down here, anyways. Heck, she was lucky enough to be able to get out of here once she finally graduated high school, she reminded herself. *Just two more years.*

She was in Genie's grade, but actually a year younger. Her mom was always proud of her, pushing her every inch of the way. Her dad always kept both Cassie and her mother grounded and focusing on the bigger picture. He was the reason Cassie could play sports and have time on the weekends to be a typical sixteen-year old kid.

"Mom? Going out for a bit. Can I take your van?" Cara's old minivan was a classic icon in town. White, beat up, and outdated, everyone in town recognized it whenever it pulled into a parking lot or driveway.

Elbows deep in dough, Cara called back that it was fine and to be home by nine. The sun was starting to set already, but that was standard for Illinois winters. Cassie thanked her, grabbed the keys and headed toward the train tracks just off the freeway. A similar, old fashion ticket stand that mirrored the one in Riverbend stood several yards from the actual train tracks with a small parking lot next to it. Cassie parked the van and waited.

The red Riverbend trolley exited the highway and turned toward town. As it pulled into the small parking lot where Cara's minivan sat, Cassie unlocked the doors and waved at the familiar faces peering at her. Genie, Billy, and Aubrey stepped out and made their way toward Cassie. The trolley driver yelled, "Last shuttle time is eight forty-five, don't miss it!"

Billy nodded and gave a 'thank you' wave.

"Hear that, Geenz? We got two hours. So whatever ya got planned, it's gotta be done by then," said Aubrey.

Genie smiled and said, "Yea, yea, got it. We'll make it back, fear not," and pulled open the side door to the mini-van. "Thanks for the lift, Cass."

Cassie grinned. "No prob. It's just across the tracks, we'll be there in seconds," and pulled out of the lot.

Moments later they bumped over the train tracks past the freeway. Billy wasn't sure at first what they were heading toward. There were a few acres of land strewn with bare trees, overgrown brush, and splotches of dead grass. The already-worn road turned into a gravel drive that diverged after several yards. One led to a smaller, more updated home, but it still looked like no one had been there in some time, years perhaps. But that wasn't the drive that Cassie turned onto. Instead, she veered left and took a crumbling path toward a large mansion. A small, white cloud of dust kicked up behind the van as they coasted along. He saw a tired looking structure with faded white paint over the splintered slats. The shutters framed most of the windows, but some seemed to have been removed or knocked off over time. These were dark blue on the upper level and light blue on the bottom floors. Billy noticed the paint was chipped on them too and the wood, decaying. As they emerged from the van and made their way up the dirt path, Billy wondered if the tattered front porch would hold up with them walking over it.

On the porch, Cassie paused before nearing the front door. She took a few steps to the side, surveying the dusty area. Billy watched her shiver as a chilling breeze swept through, tousling some dead leaves and twigs across their feet. He noticed with each step any of them took, a groan or creak followed. They all jumped back when a second gust of wind caused an eerie howl to echo through the broken windows and slats of the mansion.

"This is crazy," Genie said, breaking their silence. "What is everyone so afraid of? The house is ancient. We're just being paranoid because we watch too much TV."

Cassie shook her head. "This place shut down like, thirty years ago because the town dubbed it dangerous."

Genie rolled her eyes. Cassie treaded on her nerves and if they were going to investigate this house, they'd have to do it before it was too dark to see. "Did anyone bring a flashlight?"

Aubrey and Billy exchanged glances. "Geenz, we didn't even know where you were taking us. Ya think we have a light on us?"

"I meant Cassie."

"Uh, Mom probably has one in the van."

"Then go. Get. It."

All patience lost, Billy thought, *But at least she stays cool, even when she's pissed.*

Once Cassie produced a flashlight from the van, they again stood on the porch, musing over the best way to break into the house. Genie grabbed the flashlight from Cassie and started toward a partially shattered window to the right of the door. She climbed on the fence that surrounded the porch, and steadied herself as the beam wobbled under her weight. Once she found her balance, Genie raised the flashlight above her head, intending to smash the remaining glass from the window. Before she had the chance to lower her arm, the main door swung open with a loud moan. Genie, arm still raised, turned back to the gaping group still stationed behind her.

"Well?" she asked, "We going in or not?"

"Not," replied Aubrey without hesitation and turned to leave.

"Oh c'mon, it'll be fine," said Genie, jumping from the loose beam, blocking Aubrey's path.

Billy had felt uneasy at first, but now his stomach churned to the point of nausea. A prickle from the hair on his arms standing straight up wasn't coming from the winter air. There was a cold chill on the back of his neck, so present it caused him to whirl around, as if someone placed an icy hand there. He wondered if the others felt similar things, but decided it best not to ask just yet. Genie grabbed Aubrey's shoulders and spun her toward the open door. She shuffled her forward and through the entrance.

Genie was already inside by the time Billy collected himself. Before he had the chance to protest, a glimpse of her blonde hair vanished into the dark foyer. Cassie stared at Billy, waiting for him to follow. Billy sighed and entered the mansion. Crossing her arms over her chest, Cassie followed him.

Billy and Genie stepped through the cluttered entry. *Whoever was there last definitely left in a hurry*, thought Billy.

"Cass, what's the deal here?" Genie's voice echoed as she brushed the dust off of a counter that stood just before another doorway. "There are brochures, a sign in sheet...was this place that big of an attraction?"

"Guess so," replied Cassie, catching up to Aubrey and linking arms with her. "I think, like, stuff moves around and it is not done by anyone. It's known to be possessed. So, like a real-life Halloween house where you're guaranteed to see something crazy happen."

"That sounds horrifying, can we please leave?" cut in Aubrey.

Genie shook her head, shuffled a stack of faded papers on the counter, and said, "Nah, we're gonna investigate a bit."

Aubrey sighed. "I'm not going past the counter."

Cassie straightened up and added, "And I'm not letting go of her, so guess I'm staying here too."

"Great, you two chickens can stand watch. Technically, we are trespassing, so if shit hits the fan, give us a heads up, ok?" Genie marched past the counter and turned into another room cluttered with draped furnishings.

She squinted to see better in the room's dimness. Billy stumbled after her. He tried to avoid knocking over anything from the shelves. He noticed it looked like a formal living area of some kind, but his eyes weren't able to make out everything just yet. He focused on Genie, who made it through the first room and was about to enter the next one. "Geenz, slow up, dammit. It's not an obstacle course. We can at least pretend to be concerned for our safety."

Still moving at a fast clip, Genie called back, "It's getting dark and I want to see the whole place. Besides, for something that's supposed to be alive, this is one static house."

Before the word "house" left her mouth, they heard a tap. Then another. *Rapt-rapt.*

Genie stopped and spun around to face Billy. Billy, a little winded, caught her by the arm and whispered, "Probably just Aubrey and Cassie. C'mon, let's see what all the hype is about this place."

Genie tried to resume her march, but Billy kept a firm hold of her forearm. They walked through the second room. Billy thought it was similar to the first, but a bit more casual. With his eyes now able to make out its constructs, he again noted covered furniture, a coffee table, and an end table. Everything had a white sheet over it, but he could tell what was what, for the most part. They passed a rocking chair just before exiting through a pair of saloon-style doors.

This led them into a long hallway. Genie picked up the pace. They reached the end of the hall where she took a quick turn into a room. It had a single doll on a shelf. She ignored this and went through another doorway that led into a sunroom. At least Billy assumed it was a sunroom since it had a large picture window along the outer wall. He jumped initially when he caught a glimpse of himself. The walls were lined with mirrors. In front of the mirrored walls stood shelves and hutches. He glanced side to side and realized the shelves displayed an array of dolls from all different eras. Some looked just like the ones his mom kept somewhere in their attic from her childhood. Others looked like they would disintegrate if Billy so much as sneezed in their direction. As if they responded to his realization, on cue, each doll turned to face Billy and Genie. Billy saw several of the dolls with moveable eyelids blink in their direction. As they stepped forward, the dolls watched them. They maintained eye contact until Billy and Genie exited.

Billy's heart thundered in his chest. He wondered if Genie felt the same. He expected at least one, if not both of them, to scream when the dolls turned toward them, but it was such a shock, neither did. "She can't kill a spider in her bathtub, but this, this is something she handles with serenity," mumbled Billy under his breath, shaking his head.

Rapt. Rapt.

Billy squeezed Genie's arm without realizing it.

Rapt. Rapt.

Genie looked thoughtful. "It sounds like it's coming from that closet," and pointed to the end of the hallway.

Billy realized that they were back in the same hallway. *The hallway must wrap around the entire downstairs*, mused Billy.

Several other rooms stemmed off the main hall from what he could see, and he guessed those rooms were connected to a few other rooms further back that would merge back to the hall again. *Eventually leading back to the entrance. It makes sense*, he thought, *that if this was a museum, people would need a path going in and out. But it would be easier if we could see a thing or two.*

Genie used Billy's grip on her arm as a guide and led him toward the closet. At least, Billy assumed it was a closet. Most of the rooms didn't have doors, and the ones that did were propped open with a chair or some type of antique item. The closet, he settled on calling it, had a much smaller door than the ones attached to the rooms. How Genie even noticed it, he'd never know.

Rapt. Rapt.

The two stood and faced the splintered, wood door. Genie reached out and pulled the rusty knob. A low groan escaped from the hinges as the decayed piece of oak swung outward. Billy coughed at the plume of dust that followed, releasing Genie's arm. He studied the small enclosure. It didn't appear to be much of anything. He saw a broom and dustpan leaning up against the back wall. A bucket filled with some old spray bottles and a few aged rolls of paper towels sat in front. Genie kicked those items to the side and stood within the shallow, vacant room. Billy watched her reach to her left, feeling around. "Turn on the flashlight, Geenz," he offered.

She rolled her eyes, flicked it on, and continued to fumble through the illuminated area. "Not much here. Except...," her voice became muffled.

Billy saw her silhouette slip to the left, then a couple of thuds, as if she were dragging something. "What'd ya find? Does the closet go that far over?"

He answered his own question as he leaned over to see a small additional compartment and Genie moving a ladder back in his direction. "Ouch!" she yelled. Then, "Damn splinter," as she shook her hand.

Genie positioned the ladder against the back wall, and once it seemed steady enough, began to climb it. Billy took the light from her and aimed it at the top of the ladder. There, he saw another opening. It wasn't quite an attic; it looked as if someone could've built a stairway there, but didn't. "Oh, I get it! It's the upper level!" exclaimed Billy.

"You catch on fast."

"Well, you weren't exactly cluing me in."

"Didn't it strike you as odd that there were two stories to this house, and no elaborate staircase, or really, any obvious way to get upstairs?"

"Honestly, it didn't even cross my mind."

Now at the top, Genie put two hands on the second floor surface, slid herself on it in a seated position, legs dangling. She leaned forward and said, "Well I did. What on Earth would be up here that someone would want so inaccessible?"

Billy started his ascent. "Not sure. And not sure I want to know." But he climbed toward her anyways.

Once Billy reached the opening, he saw that it did lead into another room. It wasn't designed as a display room, like most of the ones downstairs, but instead, like a lounge area or a loft. Billy walked toward a covered couch and sat down. He saw several other pieces of covered furniture all facing the center of the room. Genie took a few steps toward a closed door opposite from where they entered, when her foot smashed through a floorboard. She shrieked and tumbled forward. Billy rushed to her side. He pulled her up as she dislodged her foot from the splintered wood. She was shaking.

"Billy," she whispered.

"Hm? What, you ok? Think it's broken?"

"No...but...something has my...my...ankle."

Startled, Billy glanced down at the busted up flooring and around Genie's victim foot. He couldn't see anything.

"Nothing? It feels like something cold is gripping it."

"Probably just pain. It's drafty anyways, and your jeans must've rolled up enough to feel the cold."

Genie didn't look convinced, but they were out of daylight and needed to get on with their exploration. "Just be careful where you step," said Billy as he pulled her away from the debris.

The pair attempted to cross the room several more times, but the floorboards failed to hold their weight, or at least creaked enough to send them reeling back onto sturdier ground.

"It's almost like something doesn't want us past that door," said Genie, cocking her head to the side.

"Well, then by all accounts, we really ought to try harder to get over there," said Billy.

Using the furniture like the game "Don't Touch the Lava," they climbed over two of the chairs, a couch, and finally, crouched on a small, wooden table close enough for Genie to reach the door handle. The two peered into the dark room. Neither wanted to step onto the floor, but finally, Genie put her foot down. She cautiously shifted her weight with the second step, then the third, until she stood in the middle of the next room. Billy called to her. "Geenz, I'm good where I'm at. Shine the light around and just give me a play-by-play."

She sighed and called him a wuss, but beamed the light over the area. It was a bedroom, one that no one seemed to have entered for quite some time, she relayed to Billy. There was a strong smell of cedar that Genie followed to the foot of the bed. No coverings were placed over the bed, and it stood decorated in aged, cream-colored linens with a lace bed skirt. Iron head and footboards enclosed the bed, and at the end stood a cedar chest. "There's a big ole' bed in here," she called to Billy. "And, um, a dresser, a night stand...there is a candle on the nightstand next to the bed that hasn't been lit. There's this ancient looking silver lamp on the dresser, an oil lamp maybe? And I think there's a cradle in the corner of the room, but to be honest, it's giving me the creeps and I don't want to check it out."

Billy laughed. "Finally, something scares you and it's a baby's bed. Swear to god, Genie."

"Ok shut up. I'm opening the chest."

"Wait, what?"

"This cedar chest," he heard her voice lower and the creak of a hinge. "Weird. There's just a few dolls in here."

"They moving?"

"Not presently."

Billy thought for a moment. "Hey, since they're likely ones that won't be missed, we should totally take them back with us; freak people out."

"You should be an example, Billy! Think of it, a coach, instigating such madness!" Genie laughed and scooped up the dolls from the chest.

She placed them into her oversized canvas purse that she always carried. She took one for Cassie, one to scare Aubrey with, and one because she wanted it. The dolls for Cassie and Aubrey could've been sisters. They looked so real. Both had dark skin, black hair, and black eyes. They wore vibrant dresses with wraps around their shoulders and heads. "Probably worth a fortune," mumbled Genie.

The one Genie took for herself was less flashy. This doll also had dark eyes, but the skin was milky white and the clothes were hand sewn. It wore a plaid dress, stockings, and shoes. The golden hair was pulled back, and Genie brushed a wisp of hair that came loose away from the doll's delicate face. Their size and life-like appearances reminded Genie of her American Girl Dolls she grew up owning. But these were definitely not from her generation.

Billy heard the chest close and Genie making her way toward the door. "Alright," she told him, "let's scare the crap outta some people."

Following that statement came the familiar crash of the floorboards splintering, but much more so than the previous crunches and snaps.

Billy heard whimpering and he jumped from the table into the room, following the cries.

He saw the glow of the flashlight, but it came from about twelve feet below them. He noticed Genie's hand holding onto the jagged edge of the spliced board, blood smeared over it. "Billy, my hand, take...my...,"

Billy flattened out onto his stomach, sliding toward Genie. The air seemed cooler to him than it did moments earlier. "Geenz, Honey, grab my hand, c'mon."

She flailed her free arm toward him, but missed both his hand and the edge of the board. She screamed again. "Oh god, oh god, I'm slipping!"

Billy struggled to catch the free hand that was waving in the air. When this failed, he directed his attention toward the other one, desperately clinging to the serrated, wooden ledge. With both of his hands, he seized her sticky, blood-soaked one. "Gotcha!" he huffed with some amount of relief.

Genie shrieked again. The pain from the shards of wood in her hand already hurt, but Billy's clasp over that same hand intensified the razor-like stabs. Genie twisted her body using Billy's grip for support, attempting to advance her reach with her free hand. She clawed at the splintered edge once more, managing to latch three of her fingers onto it. The motion was enough for Billy to lose his hold on her, as her hand slipped free. Billy yelled and lunged forward, frantically grabbing at any part of her that he could. The three-fingered grasp dropped down to two. Billy seized Genie's other hand again, but it was too bloody to keep a firm grip. Within seconds, both hands lost their hold and Genie dropped down to the first floor.

Billy watched with terror. He peered through the damaged opening, but only saw the dim beam of the flashlight several feet from where he thought Genie landed. Billy stood, used the same furniture hopping method to traverse the loft, and slid down the rickety ladder. Facing an eerily silent hallway and only the rising moonlight to help him see, he found himself in the room of mirrors. No Genie, but the dolls once again turned to greet him. He barely registered the dolls as he called Genie's name. No answer. He shuddered and fumbled back toward the hallway.

Before he exited, he paused and glanced back at the myriad of dolls staring in his direction. Some tilted their heads, then back again. Others just rotated their bodies enough to acknowledge his presence.

As he crossed the threshold out, the dolls all returned to their original positions in unison.

Back in the hallway, Billy bolted toward the saloon doors and pushed his way into the informal room. He turned around at the sound of movement on the other side of the room. His heart catapulted into his throat. Sweat clung to his neck and torso. Some muffled groans accompanied the shifting and shuffling in the corner. Billy noticed the flashlight flickering on and off. He rushed toward it, praying it wouldn't die completely. "Billy?" the groaning subsided and words now formed.

"Geenz, that you?" Billy shined the flickering light on her crumpled outline.

"Yea, I-I'm ok," she sat up, rubbing her head and smearing dark blood across her face and through her hair.

"Did you pass out?"

"No. No I landed on my feet, but then fell forward onto this end table," she said, kicking the offending agent.

Billy saw her cradling her large canvas purse. "Was that thing always that full?"

"No, Dumbass, the dolls are in it, remember?"

"All that and you still have them?"

Genie nodded. "Now let's get out of here before we get killed."

"Finally, you're coming around!"

Billy grabbed her arm and helped her stand. She limped with his help toward the formal room and then out to the main entrance.

Aubrey and Cassie were nowhere to be found. Billy felt another surge of panic. Genie called out, but no one answered her. Before Billy could echo her, a deafening rumble shook the house. It sounded like a freight train and the floors moved as if an earthquake struck. Both crouched down and covered their ears, looking around to identify the source. Billy crawled toward Genie and wrapped an arm over her.

"*Aubrey! Cassie!*" Genie screamed again.

"*The door,*" yelled Billy into her ear. "*Crawl to the door!*"

Genie started toward the ajar entrance with Billy still maintaining one arm over her. The floor continued to shake and the roar rushed through their heads. They felt exhausted from moving just several feet. Panting, Billy steadied himself, wrapped his arm around Genie's waist, and made a run for the door. Just before they reached it, the door slammed closed. The force behind it knocked them back down. "What now? Oh god we're screwed, we're screwed," whimpered Genie, still blocking her ears with her hands.

Billy winced at the amount of dried blood smeared over her face and matted into her hair.

"Ok, ok, we'll get out, we just need to think."

"What?"

"*To think*!" he yelled, noticing how hoarse his voice sounded.

"*We'll be dead by then*!" Genie's shrill reply pierced his brain even more than the cacophonous roaring.

Just then, headlights blinded Billy through the window by the door. Billy grabbed Genie again, dragging her toward the broken pane. It was the same window she had planned to smash to get them in. *Hopefully it will provide us with an exit*, he thought.

Billy turned Genie to face him, holding both of her shoulders. "We need to break the window and climb out."

Genie nodded and pointed at an iron cross-shaped paperweight on the entrance counter. "Stay here!" yelled Billy.

He dropped down and crawled toward the counter. Even though the main entrance had finished wood floors, it was dilapidated and fragmenting with each tremor of the quake. Billy felt sharp pains stabbing through his hands and knees as the splinters drove into his skin. He tried to tuck and roll, but this took more effort than he anticipated. The movements of the house worked against him in every direction he tried to move. Billy pulled himself up by the corner of the counter, grasping the Celtic cross paperweight by its wide base, then turned back toward the window. Genie remained crouched by the door. He heard pounding on the other side of the door along with more shouting. Genie grabbed the handle and started pulling at it. She slammed her other fist against the door, but it remained closed.

A silhouette appeared at the window. It motioned them to move back. Billy saw this but kept crawling to Genie. The shadow smashed the glass, scattering thick shards over the entrance. An arm reached in and offered a hand. Billy dropped the cross, reached forward and grasped Genie's shoulders. He turned her in the direction of the window and pushed her forward. The broken glass crunched beneath their feet. Whimpering, Genie reached for the hand and felt it lock onto hers. The figure pulled Genie up and out the window. "Uncle Alex?" Billy heard her cry.

Alex didn't say anything. He guided Genie down to the porch, then popped his head back in and called for Billy. Billy grabbed Alex's arm and climbed out the window. When he regained his balance, he heard Alex yelling at them to get off the porch and onto the lawn. Feeling like he was on autopilot, Billy again grabbed Genie and ushered her down the creaking steps, Alex following behind them. Billy looked up to see Aubrey and Cassie sitting in the back of a squad car. It took him a second to register it, but then, "Ah, Cassie's dad," he said.

Genie nodded. "We're still dead, though."

"Indeed you are," Alex placed a hand on both of their shoulders. "Genie, Honey, Kat's got to be worried sick about you. And Billy is it? Yes, of course it is. You're in charge of these kids, how on Earth did you wind up here?"

When neither responded, Alex sighed and said, "Tell ya what, let's go back to my house and get you two cleaned up. Genie, you look like you could use a band-aid or two."

Genie joined Aubrey and Cassie in the back seat. Billy plopped into the front. Alex joined them, started up the car, and drove off. Aubrey and Cassie explained on the way there that after five minutes, they freaked out, took the van, and drove to Cassie's house. They were worried about them, they assured Genie and Billy, but couldn't wait it out. When Alex found out where they'd been, he took them back over in his squad car to make sure everyone made it out alive.

"Not to pour salt in wounds, Kids," Alex added, "but I needed everyone involved to know how dangerous the house is. These two came back with me because I figured you'd wind up proving it somehow, and they needed to see it firsthand."

"I thought you said the house wasn't dangerous, Cass," said Genie, "just that stuff moved and it creeped people out."

"You don't listen," hissed Cassie, "I said it was dangerous. I said it used to be safe, but then something changed and, and, now it's not!"

"Ok, ok, calm down," said Alex. "We can all agree now, that house is off-limits. No one and nothing goes in or comes out of it. Understood?"

They all nodded and remained silent for the rest of the trip.

15

As they pulled into the Kingman driveway, Genie saw her Aunt Cara wringing her hands and pacing back and forth through the picture window in front of the house. Genie was surprised to see her there instead of at her mother's place. "Guess news of breaking and entering warrants both parents present for a lecture," she mumbled.

After entering the house and with sheepish glances from the group at Cara, Alex invited them to each take a seat around the kitchen table. Cara started wiping Genie's face with a warm dishrag and working on removing some of the matted blood from her hair. Aubrey sat next to Genie, arms crossed, and Cassie next to Aubrey in a similar pose. Billy leaned forward on his elbows, his face buried in his hands. Alex started, "First off, I'm glad you guys are all ok. Genie, I know you're banged up, Kiddo, but it could be so much worse."

Genie nodded, but didn't make eye contact. She kept her focus somewhere on the floor in front of her while Cara worked at untangling her hair.

Alex continued to reiterate the dangers of the house, their overall stupidity for going into an abandoned old home and then offered to give Aubrey, Genie, and Billy a ride back to the hotel.

"Finally," added Alex, "we've decided to keep this between all of us."

Everyone, including Cara, looked surprised.

Alex nodded, "Yea, I know, I know, why would I do that? Well, you're all almost adults...no, not you, Cassie, you're grounded until further notice. But, the rest of you have the choice to come clean to your folks without me tattling on you. You pulled a stupid stunt and made it out alive. What you choose to do after this is up to you."

Cara started to protest, but Alex held up his hand. "They're fine. They're not our kids to punish, and from a legal standpoint, no one would care enough to press charges, so to me, it isn't worth the paperwork."

Cara glared at him. "This is horrible parenting. You are friends with Kat! She needs to know what her daughter is up to!"

Alex nodded. "I'm not disagreeing with you, Carr, but I also have a trust to maintain with Genie, and if she knows I'll tell her mom on her every time she gets into trouble, she may not come to me if or when she truly needs help."

Genie glanced at him and murmured, "Thanks, Uncle Alex. I'll probably tell her anyways."

"You better!" screeched Cara, "Y-you almost got Cassie killed!"

Genie rolled her eyes. "Hardly. She was too afraid to go past the front door."

Alex waved his hands. "Enough, enough, enough! We all agree Kat should know what happened, and that information isn't coming from me. Cara, I strongly encourage you to take the same approach. As for everyone else, who you choose to inform is entirely up to you, but as young adults, and injured ones at that, I'd at least mention tonight's events."

"Terrible parenting, just terrible," muttered Cara, moving toward the sink to rinse off the crimson dishrag.

Genie gathered her damp hair into a messy bun and secured it with a hair tie. She excused herself to use the bathroom to finish washing up. Cassie stood and headed to her bedroom. Aubrey turned to Billy. "Coach, can we go? I'm so tired, and our game's early in the morning."

Billy sighed and said yes. Once Genie returned, the worn trio gathered their things together, piled back into the squad car, and Alex drove them back to Uptown.

16

Their season did not end in a championship. The spectators suspected at least one of the players to be hungover based on her tired appearance, and one of the coaches looked like he'd lost a day's worth of sleep. The team left Millerton later that day, welcoming the end of their season.

As the team parted in the school parking lot, heading toward their cars or parents' vehicles, Billy and Genie hung back.

"So," said Billy.

"Mhm."

"You gonna tell your mom what happened?"

"God no. She thinks we went on a hike in the woods nearby and I fell."

"Ah. Alright then." Billy turned to face her, "Guess it will all be just one, horrific memory."

Genie smirked. "Well, it isn't entirely over."

Billy raised an eyebrow. "What?"

As she bent forward to pick up her duffle bag, Genie whispered, "I left one of the dolls in Cassie's room. I'd pay big money to see her and her mother crap themselves when they find it."

He shook his head, but laughed anyways. "That's so cruel, Geenz."

"Yea, well, it's more to freak out her mom. Cassie's fine and all, but she needs to loosen up, and it'll never happen until Cara does."

Before Billy had a chance to interject, Genie said, "Besides, I left the other one with Aubrey. She ditched us, too. Plus, she needs a reminder of our adventure."

Genie was already on her way to his car. Billy called after her, "Not one she'd likely forget anytime soon."

With a giggle, Genie answered back, "No, no I guess not. Hurry up."

Billy trotted toward her, unlocked the car, and soon he was on his way to drop her off at home.

17

He'd always had a bad temper. This was not a secret. It'd been this way long before he'd met Kat. He tried everything: meditation, exercise, medications, counseling. None of it, however, rid him of the spiteful remarks and boiling frustrations that surfaced throughout the day. The thoughts were easier to manage. He could scream as loud as he pleased in his head, and no one got hurt. The intensity of his rage, however, took its toll on him physically. He sometimes felt pressure in his chest, flushing in his face, or tingling under his skin. At times he believed his blood truly boiled. When it became physically uncomfortable to tolerate, he'd lash out. Not intentionally to hurt anyone, of course, but sometimes the thoughts in his head flew out of his mouth. When they did, the pressure in his chest or the throbbing behind his eyes released, and he felt better.

Unfortunately, no one else around him shared in this relief. In fact, he noticed they appeared worse, as if he shared the load and took them down a notch to bring himself a touch of relief. *Selfish*, he concluded. *They're just being selfish...not helping me when I need it most.*

But he noticed it worsening recently. He wasn't sure what changed, but now, when he let some of the thoughts free, he felt almost trance-like. He had no control over what he said, and when it was finished, he had to question whoever was around to help piece together a replay of what took place. His thoughts were cut short by the sound of a crash. Huey, the cat, managed to knock over a plant from the windowsill and the dirt and broken ceramic pieces now accompanied it on the floor. The pressure in his chest started to swell. Not wanting to deal with the discomfort, he broke into a rant, scaring the cat into the other room and out of sight. His verbal obscenities were so loud that he didn't hear the faint sound of the front door opening and closing as Genie slipped out.

***

Sometime after four o'clock, Calvin heard a soft knock on his front door. He just returned from work and was about to heat up some pizza rolls. "It's open," he called out, sliding the metal tray into the preheated oven.

The front door creaked and Genie walked in. "Uncle Cal?"

"In here, Kiddo. Making a snack if you're hungry."

Genie walked into the kitchen. Cal turned to face her and saw her eyes were outlined in red. "Hey, there, you doing alright?"

"Yea, yea, just some allergies."

"Ah. Uh, well here, here, have a seat." Cal pulled a chair from the table and Genie sat down, placing her bag on the chair next to her.

"Because it's a Friday," Genie informed Cal, "Aunt Elle and Mom are out shopping."

She told him that she'd been home briefly from school, but needed a change of scenery. When Cal asked if Walt was home, Genie dropped her eyes and gave him a quick nod. When she finally looked back up, Cal noted the increased redness in her eyes. "I see. Well, does he know where you are?"

Genie shook her head no, and made no indication that she planned to tell him. "He'll figure it out," she managed to mutter.

Not quite sure what to make of it, Cal gave her a glass of lemonade and told her they had a few more minutes to go on the pizza rolls.

When the timer dinged, Cal transferred the rolls to a plate, warning Genie to be careful because they were hot. He tried to keep more of a conversation going with her, but she was uncharacteristically quiet. Finally giving up, Cal joined her in a silent staring contest with the steaming pizza rolls, waiting for them to cool.

After Cal inhaled several pizza rolls and Genie nibbled at part of one, several thuds echoed through the living room. Genie jumped up and backed toward the corner of the kitchen. Cal raised his eyebrows and mumbled, "What the...?"

Yelling started from the other side of the front door, along with persistent banging. Calvin walked into the living room and saw Walt through the peep-hole. Calvin shook his head and started to unlock the door. He barely clicked open the deadbolt when Walt shoved the door and pushed his way inside. Calvin stumbled back several steps without falling over. Walt stood in front of him, both fists clenched and face beet-red.

"Where is she?" he sputtered.

Calvin saw spit fly from his mouth when he spoke. Blinking, Calvin asked, "Who?"

"Who the hell ya think? My kid! She been here? And if my wife's here too, you better say something!"

Calvin scratched his head. "Uh, Walt? Man, what's going on?"

Calvin searched Walt's face. The round, flushed cheeks puffed in and out with each breath. His green eyes blazed with a wild, dark glare. The peppered hair on Walt's head stuck out in all directions, as if he'd raked his fingers through the strands starting at the back of his head. Sweat beaded over his maroon countenance. To Calvin, it was Walt, but at the same time, it wasn't.

"Look," growled Walt, more spit flying forward, "I'm only going to ask you once more. Where is she?"

He usually stayed neutral, and he was almost always the peacemaker, but Calvin couldn't let Walt near anyone in this state. He crossed his arms over his chest and mutely stared at Walt.

Walt snarled and lunged at Calvin. He attempted to wrestle him to the ground, but Cal tucked and rolled to the side. Despite Cal's increasing waistline and not-so-toned upper body, he remembered how to fight. His boxing record in college still held, and some things he felt he'd never unlearn. When Walt lumbered toward him to strike again, Cal jumped into his fighting stance. He raised his left fist to guard his face and shot two quick jabs into Walt's chest. The blows sent the flushed hulk crashing to the floor. Walt sat and blinked a few times. He looked up at Calvin and asked, "Cal?"

Not dropping his fists, Calvin replied, "Yes, Walt?"

Walt wiped his face with his hands and ran his fingers through his hair, smoothing it back down. He shook his head, drew in a few labored breaths, and asked, "What the hell just happened?"

"Well, I was hoping you'd be able to fill me in on some of that."

Another deep breath. *God, he's out of shape*, thought Cal.

Walt glanced at his chest, then back at Cal. "Did...did you punch my chest?"

"Twice, I'm afraid."

Nodding, Walt said, "Well, that worked. Thanks."

With a sigh, Cal lowered his fists and reached down to help him up. Walt waved him off. "No, no...let me...just...catch my breath."

Cal found the closest chair and sat down, leaning forward with his elbows on his lap. Walt slumped against the wall behind him, closed his eyes, and continued his loud breathing. From the kitchen, Calvin heard soft footsteps moving toward the living room. Genie appeared moments later and stood next to Calvin. "He's getting scarier and scarier," she whispered.

Walt opened his eyes and focused on Genie. "Hey, Sweet Pea," he said.

Genie didn't reply.

"I--I didn't mean to frighten you, Honey. I think I just needed to get out of the house."

Walt started to stand. Cal jumped forward and helped him to his feet. "Fresh air and a couple of blows to the chest," muttered Calvin. "Man, what the hell was that?"

"I don't know," Walt shook his head. "Honest to god, I don't. Something sets me off and I see red until it's over."

"Well you better get on top of whatever it is, before you hurt someone."

"Never have. Docs say I'm fine. I've seen plenty of em since this is getting worse."

"How long?"

"Few weeks now. I've always had a temper. But, but the blinding rage is a new offset."

Walt shook his head. Calvin knew he was calm enough to go home and hoped nothing else set him off that night. Genie went back into the kitchen, grabbed her bag and returned. "C'mon, let's go before Mom comes home," she said. She grabbed his hand and pulled him out the door. "Thanks, Uncle Cal," she called as Cal closed the door behind them.

"Seriously," said Cal to himself, "what the hell was that?" and made his way toward the fridge for a beer to accompany his pizza rolls.

18

"God help me," smiled Kat, "I know the pumpkin spice craze is getting ridiculous, but I cannot get enough of this stuff. It's like legal suburbanite crack."

Elle smirked and sipped her latte. She went with vanilla because as much as she loved pumpkin stuff, the lattes seemed to overdo it with the syrup.

"Speaking of addictions," Elle nodded toward the shoe department. The two headed in with the intent of shopping for others, but knew full well they would leave with at least two new pairs for their own collections.

As Kat examined a pair of classic black pumps, presumably for Genie, Elle inquired about Genie's recent attitude and overall demeanor.

"Not quite sure what ya mean," replied Kat, half listening. "And these are on sale too...hm, if they come in another color...?"

"She just seems a little less, you know, herself. The spunk isn't there," Elle said.

"Well, who could blame her? Junior year is when all hell breaks loose. The SATs, ACTs, LMNOPs, whatever it is, you name it. They take it. And she's applying early to schools, she is in some advanced courses...you try staying perky and positive all the time with all that."

"Does she talk to you guys? Like, if she were really stressed, does she come to you or Walt with personal stuff?"

"Of course she does, Elle, I'm her *mother.* Walt, not so much. That temper of his sets its own boundaries with her, and I think she judges her timing daily with stuff to bring his way."

Kat started saying Walt's name as if she were sucking on something sour. *She damn near spits the name when she says it,* Elle noted.

"I'm guessing you two are in a cold phase."

"Hey, we go through seasons of love and hate just like everyone else."

"Right, but you seem to embrace more volatile transitions."

Kat rolled her eyes. "Well we can't all be in the perfect relationship, Ellbea."

Elle saw the frustration, but she wasn't feeling the frustration, at least not directed at her. "Kat, hey, are you--are you crying?"

"God no. Damn dust from the shelf," said Kat, as she rubbed her eyes with the back of her hand and kept rummaging for a pair of heels. She picked up a pair of clunky brown clogs with faux leather and buttons on the sides. Something Elle thought were too ugly to even consider.

"Besides," she went on, "he's just so, I don't know, unpredictable. Well, he always has been, but lately, I don't know. It's getting worse. It'd be easier if I had at least five minutes of mental preparation when he goes and blows a gasket."

"Sort of comes at ya from left field at any given moment, huh?"

"Don't pretend like you even have a clue about baseball. And yes, despite your ignorance, that's exactly what it is."

"You hit a ball and run the bases. Yea, that was tough." Elle set down the red pumps she had been examining for the past minute. The logical, financially savvy part of her brain won the argument with her ever-so-pleading fashionable side. The two never seemed to get along.

Kat remained silent for a few moments. She still had the hideous clogs in hand, but was not looking at them. Well, she pretended to be eyeing every aspect of them, but Elle could tell she was miles away from assessing crappy merchandise.

At last, Kat glanced at Elle, who realized she'd been staring at Kat for the duration of the silence. "Let's go. I'm not finding anything worth a dime in this place," said Kat.

Elle nodded and grabbed her coffee cup, which now contained what she could only imagine was mostly vanilla syrup. The two split to their own cars and headed home to finish out the evening.

19

Cara stepped into the kitchen and clicked on the overhead light. She followed the fluorescent glow toward the laundry room, and flipped the light switch there as well. She wasn't sure why, but she felt uneasy the last few weeks. Dark rooms seemed occupied, shadows crept across the walls, and she kept seeing something out of the corner of her eye. Cara started to load the washer. *Reds tonight,* she thought. *Cold water only. Maybe I can add some very dark colors, too.* A faint yell broke her train of thought.

Stepping out of the laundry room and looking back into the kitchen, she couldn't see much beyond the fluorescent glow. The hallway leading to the kids' rooms remained unlit. To the left of the kitchen, the living room stayed dark and silent as well. "Cass? That you?" called Cara.

No answer. Justin was at a friend's house and Alex was on patrol. *Cassie could be home,* she thought.

She closed the washer and started the cold cycle. Another whimper from the hallway sent a shiver up Cara's spine. "Cassie? Everything ok?"

No response. Cara passed through the kitchen and clicked on the light to the hallway. Darkness. She clicked the switch several more times, but the dead bulb refused to illuminate. Now the hair stood on the back of Cara's neck. She used her hand to guide her down the narrow hallway until she reached Cassie's door. With a soft press, the door opened and Cara stood to face a vacant bedroom. Flicking on the purple lamp at the edge of Cassie's desk, she glanced around the bedroom. No radio, no forgotten cell phone, no iPad left playing a movie, no source of the sound. *Maybe just the wind,* Cara thought. *It's an old house. Wind and old structures create quite unsettling symphonies.*

She turned to click the lamp off, but again, something moved out of the corner of her eye. Cara spun around, but didn't see anything in motion. Sitting on the nightstand next to Cassie's bed was a doll Cara hadn't seen before. The doll had mocha-colored skin, dark hair gathered into a bun, and quite eccentric fabric that formed a dress. The dark eyes stared back into Cara's hazel ones. Another chill electrocuted her fragile frame. She had no explanation to why this doll instilled such an eerie sensation, but she backed out of the room and closed the door behind her. She planned to ask Cassie about it once she returned home.

"I don't know, I told you!" Cassie sat on the corner of the bed later that night with her mother standing cross-armed in front of her.

"I don't like your tone, young lady," snapped Cara.

Cassie stood up and pushed passed her, attempting to leave the room. Cara caught her arm and guided her back to the bed. "I'll ask you again. I can do this all night, Cassandra. Where did you get the doll?"

Cassie pulled her legs toward her chest. She didn't have a clue as to where the creepy thing on the nightstand came from. It looked old and smelled faintly of mildew. "I swear to you, I don't know. I'm just as freaked out by it."

"Are you?"

"Mom, this is the first time I'm seeing it."

"You sure you didn't steal it? Those other kids are a bad influence, Cassandra. If you stole this or tried to--,"

"Tried to what? What would I have done with a creepy-ass doll from a jillion centuries ago? Huh?"

"Don't you raise your voice and for gosh-sakes watch your language!"

Cassie hugged her knees closer to her chest. She stared at her mom and waited for her to speak.

Finally, Cara said, "Alright, fine. If you won't admit to anything, the doll stays with you. Keep it in your room with your stuff, and in your sight. If I find it tucked away, I'll take it back out and you'll lose your phone for that day."

Cassie shook her head. "I just told you it scares me, why would you--?"

"To teach you to stop fooling around and that your actions have consequences!" she said, proudly echoing the words her mother once used to correct her.

She then turned to leave. As soon as she exited the room, the door slammed behind her and the lock clicked.

"Y-y-you won't get dinner tonight! You think a locked door can prevent further punishment?" Her stammering threats went on for another five minutes.

Cassie remained silent and glared at the closed door, fists clenched at her sides. Behind her, she heard a soft thud. Spinning to see the source of the noise, Cassie saw the doll now laying on its side. Its legs were still placed in a seated position with the arms stretched out in front of it. It looked like it was reaching for a hug, only sideways. Cassie climbed over the bed and repositioned the doll upright. She sat on her knees and watched the doll for a few more minutes. Outside the bedroom door, her mother's voice quieted and she heard her slamming dishes around in the kitchen. Cassie felt the urge to yell, "real mature," but decided against it. She knew when to pick her battles. Besides, if she kept her cool, eventually she could get her dad's defense, and that proved most effective.

The doll remained motionless. The dark eyes stayed in a fixed gaze and the arms and legs frozen in their placement. Cassie sighed and made her way over to her desk. She opened her physics book and started on her reading assignment. "James Prescott Joule," she murmured, scanning the introduction. "Conservation of energy...Einstein factored in mass as a form of energy...energy cannot be created or destroyed...," she paused to write down the equation.

Thud

Cassie whirled around again. The doll was back on its side without anything else out of place. Cassie's hands started to shake. She stood, half-expecting her legs to give out on her. She moved toward the door, and unlocked it. The doll's eyes seemed to follow her every move. Then, a blink. *A blink? How?* Her heart plunged into her stomach, then made up for the pause with rapid, subsequent beats.

Suddenly, the doll's limbs began rotating in half circles, forward and back. This caused the doll to rock into a bear-crawl position and move forward with each semi-rotation of the arms and legs. It was a slow, but steady movement that allowed the doll to transition from the nightstand onto the adjacent bed. Seconds later, Cassie found herself staring at a doll on all fours, now at the edge of her bed, staring back at her. Cassie froze. Terror seized up every muscle in her body and she could not move. With a final motion, the doll's arms swung forward in unison, pushing itself back into a seated position. The legs once again stuck straight out and the arms reached forward. The eyes still stared, and Cassie stared back. Another blink from the doll and Cassie's fear-induced paralysis broke.

Keeping her eyes on the doll, she opened the door and backed out, closing it again behind her. Once shut, Cassie broke into a sprint toward the kitchen. She flew by her mother who tried yelling at her again. She stumbled into the rec room and grabbed her coat off the chair right before ducking out the door leading into the garage. Form there, she maintained a steady sprint to her grandmother's house. She'd have her dad pick her up once he finished work, and at this point, Grandma Cass's house looked like a good safe haven.

Puzzled and still irritated, Cara marched toward Cassie's bedroom. She found the doll at the foot of the bed, laying facedown. Cara sighed and muttered, "How very grown up, Cass. Just throw things around when you're upset. Very. Grown. Up."

She kept grumbling and returned to some unnecessary banging of pots and pans around the kitchen.

20

"Geenz, what's up?" Aubrey answered her phone as she flopped back onto her bed and stared up at the fan slowly rotating above her.

"We going out tonight?" Genie asked. "I gotta get out of the house, my parents are driving me nuts. They won't stop fighting."

Aubrey rolled onto her stomach and propped herself up on both elbows. "Sucks. Yea, I'm around."

"Want to go to the movies?" Genie could hear her dad walking into the kitchen and closed her bedroom door. She knew what would follow, and really didn't want to hear whatever fight he'd pick for tonight's pre-dinner entertainment.

Aubrey said yes, and hung up. She sat up, but stayed seated on her bed. She saw something move from the corner of her eye. She whipped her head around. Nothing. *Well, nothing moving*, she concluded with a sigh. *Probably just shadows from the trees blowing outside*.

She got up, closed the blinds to her bedroom, and headed downstairs to get some dinner.

Genie paused and pressed her ear against her bedroom door. She heard her parents talking, their voices increasing in volume with each passing moment. Genie felt her appetite wane. She slipped back to her desk and pulled out her iPod and headphones. Inserting the earbuds, she piled up a few pillows on her bed and slouched into them. Moments later, she fell asleep.

Genie took a couple of steps forward, surveying her surroundings. She saw a vast field filled with stalks of wheat and corn blowing from a crisp breeze. A cloudless, blue sky stretched as far as she could see. No buildings, homes, or silos; nothing but harvest-ready crops stretched before her. Genie took a few more steps, turning around, but not seeing a change in her setting. The golden rays of the sun created an orange tint to her scenery. *Sunset*, thought Genie, then noticed a table and chairs a few yards away.

She proceeded toward the furniture, curious what it was doing out in the field. As she approached the table set, she saw a small doll seated in one of the two chairs. Squinting her eyes and using her hand to shade her vision, she noted the doll's golden curls and faded dress. The doll appeared larger and larger the closer Genie got. By the time she sat facing the figure, the doll no longer seemed like a doll. Genie tilted her head, noticing the milky white skin and dark eyes. The lips on the figure began to move, but Genie couldn't hear what they said. "What?" asked Genie.

Moving again, a whisper escaped the merlot painted lips. The rest of the figure remained motionless and the eyes locked onto Genie's. Genie felt her body relax and lost the ability to move her arms. She tried to look away but she realized her eyes remained locked in position. Heart racing, Genie tried to scream, but that part of her body failed, too.

"Genie!" Her father's voice echoed across the plains. She jumped, then her world shook.

"Genie! Get up. We've been calling ya for the last ten minutes," said Walt, giving her shoulders another shake to ensure she was conscious.

Genie gasped and gripped both of Walt's forearms. She felt her hair sticking to the back of her neck and face. Her dad released his grip once she did this. Genie glanced at her earbuds lying next to her on the bed. "H-how long was I asleep?" she asked.

"How the hell should I know?" grumbled Walt. "What I do know, is that you should be doing homework and should be making a prompt appearance when we call you for dinner. Not daydreaming like a--,"

"*Walt*!" Kat's voice sliced through Walt's rant and he paused, looking back toward the door.

Kat shouldered him away from Genie and pressed her hand over Genie's forehead. "My god, Honey, are you sick? You're soaked!"

"I'm fine," said Genie, trying to get to her feet.

Kat had her sit back on the bed and ran to get the thermometer. She pulled Walt out of the room so that Genie could change her t-shirt and fix her hair. Plus, she figured Genie had enough fatherly interaction for one night. Once Kat returned to Genie's room and checked her temperature, "cool as a cucumber," the two made their way into the kitchen. Walt was already on his second helping of beef stew. Genie took a few quick bites and returned to her room to finish up her homework. As she opened her math book, she heard her parents' voices again, volume increasing with each passing moment. She closed her eyes in hopes to tune them out.

Moments later, Genie found herself face to face with the porcelain figure. This time, when the lips parted, Genie heard the words that left the maroon mouth. "Take me home."

Genie glanced around but saw nothing beyond the crops and tall grass. The vacant horizon gleamed in the dwindling sunlight. "Where's home?" Genie tried to ask, but again found her body frozen. At least she could think. At least her mind stayed with her.

The chime of her phone snapped her out of the dream. The familiar dampness clung to the back of her neck. She fumbled to locate her phone. It was a text from Aubrey saying she'd pick her up in a few. Genie sighed and got up to change her clothes.

21

"Where's Genie?" asked Walt. "I thought she was doing homework."

"Out with friends," responded Kat from the bedroom. She sat cross-legged on the bed folding laundry while watching syndicated reruns. She couldn't get enough of them, and she dared anyone to try and stop her from doing otherwise.

"Couldn't pick anything better to watch?" Walt stood in the door frame, pursed lips and head tilted up slightly.

"Sorry, this is all we bought to watch for the year. Besides, I left you the big screen to do with it whatever you want. Enjoy."

"Why do you hate me?" Walt crossed his arms over his chest.

Sucking in a slow breath, Kat ventured with, "Hate you? I don't hate you, Walt."

"Really? Because every time I enter a room, or a conversation with you, I get anger laced with sarcasm. And it's not the funny, dry stuff you usually throw out. No, no, it comes loaded with scorn and resentment."

Kat paused with consideration. "Well said, Walt. That's exactly how I intend stuff these days. At least it gets through to you."

"Now, see, that's not fair, Kat! I want a genuine conversation, and you're doing it again. Why not get literal and just throw shit at me?"

"Because our 'shit' is far too valuable to waste on me possibly knocking your teeth in. Don't get me wrong, I'd enjoy it, but afterwards I'd feel upset that my 'shit' would be broken."

Walt took a deep breath. He was really trying this time, and for whatever reason, Kat seemed to give up on that tonight. "Ok, Kat, final shot; talk to me. What's wrong?"

"Presently, nothing."

Walt audibly sighed with frustration.

"But that's just it," she went on, "there usually isn't anything, then suddenly out of the blue, you blow a gasket over something random. Or, at least it seems random to me."

"That's ridiculous, I never get upset over something unless it's worth getting upset over!"

"Even still, it's never a calm conversation, when a lot of times it easily could be."

Walt looked thoughtful. "Give me an example."

Kat despised this request, often because if she couldn't produce a situation that he recollected, he'd dismiss the whole issue. If he could remember it, he'd often readdress the fight itself, rather than the big picture. "Childish, so damn childish," muttered Kat.

"What?"

"Nothing. Ok, how about the night when you screamed at Genie because the cat puked on the carpet?"

"Yea? What about it? She was right there. She could've prevented a mess and she didn't. It's her cat and her responsibility. You're too easy on her, Kat."

Kat sighed. She was too tired to deal with her frustration. It was always the same thing. He pushed her until she snapped, then he'd get upset that she was acting pissy, then he'd break down why she had no right to feel the way she did, and she'd end up being the one to apologize. Except for this time; this time her apology was dripping in condescension. "You're right Walt, one day I'll be great like you. But until then, accept my faults and know deep down, I'm striving one day to be perfect in your eyes."

That did it. What happened next, neither is too sure of. What they both surmised after discussing the events later the following day, was that Walt took his forearm to their dresser standing to his left. He crossed his right arm over his body and in one move, flung all the contents on top of the dresser across the room. Unfortunately, it wasn't a large room. Kat still sat on the bed facing the dresser. She did her best to cover her face, but the initial item Walt sent flying was an iron owl-shaped book end. This didn't get much momentum, but it got enough.

The metal bird drove its beak into the corner of Kat's eye. She screamed, both out of pain and fear and ducked for cover next to the bed. Once on the ground, she decided it best to hide under the bed. She could hear Walt yelling and launching things around the room. A vase smashed against the wall behind the bed. Another shatter sounded that Kat knew to be the glass from a picture frame. The destruction pressed on as Kat's world darkened from a throbbing headache and the inability to keep open her weighted eyelids. That's where things became hazy to Kat and clear to Walt.

Walt stood in the door frame with a bloody right arm along the side, where he had made contact with everything on the dresser. "Why does everything we own need to be metal or glass?" he growled.

He glanced around the room, looking for Kat. He noticed the trail of disrupted blankets leading down the side of the bed. He found her, barely conscious underneath it. "Kat? C'mon, wake up!"

Rage turned to panic. Walt dragged her out over broken glass by her arms and placed her on the bed. "Walt? What—?"

Kat's eyes opened and her mind picked up where it previously left off. She screamed again, and Walt saw a fear in her eyes he never thought would be meant for him. She coiled and kicked him square in the chest. As he stumbled back, she rolled off the edge of the bed and half crawled, half ran out to the hall and into the kitchen.

Shaking, Walt stood up and followed her.

After convincing her to put down the butcher knife, and no, he really wasn't going to hurt her, and dear God, should we go to an ER, the two sat across from each other with a glass of scotch between them.

"We need help."

"Yea....yea I suppose we do," agreed Walt.

"What were you thinking? When you threw that at me?"

"I wasn't. You infuriate me sometimes, Kat! I blank out and come back only when it's over. And sometimes it's just words you tell me I said later that I don't remember even saying, but tonight...shit, what if it gets worse?"

"It is worse. Much worse. I'll tell you one thing, you lay a finger on my daughter, and we will be out of here before you come back to reality to realize it." She meant every word of that statement.

"Our daughter, Kat, our daughter."

"You're really not in a position to argue."

"No, but that is one person that I never intend to lose."

Kat sighed and raised the chilled glass of scotch to her right temple. He missed her eye, and she was thankful not to have to deal with any vision loss.

"I'm calling Elle," said Walt. "You need someone to look at you."

"Don't you dare," hissed Kat. "She *cannot* know about this."

Walt looked bemused. "You tell her everything. Won't this be the highlight of happy hour gossip tomorrow after work?"

"She's off tomorrow, and no, I tell her most things, but I leave some stuff out. She doesn't need to resent you."

That stung, mostly because Walt knew the extent of his temper, and saw in full, the toll it took on Kat. Still, he blamed her for it.

"Ok, we will tell her you fell."

"Oldest lie in the book. She'll know what happened without either of us telling her. I'm telling you Walt, she's a human lie detector, or something."

"Ok, ok, but we need you looked at."

They went back and forth for another ten minutes. Kat's headache intensified and Walt finally shot Elle a text stating, "Kat hit her head and won't let me take her to see a doctor. Will you come take a look at her?"

He half-smirked at the message. Genie would've given him hell for taking up so much space. "Why write a novel when you can send a message in less than five words?"

Of course, it did help to know what half those abbreviations meant. *Kids these days.*

22

Close to midnight, Aubrey realized they blew Genie's curfew. Genie already had a few drinks in her, as did Aubrey. Billy showed up somewhere in the last hour and Aubrey laughed at how un-hidden their relationship was once both of them had a little booze in their veins. Hanging over Billy's shoulder, Genie slurred something. When she repeated herself, Aubrey realized she was asking if she could sober up at her place. Aubrey's parents worked odd hours and Genie knew there was a good chance they could get away with it.

Billy gave her a kiss on the cheek and Genie turned to him, laughing, and returned it with a bigger one. Aubrey rolled her eyes and took her turn to bowl. Why they bothered continuing to play, she'd never know, but it was one of the few places in town that didn't check I.D. Besides, even if someone decided to, they could easily ask a nearby player to grab them a pitcher or two with the promise of a free drink in return. *Split.* Aubrey cursed under her breath and threw a gutter-ball on her next turn. Even with the new Friday night hangout place after the movies, she had yet to improve her game. "Double damn," she said.

Now sitting on Billy's lap, Genie finished another beer and laid her head against his chest. Billy twirled a lock of her blonde hair between his fingers and kissed the top of her head. "Guys, are we calling it a night?" asked Aubrey.

Genie stood up, slightly unsteady with her first step. Billy grabbed her arm and they made their way toward the front entrance. "You're taking an Uber to Aubrey's," he told Genie, and in the same breath, "No one's driving home."

Aubrey rolled her eyes. "And what do we tell my parents when they find us home without my car?"

Billy shrugged. "Say I drove you guys home and I'll swing by for you tomorrow to pick it up. Keep it simple. It'll be safe here in the parking lot."

Genie nodded and pulled up the Uber app; it was faster and cheaper than hiring a cab. Plus, they'd have a driver in minutes. She put one for Aubrey's address and one for Billy. "We're set," she said, locking her phone and pushing her way out of the bowling alley's front double glass doors.

The cool air felt refreshing, and the wind quieted for the time being. Aubrey zipped up her coat and Genie wrapped her scarf around her face. Billy shoved his hands into his pockets, but stayed close to Genie in case her balance decided to take the rest of the night off. Soon the cars arrived and the girls and Billy parted ways.

Making it into Aubrey's room, the stumbling pair collapsed onto her king-sized bed. They had kicked off their shoes and left their coats somewhere near the front hall, but decided they were too tired to change into anything else. Aubrey had a small remote control near her bed for the light. Once they were settled, she dimmed it, leaving enough light to see the layout of the room. *Mostly for Genie's benefit*, Aubrey figured, as Genie had far more to drink.

Aubrey wondered if she'd even remember making it back to the house. After a few minutes, Genie rolled to face Aubrey, and whispered, "Don't hate me, kaaay?"

Aubrey rolled her eyes. "What'd you do now? You better not have pissed yourself."

Genie giggled. "Nooo. Stupid. I meant the...," her voice rang into laughter.

"Look, I'm going to sleep. Stay if you want, otherwise call another Uber in an hour once you've sobered up some." Aubrey rolled to face the wall.

"Au*breeey*."

"Swear to god, ya drunk ass, go to sleep."

"Fine you'll never know where I hid it, then."

"Hid what?"

More laughter. "You'll never know," Genie said in a sing-song voice.

Aubrey sighed and sat up. She scanned the room, but didn't see anything out of place. She was certain Genie wouldn't remember much of this, so she said, "I'll find it tomorrow. G'night."

Genie sighed with a final "Ha!" then rolled over and stayed quiet.

Aubrey shifted to lay flat on her back. She stared at the ceiling and watched it slowly move out of focus. The room grew darker as her eyes grew heavier. Moments later, she dozed off.

Ba-bump

Aubrey rocketed upright, searching the room for the sudden noise. Genie was no longer next to her. Aubrey surmised she sobered up just enough to order a ride back to her house. *Doubtful she'll be sufficiently quiet to sneak into her house undetected.*

Focusing on the closet, Aubrey squinted her eyes. It seemed to be where the sound originated, but she was asleep, so it was hard to know for sure. Silence followed. Aubrey glanced at the lime-green glow of her digital clock on her dresser. It showed 3:43. She sighed and reluctantly slouched back into her pillow. She stared at the ceiling and watched it grow darker and darker.

Thump. Thump.

Jumping off the foot of the bed, Aubrey stood in the middle of her room, searching for the cause of the disturbance. Her adrenaline coursed rapidly throughout her body. She dropped to her knees and looked under the bed, using her cellphone as a flashlight. Finding nothing unusual, she stood and lit up the corners of the room. Nothing out of place. To Aubrey, it sounded as if something fell. *The closet.*

She shivered and moved toward the door. With shaky fingertips, she touched the knob and pulled it toward her. The door opened, revealing some laundry, hanging clothes and several shelves of cluttered collectables. Using the light on her phone, Aubrey scanned the small space, not seeing much out of place aside from the expected mound of her dirty clothes. As she lit the hanging clothes in front of her something shifted out of the corner of her eye near the bottom of the shelves. Aubrey jumped back with a shriek.

Shining the light over the perceived movement, Aubrey noticed a doll lying flat on its face. This surprised her. Most of her dolls she donated to charity years ago. The few that she held onto were in storage. But the doll on her floor looked about the size of her American Girl dolls. With her foot, she kicked the doll onto its back and used the light to examine it. "Not one of my American Girl dolls," she murmured.

This doll had dark skin and black eyes. The hair, she could tell, was long, but pinned on top of its head. The dress was purple and green shrouds of fabric wrapped around the body. It looked old. Genie's sing-song voice saying, *you'll never know*, suddenly echoed in her mind.

"Crap," grumbled Aubrey, sitting the doll upright and placing it on a higher shelf among the rest of the clutter. "Guess you'll have to hang out here until I find out where you came from."

She assumed the doll fell from wherever Genie originally placed it. She wasn't sure about Genie's angle for this prank, but she didn't find it funny, especially with what happened at that stupid hick-town mansion. Aubrey wondered momentarily if the doll came from there. She couldn't recall if Genie left with anything. She hoped not, and felt too tired to think about it. She'd re-hide the damn thing in Genie's house once she got some sleep. "Drunk-ass," she muttered, shaking her head as she returned to bed.

23

"Ah...damn."

"Ellbea? Hon, what is it?" Cal was in the living room reading his copy of the latest Pulitzer prize winning novel. He was at a good part, but Elle's voice brought him back to reality.

"Apparently, Kat hit her head and according to Walt, won't go to an ER to get checked out."

"Well, why would she? She's got you here."

"Me and my x-ray vision. If it's bad enough for him to text me...,"

"It's probably nothing. Go over there."

"I'm just worried. The way those two have been going at it the past few weeks, one was bound to snap. If it was Walt, it'd be physical instead of emotional."

Cal nodded. Kat snapping would consist of either plotted murder that would never come to fruition, or an impromptu vacation far away without so much as a postcard stating where she was. Walt, on the other hand, would likely explode.

Elle stood in front of Cal and said, "I'm going over there. I'll be back at some point."

"Want me to go with you?" It was a semi-sincere offer, but Elle nodded. She knew Cal would be able to run interference with Walt so she had at least a chance at getting the full story out of Kat.

Elle threw Cal's shoes at him and started putting on her own. The worn-down running shoes had seen better days. Formerly bright neon pink, Elle ran the shoes into a new state of decomposition. *Literally,* thought Cal. Mud and blood dyed with grass stains; they looked like she ran them over with a lawn mower several times. She finished lacing up the sad-state of apparel and walked out the front door. Cal was close behind her, locking up as they trekked three houses down to sort through the night's excitement. *We really need to get her new shoes,* thought Cal, as he watched Elle move ahead toward the Muller's house. *And why does all the nonsense kick up on a Friday night? Doesn't anyone relax anymore? Damn their tempers. She always seems to push him and then, bam. Something. Course I'm just assuming now that there was a fight. She might've tripped over the cat, for all I know.* His thoughts were interrupted by Elle yelling at him to hurry up.

"Well, for god's sake, Woman, you're practically sprinting."

"Hey, I don't know what we're walking into. She could be unconscious for all I know."

"He probably would've led with that in his message if so," said Cal. "Besides, they're both marginally intelligent adults. Don't you think they'd exhaust all options on their own before reaching out to us?"

"Well, technically it was me, but I'm roping you in, too."

Cal smirked, "Damn skippy."

Elle gave him a hard look. "Now don't go assuming this was a fight. We've gotta be open and supportive and--,"

"Yea, yea, I know, geesh, just go in."

Without so much as a tap on the door, Elle pushed it open and Cal noticed her immediate anxiety. She had a nervous habit of pushing back the cuticles of her pointer fingers with her thumbs, in sort of a rolling motion when she was stressed or ruminating. It was a subtle movement that most overlooked, but hard to miss after being with her for fifteen years.

Cal reached out to put a hand on Elle's shoulder, but she quickly brushed him off and headed for Kat's bedroom. Cal hung back, looking around the living room as he strolled through it and into the kitchen. "Feel the room," Elle would often tell him. "It'll feel heavy after a fight."

God, she could be such a hippie. Well, thought Cal, *it feels like 70 degrees, low humidity, and a well-lit kitchen.*

From the bedroom, he heard Elle firing off questions and Walt answering them in great detail. It wasn't hard to pick up Walt's voice from any part of the house. "Yea, she was folding clothes, and Hubris, Huey we call him--,"

"Oh for the love of it, I know the damn cat's name, Walt!"

"Right, right, sorry Elle. Um, yea, he ran up and into the pile she was folding. Dark colors today, because Genie needed her volleyball top clean and it's emerald. But Kat was worried Huey would get paw prints on the clothes. She shooed it off the bed, but caught her foot in the comforter. See, we never make the bed...well, she doesn't, and she lost her balance, and fell sideways, off the bed and hit her head on the nightstand halfway down."

"Did she pass out?" Cal knew that tone. That was the "I believe she hit her head and nothing more" tone.

Elle was a human bullshit detector. He chuckled thinking that could be her super power. The Bullshittonator: reigning terror over all tall tales ever told. He'd run that by her later to get her thoughts on the title. He redirected his attention to Walt's voice explaining that Kat lost consciousness for a few seconds, but seemed to be fine now. A few more exchanges, then he heard footsteps exit the bedroom and approach the kitchen.

"Calvin, my good man, I didn't realize you came as well! Can I get you a drink?"

Cal nodded. "Yea, I started with wine earlier, and I think I should stick to it."

"Believe we have a bottle of red open. It's a blend, that ok?"

"I'm a cheap date and a cheap drunk, pour whatever ya got."

Walt grunted with a nod, grabbed two glasses from the cabinet and poured away. He passed one glass to Cal, who instinctively swirled it a few times and took a sip. It wasn't bad. The two sat down at the table, wordless for the first few minutes.

"Walt...I gotta know...what really happened?"

Walt paused for a second. Whether it was from the wine or the stressful blur of events, Walt let his guard down enough to allow open communication.

"Believe me when I say, I don't know one hundred percent," he enunciated 'percent' with heavy emphasis on the T, "but we weren't seeing eye to eye. It happens. Hell, I'm sure you and Elle get into it at times."

"Disagreements and head injuries are on separate planes, Walt. C'mon, you know that."

"I do, I do...but all I see is a blinding light of rage when we get into it. Then I snap out of it and everyone in the room is either hiding, crying, or...well...,"

"Unconscious?"

"As it happened in this instance, yes, but I swear to you, Cal, I didn't do it intentionally!"

Cal shook his head, unable to conceal the look of disapproval that crept over his face.

"No, no you don't understand...I pushed a bunch of her shit off of the dresser. One of those things flew at her and clocked her in the head. Knocked her out cold. Might've smashed a few things into the walls, too."

"Shit, Man," muttered Cal.

Walt glanced down into his wine. Cal tried throwing him a bone. "Hey, I'm glad you didn't just clobber her over the head. Or punch her." He paused, hearing how awful that came out. He stuck his foot further into his mouth by adding, "I'm not condoning throwing things that could potentially harm someone...because you did and it did...uh, but, but I'm glad you didn't come at her and attack her on purpose."

Walt accepted the attempted consolation, along with thanking God that Genie was not home. *Where is that kid, anyways? It's well past midnight. She is usually home by now.* Course, he was glad she still wasn't.

Just then, the back door swung open and Genie stumbled through it. She seemed to be using it as a support, but when the door moved from her weight, she lost her balance. Cal noticed this and hoped Walt didn't. Last thing he wanted was another explosion. Fortunately, Walt was more focused on swirling his wine glass, lost in a tornado of thoughts.

Cal jumped up to greet Genie. "Sweetheart, how was your night?"

He mumbled because he knew if she was like any teenager with a drop of alcohol she'd...

"*Oh my gaaawd,* Uncle Cal! Wow you guys are here? I had noooo idea. What—what's uh...why are you here? So laaaate?"

"Shhh, Honey, your Mom had a little bit of an accident and she called your Aunt Ellbea to check her out."

"*Shhhit* is she ok?"

Wow, she's loud, thought Cal, quickly guiding her by the table and out of the kitchen.

Walt glanced up. "Pumpkin you feelin' ok?"

Genie seemed to sober up enough to lower her voice. "Yea, Daddy. Just tired. Gonna head...," she pointed with a determined glare through her smudged make up, "thatta way," and headed toward the bedrooms.

Her room was next to Walt and Kat's. Cal decided it best to accompany her. He figured the girls were either in detailed discussion about tonight's events, or Elle was kept completely in the dark and they were off topic to ensure it stayed that way. The latter, Cal found out later from Elle, was accurate.

A soft knock on the bedroom door sounded. Kat's headache kept a constant seven out of ten; some stupid pain scale Elle kept asking her about. She couldn't tell her what happened. Not yet. She wasn't thinking clear, and she didn't want Elle to jump to conclusions over Walt. She was a little peeved that Walt called the Conways over, but at the same time, relieved to be with Elle because it meant an end to her and Walt's 'discussion.'

"Come in," answered Kat.

"Mom? Mom, oh my gaaawd. Are you ok?"

"Genie, Honey, c'mere." Kat motioned her over.

Genie stumbled toward her mom in a zigzagged pattern. Until then, Cal had her propped on his arm for support.

"Oh lord, what the hell did you drink?"

Genie looked genuinely shocked that Kat knew her level of sobriety, or lack thereof. "Wha-what?"

"Genie, we own a bar. Your father and I both went through college. Your adopted aunt and uncle drink like fish."

"*Hey*," shouted Elle and Cal in unison.

It would've been cute if Kat wasn't in so much pain.

"We do *not* drink like fish," said Elle.

"Yea, we drink like sharks! Those are way cooler!" added Cal.

Despite her best efforts, Elle busted out laughing. "Idiot," she managed, shaking her head.

Kat returned her focus to Genie.

"Sweetie, I'm not mad, just, fill me in. What'd you have? Where were you?"

"Bowling alley, again. I thought I told you that! They serve alcohol. We had some pitchers of Bud Lite."

"Panther piss?" said Cal.

"Not now!" Kat growled. Back to Genie, "Honey, we've had a bit of a rough night. You think you'll be ok sleeping it off?"

Genie was looking fairly pale, maybe a little green. *Her world must be spinning*, thought Kat.

Kat shot Elle a pleading glance and Elle immediately jumped in. "Hey Kiddo, come stay with us tonight. We have plenty of Zofran, Aleve, and Claritin; the holy trinity of hangover cures."

Genie nodded, not in a state of mind to argue. *She's ready for bed and possibly some water*, noted Kat, "C'mon, Love, go with those two. They'll set ya up and we'll have breakfast for all of you tomorrow."

"Only if you're up for it, Charlotte Mack," winked Elle.

Kat was in too much pain to get angry. "Whatever, get out before I throw ya out."

With Genie between them, Elle and Cal walked the short distance back home, gave Genie medication, and got her settled in their guest bed.

"Holy shit, this has been a long day," exhaled Elle as they settled in bed themselves.

Cal debated filling her in now or tomorrow. "Elle, Babe...the day's not done yet." And he started from the beginning.

"No wonder she wanted Genie out of the house."

"Yea...I think it all seems worse now because of how late it is."

"It's still bad, Cal, you know that. Actually, it is getting worse. They've always had tempers, but this is different."

"Let's get some sleep. Keep an ear out for Genie, she still might hurl."

"I left a plastic basin by her bed. We're covered."

"I love you, my super lady." He leaned over and kissed her forehead.

"Love you too, Cal."

Three houses down, Kat slipped into a deep stupor. Walt remained seated at the table, polishing off the bottle of wine and then, opened another. He finally fell asleep, head atop clasped hands, slumped in his seat.

24

"So, how's the perfect woman, Bacon?" RJ's voice startled Billy and caused a small splash of coffee to sting his hand.

"Ah, Boss, you scared me," Billy grinned, shaking his head.

"Sorry about that. Here," RJ handed Billy a paper towel and proceeded to move toward the Keurig for an afternoon decaffeinated brew. "But seriously, how're things? You've been quiet lately."

Billy shrugged. Genie's boldness and manipulative tactics in Millerton flashed in his mind, followed by the recollection of her falling through the floorboards and how close they came to never leaving the Doll House. "She's fine. We're fine."

"Uh huh," RJ started the machine and coffee poured into his mug.

"I think I'm newer to relationships than she is," Billy continued. "I think she knows more about them than I do."

RJ chuckled. "Well, that's probably an understatement."

"I mean, she knows how to get what she wants, when she wants it," he paused, remember Genie roping Aubrey, Cassie, and him into the Millerton adventure. "Not just with me, but with everyone. She's smart, and she uses it to help others see things the way she does, and before you know it, you're doing something you wouldn't have even considered otherwise."

"Perceptive," RJ nodded and sipped his coffee. "Very perceptive, Bacon. Now, is this stuff bad stuff or just typical teenager stuff?"

Not wanting to divulge details about the Doll House, Billy shrugged again and smiled, "She's a typical teenager in a few aspects still, I suppose."

RJ shifted his weight and took another sip from his mug. He waited to see if Billy would expound further on that statement. When the silence started to feel uncomfortable, Billy added, "It's fine, really. I think I'm just a little more naïve than her, if you can believe that."

"I can."

"Thanks."

"It's not an insult, Bacon. You're no longer dealing with a kid on your team. If she's as mature as you say, then she also knows how to play the game a little. She doesn't sound like some innocent doe-eyed deer. She sounds like a bit of a firecracker."

Laughing, Billy nodded. "That's exactly what she is."

"Nothing wrong with it, but don't be stupid."

Billy smiled and nodded. "Yea, will do. Thanks, Boss."

Raising his mug as Billy left the break room, RJ said, "No problem," and chuckled to himself.

25

Another week passed. On Friday night, Aubrey dragged herself upstairs to her bedroom. She flopped onto her bed, face up, staring at the ceiling fan's slow, rotating blades. Without volleyball practice, she had more free time, but felt sleepier and more drained at the end of her school days. Her parents were downstairs. *Probably making dinner.*

Rolling on her side, she propped herself onto her elbow and started scrolling through her phone. There were a few texts from Genie, which she blew off with a "**busy tonight. c-ya tomorrow**" reply. She sighed and glanced around the room. "What the...?"

Aubrey sat up, staring at the doll seated on her dresser, facing her. The thing looked so real. How did it get there? She stood and approached the dark-featured figure. She didn't know what she found so startling about the thing, but she trembled as she edged closer to it. With one finger, she poked the doll in the midsection. Nothing.

No movement, no signs of life. Aubrey sighed and laughed. "What, like I thought it would move?"

She shook her head and headed to the bathroom. Bubble baths were her latest addiction. She grabbed a bath bomb from the cabinet and started filling the tub with warm water.

Closing the door, she kicked her clothes to the corner of the bathroom. Dropping the bath bomb into the tub, Aubrey watched swirls of pink effervescence fuse with the clear water. Bubble gum and floral aromas rose with the steam. Once the fizzing stopped, she climbed in and turned off the faucet. Sinking to a spot where the water covered most of her body, she played with the pink bubbles a bit and then felt herself drifting off.

When she opened her eyes again, Aubrey only saw the wavering outline of the bathroom ceiling, tinted pink. She felt her body, but couldn't move it. Was she still sleeping? Within seconds she also realized she was holding her breath, unable to let it out or draw in another. Panic gripped her as she struggled to come up to the water's surface.

Frozen and still submerged, her horror amplified as a figure passed in front of the shimmering view of the ceiling. When the water stilled, Aubrey recognized the dark hair and life-like appearance of the same doll she had left sitting on her dresser less than an hour ago. The wavering image appeared to tilt its head from side to side, but the rest of the body remained motionless. Unable to come up for air, Aubrey's vision faded until nothing but the imprinted image of the doll's silhouette burned into her mind. Then, complete darkness.

26

On Monday morning, RJ skimmed the paper at his desk as he sipped his coffee. A headline caught his eye: *Local teen drowns: suicide suspected.* He frowned and flipped to the story to read further. He saw:

Pinecrest Park, IL. 01.10.2015. Aubrey McDowell (18) passed away at 16:00. McDowell was discovered submerged in her home bathtub. Paramedics arrived on scene and transported McDowell to St. Michael's Hospital where she was pronounced dead. Police suspect suicide. No evidence of foul play or bodily detriment discovered on initial intake. Police will not comment on official cause of death until they receive a full autopsy report. McDowell, a senior in high school and member of the Pinecrest Park High School volleyball team was well liked in her community. She planned on attending junior college next fall to study communications. She is survived by her

mother, father, and older sister. Arrangements for the services will be announced later this week.

RJ let out a low whistle. When Elle popped in, he tossed her the folded paper. She scanned it and let out a small gasp. "This is horrible! Why do I come to you to ruin my day straight out of the gate?"

He shook his head. "Tragic. Drowning's one of the worst ways to go. I find it hard to believe a that kid would choose that route to end things."

"Right? Maybe she fell asleep."

"More likely, but I'm not sure I'm sold. In any event, figured you'd wanna know. Billy coaches at that school, one of us should probably tell him if he doesn't know already."

"I'm on it."

Before Elle turned to leave, Billy pushed by her and joined them in RJ's small quarters. "Billy, hey--," Elle's voice trailed when she saw his bloodshot eyes and untucked, wrinkled scrubs. "You heard?" she murmured.

"Yea," Billy sniffed and rubbed his eyes with the back of his hand. Elle wrapped him in a hug before he could say much else.

"Need the day off, Bud?" asked RJ.

Elle felt Billy shake his head and mumble, "No, I'll be ok. Just, I can't believe it." He stepped back and grabbed a tissue from the box on RJ's desk. "Genie's holding up better than I expected. We found out last night. Guess Aubrey, uh, passed away Friday evening." He took in a shallow breath, then continued with a shaky voice. "Genie's mom found out from Aubrey's mom. Genie called me right after."

RJ stood and clapped Billy on the shoulder. "Let me know if you need anything," and stepped out to see his first patient.

27

The long Illinois winter kept its slow pace. Weeks passed after Aubrey's death. Police ruled it as a suicide, but her parents refused to believe it. However, because of the official ruling, no further investigation pursued. Genie felt the tension in her home continue to escalate. Her parents constantly argued, and she felt the need to escape whenever possible. One night, in the middle of the week, her father's temper spiked again and as usual, without any warning. Genie retreated to her bedroom, turned up her radio, and waited for the storm to pass.

A soft tap caught her attention over by her desk. She glanced toward the sound and saw her backpack hanging from the chair. Sitting up on her bed, she surveyed the rest of the bedroom. Everything on her desk appeared as it did when she came in. No open window, *but why would there be, it's January*? Her closet was ajar with two weeks' worth of laundry spilling out of it. *Maybe the cat was in there playing with one of the shoelaces*?

She stood to check. No cat. With a sigh, she turned back to her bed. Positioned exactly where Genie was, sat the porcelain doll she'd snagged before leaving the mansion a few months ago. Genie shook her head and rubbed her eyes. The doll remained in its place; motionless but staring directly at her. Genie's heart thumped faster. Her legs felt like their muscles were about to betray them. *Maybe I had her next to me on the bed and she fell forward when I stood up*.

Shaking, Genie lifted the doll and placed it back on the shelf near the back corner of the room, opposite from her desk and chair. She then sat on the edge of her bed, radio still blasting, and watched the doll. Several hours passed, and with each one, Genie slowly advanced into a position closer and closer to laying down and falling asleep. Finally, in the early hours of the morning, she slipped into a world of dreams.

One dream seemed all too familiar. She found herself in a vacant wheat field. *Right after harvest season*, she decided, as the crisp air brushed against her face, leaving her with a chill. She looked down and saw herself dressed in pants and a sweatshirt. *Typical autumn attire*, she smiled.

Looking around the vast land, she saw a wooden table stationed several feet in front of her with two chairs. She walked toward the table and took a seat, staring at the empty one in front of her. Suddenly, the figure of a young woman appeared. The woman had a slender build, with dark eyes and straw-colored hair. Her skin was white and smooth. "Just like porcelain," Genie said aloud.

"Yes," agreed the figure, "Just like porcelain."

A breeze rustled through the stalks of wheat surrounding the two with a soft whistle. The figure remained expressionless, but it—*she*? She could speak. She didn't do much more than that, though.

"This is where I belong," said the figure. "I was going home. You interfered. You must leave."

Her gentle, melodious voice uttered each phrase like the start to a lullaby. Genie glanced around, puzzled. "This? This field is home? Where are we?"

The figure ignored her. "You took me further away. I simply wish to return home."

Trying again, Genie asked, "Well, where is home?"

"This is my home," repeated the figure in the same sing-song way.

Genie wasn't even certain the figure had heard her question, although the response was appropriate. Genie was about to ask who the figure was, but noticed an embroidered name on the collar of her faded dress.

"Lucy," said Genie.

The figure stayed still, except for her crimson lips, which parted only slightly when she spoke.

"Lucy? Is that your name?" Genie tried again.

No response.

Genie tried to stand, but found herself unable to move. Stuck. The only things moving on Genie's body were the necessary systems to keep her body alive. Even her eyes were locked in focus.

"Your lungs. Those must stop," and as the figure sang this, Genie began gasping for air. She instinctively tried to clutch her throat, jump to her feet, anything. But, her body remained frozen.

As she drew in raspy breaths, unable to get more air, the figure chanted, "Your heart. It must desist."

Genie felt a sick dropping sensation in her chest, like she was on a roller coaster. This time, however, the feeling never stopped. She felt the blood drain from her face. Her arms and legs felt limp, and her breathing ceased. The world grew darker fading at the corners of her eyes. With her ragdoll form and head now hanging to the side, the last burning image Genie Muller saw was the figure, seated across from her, and staring back. She heard, "And now, your mind must sleep."

Then darkness.

28

Kat only had a hazy, fragmented recollection, but even that much she wished she could erase. She replayed pacing around the house. An eerie, chilling stillness embraced her. Her mind had snapshots of the kitchen, the living room, all appearing as they should, but the feel--*why did it feel so off*? She felt her stomach knot and her heart launch into a gallop. The prickles that ran down her spine caused a violent shiver and she found herself sprinting...*but where? And still, why?*

Sprinting to Genie's room, skidding a little past the door and catching the handle to pull her back. She shook the doorknob and, in her haste, lost two fingernails. She then shouldered through it, even though it wasn't locked. Time froze. This snapshot she could revisit without the haze, without question, with full clarity. This picture embedded itself in her mind forever.

The room was more disheveled than usual. Genie always liked things somewhat in order. Even in the dim light, Kat saw that several papers and books were knocked off the desk. The chair next to her desk was tipped back, and yesterday's previously folded laundry littered the floor. Kat's eyes followed the trail of clothes to the bed. The bed wasn't even made. The pillows were also tossed to the ground. The mattress laid partially askew and part of the comforter was torn. Lying face up on top of the asymmetrical wreck was Genie.

At least, Kat knew that's who it should be, but no other familiarity of her daughter lay there except the clothing and hair color. She later explained to Elle that it was her, but it felt empty to be near her, like she found Genie's shell. The shell exhibited two crystal blue eyes with an icy, distant stare. Her partially opened lips were tinged with a similar hue. Genie's right arm froze in an arch over her head and her left, across her chest. Both legs were stiff and straight. A blue tint started to take over her skin. "Cyanosis," Kat could hear Elle's voice explain once during a medical show about postmortem changes.

In the next series of snapshots, Kat remembered only the plunging sensation of her heart into her stomach and her chills changing to sweat. She remembered her throat burning from screaming and somehow her legs carrying her over to Genie. Her hands attempted chest compressions and with shaky gasps of air, her mouth and lungs pushed oxygen into Genie's lifeless lips. There was a moment Kat actually thought she had saved her, but a vital Genie did not follow the eruption of vomit that her stomach expulsed. Kat's mind also must have had the sense to dial 911 on her phone at one point. She couldn't remember that part at all, but it must have happened since her ears heard the front door clamor open as the paramedics entered the house. Kat's body met the medics as they rushed into Genie's room to revive the cold shell that so closely resembled her daughter. The following twenty-four hours beyond that, Kat retained no memory of.

Elle heard sirens as she and Cal sat down to a classy snack of Cheetos. The mac and cheese simmered on the stove and Elle secretly loved using Cal's cooking as an excuse for her favorite fourth grade foods, save the wine of course. Halfway through the bowl, the house phone that neither knew why they kept interrupted their absent-minded munching. Cal reached over and answered. "Yea? Whoa, whoa, slow down--Kat?"

Elle noted Cal's tone and immediately yanked the phone from his Cheetos-stained fingers. He lingered close to her as she tried to calm down her incoherent friend.

"*Genie, oh god it's Genie, she's gone. She's gone! They took her. I want my girl!*"

"Kat? Honey, slowdown, who took her? Where are--?"

"*Ambulance. Blue, she turned blue! I knew it was bad but not this, not this bad. She'd never do it. Why would she-why would sh--sh--she do--,*"

"Do what? Is Genie Ok? Are you at home?"

At this point, Cal sprinted out the front door toward the Muller home. He saw the ambulance loading up a stretcher and pulling away. Running back home and between breaths, he relayed this to Elle. She hung up and called Kat back on her cell as she and Cal jumped into the car and drove off to St. Michael's Hospital.

RJ's peaceful, postprandial stupor was cut short by the shrill sound of his cell phone blaring across the room. Spencer was long gone, likely playing video games in his bedroom. His quality headset blocked virtually any sound beyond those games from entering his head.

RJ rolled over on the couch, catching himself with one arm prior to succumbing to gravity's full effect. He fumbled for the phone and squinted to see Billy's name light up on the iPhone's screen.

"Bacon, what can I do ya fo–,"

Billy cut him off with gasps and what RJ believed to be muffled sobs. "She–she–I can't...I think she...she's gone, Boss. She's gone."

"Who, Billy? Talk to me, what happened?"

At this point, RJ felt a linguistic analyst would have a run for his money attempting to decipher Billy's tale, but RJ did his best to keep up. By the time he hung up the phone, he was in the process of putting on his coat and heading out to check on Billy. In route, he phoned Elle.

Elle sat in her living room with a glass of wine in hand. Cal sat across from her, elbows on his lap and chin resting in his hands. Neither had much to say, but they couldn't sleep. Kat and Walt were back at their house. Elle and Cal felt it best they leave them be for the night. Elle's ringtone broke the silence.

"Hi there," Elle whispered.

"Hey, Princess," came the familiar tone.

"RJ. Oh god. You heard?"

"On my way to check on Billy. Spence is home on his own, so if he needs something and can't get to me, I told him to call you."

"Not a problem. How's Billy?"

"A complete wreck. How're Kat and Walt?"

"Even worse," Elle stood up and strode back and forth across the living room.

They chatted for several more minutes, assuring one another that they were ok. Elle hung up and turned to Cal. "Should I go...?"

"No."

"But Kat...,"

"You can't fix this one, Ellbea. And Honey, this is going to hit you hard too. Just, sit," Cal said as he moved over, making a space for her on the giant armchair.

Elle hesitated, then wedged her way into the spot Cal created for her. She took in a deep breath, put her head on his shoulder, and started to sob. Cal tilted his head away so that she wouldn't see the stream of tears that began to trickle down his face. They stayed there for the rest of the night.

30

To Elle, the few weeks following Genie's passing blurred together. The town collectively mourned as well. Cara and Alex remained in town a few days after Genie's funeral. Cassie had a hard time handling everything that took place, so Alex determined that given the recent events, time away from Millerton would be beneficial. Justin was up north for baseball camp in Chicago as it was, so the three stayed with the Conways.

The morning before the Kingmans headed back to Millerton, Elle hosted brunch. Kat and Walt stopped over to join. Elle stood by the stove making pancakes and Cassie, next to her, watched and chatted. Kat and Cara sat at the table talking in soft tones and Walt, Calvin, and Alex appropriated the living room to watch some football.

"Auntie Elle?" Cassie started.

"Yea Cass?" Elle poured more batter onto the skillet and turned toward her.

"You know when you guys came in for that volleyball tournament?"

"Mhm."

"Well," Cassie folded her arms across her chest and shifted her weight, "This is gonna sound sort of crazy, but...," she paused.

Noticing the batter starting to bubble, Elle flipped the pancake, creating a sizzling sound in the pan. "What's up, Cassie?"

"We went to that house. That Doll House."

Elle stopped. She set the spatula down and turned back to Cassie. "Who's 'we'?"

"Um, me, Aubrey, Genie, and uh, her boyfriend. Or coach, whatever."

"Anything happen while you guys were there?" Elle felt a familiar knot tying in her stomach. She waited for a response, but Cassie just glanced down at her shoes.

At this point, the pancake started to smoke. Elle didn't notice, but the smoke detector did. "Ah shit," said Elle, flipping the charred cake into the wastebasket and turning to wave a dish towel at the alarm. Kat and Cara jumped up to see if they could help. They couldn't, but the noise alerted them nonetheless. Once the shrieking alarm silenced, Elle turned back to Cassie. She ignored the fact that Kat and Cara were now close by.

"Cassie, at The Doll House, did anything unusual happen to any of you guys?"

This caught Kat's attention. "What? What did you just say, Elle?"

Elle sighed. "The teens hit up The Doll House when we were in Millerton."

Kat normally had a short fuse and given the events of the past week, that fuse became nonexistent. Elle expected rage, ire, items to be thrown. Instead, Kat burst into tears. Cara raised her eyebrows. *Must've been expecting the same thing I was,* thought Elle.

In attempts to quell the situation, Cassie did something out of character; she lied. "Aunt Kat, Aunt Kat, I'm so, so sorry. We just wanted to see it. We didn't even go inside, we just walked around it and looked through a few of the windows."

Kat's sobbing slowed. She drew in a few deep breaths, and reached for the tissue box on Elle's counter. Cara, not wanting to upset her further, remained silent. Cassie had told her mom all that she had witnessed that night, which turned out, wasn't much. But Cara knew Genie and Billy were in the house and would've likely been killed if Alex hadn't shown up to drag them out. She decided now was not the time to share this with Kat.

As Kat calmed down and resumed her seat back at the table with Cara, Elle glanced at Cassie and clicked on the fan over the stove. The steady whir blended with their low voices.

"Cass, what really happened?" She added another circle of batter to the pan.

Cassie took a step closer to Elle. "Well, we all did go there, and it was pretty creepy. Aubrey and I decided we didn't want to go further than the front entrance. Genie was kinda mean about it. Then, she and Billy left us to go explore the house."

Elle flipped the pancake and nodded. "So, did you see anything happen while you were there?"

"Aubrey and I waited for a few minutes, but then, she felt something cold on her arm. I was holding onto her other arm, so when she ran out of the house, she pulled me with her. When we got outside, we waited on the lawn for a few more minutes. Then we heard Genie scream from the upstairs."

Elle tilted her head, bemused. "Upstairs?"

Cassie nodded. "Yea, I didn't know that there was a way up there, but we saw the flashlight shining in the upper window."

Elle added the finished pancake to the others plated on the counter and began adding strips of bacon to the hot pan. They hissed and popped on contact with the metal.

"Anyways," Cassie continued, "We thought they might need help, but we were too afraid to go in and try to find them."

"That probably saved all of your lives," murmured Elle.

"We drove the van back to the house and Dad was there. We barely mentioned the mansion and he jumped up, put us both in the back of his police car, and drove us over there. He went so fast! Like, this spooked him, too," said Cassie.

Nodding and turning over the bacon, Elle said, "It's a dangerous house, Cass, and your dad knows what it can do to people."

"Yea. Well, when we got there, Dad made us stay in the car, but I saw him break one of the windows and pull Genie and Billy out. He was yelling and banging on the door before that, but couldn't get in, so he used something on the porch to shatter the glass."

"Quick thinking on his part. Let me ask you this, Honey, does your mom know about all of this?"

"Yea. But after Dad took us back to our house, he made a deal with Genie that he wouldn't tell just to get her in trouble. Mom didn't really like that idea, but Dad said that he wanted Genie to be an adult and tell her mom on her own. Plus, something about him wanting her to come to him if she got into trouble again."

Elle mulled this over a moment. "I suppose I get where he's coming from," she replied. "But, you initially said, 'this is gonna sound crazy'; is there more to this?"

Cassie shifted her stance and glanced back at the floor. "Uh, well, ever since that night, I don't know, our house just feels...tense."

"Tense?" repeated Elle.

"Uh huh. Like, me and Justin fight more. Mom and Dad argue over little things. Mom spends more time at Gramma Cass's. And, um...,"

"C'mon, Cassie, what else?"

"Well, nothing I can see. But I'm afraid to sleep at night. I have nightmares and wake up all the time, afraid someone's in my room, watching me. But I turn on the lights and no one is there."

"Think you're just stressed out from everything that happened over the past month?"

"I guess." Elle didn't think she sounded convinced. "I did find something in my room though, that wasn't there before that night. A...a doll with dark skin and dark eyes. It seems much older than the dolls at the store."

"Does your mom or dad know you still have this doll?"

"I'm afraid to talk to them. Mom already thinks I stole it or something! But I don't know where it came from."

"Where what came from?" Kat's low, raspy tone came from behind them.

Cara started to stand and make her way across the kitchen as well.

"Where...where Cassie's interest in cooking came from. She asks some great questions," said Elle. Elle decided to talk with Cara and Alex later, but for the time being, didn't want to upset Kat.

Kat didn't press it further, but Elle heard her mutter, "You're a shitty liar, Ellbea."

Cara called the guys in from the living room and the group gathered together and enjoyed brunch. Once they finished and cleaned up, the Kingmans headed back home. By then, Elle completely forgot to mention to Cara and Alex about the mystery doll in Cassie's possession.

31

"Ah, crap!" Elle sat up from the couch after a power nap. It was the following weekend after all the chaos and she still felt like she couldn't catch up on rest.

Calvin sat across from her on his recliner. "What's the matter, Babe?"

Elle grumbled and rubbed her eyes, "Nothing, it's just, I meant to talk to Alex about something last week." She stumbled to her feet and made her way into the kitchen. Her cellphone sat charging on the counter. Elle turned it on and the time and date flashed January 18th, 2015. 7:45pm. She unlocked it and called Alex.

"Ellbea, hey!" Alex answered on the third ring.

"Hi Bud, listen, there's something I meant to ask you."

"Sure thing, what's up?"

"That night you found the teens at The Doll House...,"

Elle heard Alex sigh, but she went on, "I think, somehow, Cassie got a souvenir from the event."

"What the hell does that mean?"

"Don't get mad, I doubt she had much of anything to do with it, but I think one of the dolls, uh, made its way back home with her."

Alex paused. "Well, I'm working right now, but I'm on patrol. I'll swing by the house and see if that's actually the case. But, why wouldn't she say something?"

Elle sat down at the table. "Alex, you remember the house. It affects people differently. People aren't themselves. Also, she's scared. She probably doesn't want you thinking she stole it or something."

"And she told you this?"

"Promise me you'll act like you stumbled upon it, rather than rat me out. I still need her to be able to come to me...,"

"Yea, yea, I know, I know. Thanks for the heads up, Ellbea."

"You got it."

While Alex made his way back home, Kat dug up some nerve of her own. After a few glasses of wine, she mustered enough courage to go back into Genie's room. Wincing, she turned the handle and stepped in. The room appeared in as much disarray as it had the night she lost Genie. Kat moved around, with trepidation at first, straightening the bed and picking up the scattered laundry one piece at a time. Once she eased a bit, she bunched the remaining laundry into Genie's hamper. She cleared some of the items on her desk and folded down the comforter on the bed, adding the sheets to the pile in the hamper. She took care to breathe through her mouth; even the familiar scent of her late daughter was too painful to endure.

As she decluttered the space, an unfamiliar piece caught her eye. Kat stood and made her way toward the shelf in the corner of Genie's room. There sat an aged, porcelain doll. Kat frowned and picked it up to examine it closer. The doll had on a faded dress with a large white collar. The hair fell in yellow ringlets around the ivory colored face. The dark eyes were the doll's boldest feature. It wore a small backpack, Kat noticed, as she turned the doll over. It was the same pattern as the dress, and didn't stick out. She almost missed it. Everything on this doll appeared to be hand stitched. Kat took in a faint, musty smell as she held the doll. *Definitely old,* she thought. *But how? Millerton. They visited the Doll House in Millerton.*

Almost dropping the doll, Kat let out a small scream. She placed the doll back on the shelf, picked up the hamper and left the room, closing the door behind her.

Even though it was only eight o'clock on a Saturday night, Cassie also felt the exhaustive weight of last month's events. She made her way to her room and closed the door. She changed into some sweatpants and a baggy t-shirt, then powered on her laptop. Loading her Netflix account, she created an alcove of pillows and blankets atop her bed to prepare for her TV show marathon. Once she sank into a comfortable spot, she reached to her right to flick off the light. The glow of her computer illuminated the room. The nightstand next to her closet caught her attention as the theme song to *Law and Order SVU* started playing. There sat the mystery doll. "Don't remember setting you there," murmured Cassie, but soon the detective work of Olivia and Elliot claimed her full attention.

Cassie felt her eyes growing heavier and heavier with each passing episode. She slumped deeper into her pillow fortress, until she dozed off. She didn't know how long she slept for, but she woke up feeling like she needed a puff of her inhaler. She kept it by her bed for such occasions, but when she sat up to reach for it, she realized thick, black smoke clouded her entire room. Wheezing, Cassie frantically rummaged for the inhaler on the shelf next to her bed. Once she found it, she drew in two deep breaths. The smoke thickened and Cassie continued to cough. *Where was the smoke coming from?*

Her eyes darted around the room. Flames licked the bottom of her closet door and Cassie jumped up and tried to escape. But her door was locked. *Locked*?

She never locked it. Her heart skipped a beat. She tried to scream but more smoke flooded her lungs, sending her into another coughing fit. Dropping to her knees, she started to crawl toward the window. Living in a ranch house, she figured she could use the window to retreat to the backyard. Her room wasn't large, but Cassie needed all of her strength just to get to the window. Each movement sent her head spinning. She felt like her lungs were on fire and no matter how much she coughed, she could not refill them with enough air.

She pulled herself up using the windowsill. She unlatched the bottom lock, then the top and started to rotate the crank at the base of the window. It moved a few inches, then stopped. Cassie pulled her entire weight down on the crank, but it would not budge. With a final, desperate shove, the handle on the window broke free, sending Cassie falling back to the ground. She glanced back to her bed and the door. A figure stood at the edge of the bed. It was small, but person-like. "Oh god, that freakin' doll," she gasped. Cassie's world darkened. The remaining air abandoned her with each passing second. She curled into a ball, sputtering and wheezing.

Then, darkness.

Alex pulled into his driveway after hanging up with Elle. He planned to go directly to Cassie's room and remove the doll, but Cara caught him as he passed through the kitchen. "Home so soon?"

"Uh, hi, yea, just needed to check on something real fast."

Cara crossed her arms over her chest and blocked his path. "And, what, I can't hold the fort down without you?"

Alex sighed. Cara was always sensitive, but lately, she was acting over the top, even for her. "No Dear, that isn't what I said."

"You think since you're a police officer, and I'm just some, stay-at-home mother, you have to check in every gosh darn second to make sure I'm doing my job?" Her shrill tone echoed from the kitchen and down the hall.

"Cara, please. You're fantastic with everything you do here, for the house, the kids. This is something Elle mentioned--,"

"Oh, oh, ok. Now Elle gets to help out with the house. Now we have three people running the show." She started rubbing her hands together and pacing back and forth across the kitchen.

Alex rubbed his temples, took a deep breath, and then met her as she paced toward him. He took her hands, unclasped them, and said, "Let's sit, ok? Just, here," he dropped her hands and pulled out a chair from the kitchen table.

Cara sat down, keeping her eyes lowered. Alex sat next to her, facing her. They sat this way for several moments without saying anything. Then Alex started, "Listen, I know things have been, well, stressful the past few weeks. I'm sorry that they have. I need you to know I love you."

"Love you, too," she murmured back.

"We're a team, ok?" he said. "The kids need us united. Hell, pretty sure the town needs us united, if you think about it."

Cara laughed, and looked up at Alex. "Well, who else would keep everyone here sane and on their toes?"

"Only the best PTA, boyscout-leading, uniform-repairing mom in Millerton."

"Too cheesy," she smiled, but secretly loved the recognition.

"You think?" Alex knew she loved every bit of it.

Alex pulled her forward and kissed the top of her head. Silently, he prayed whatever tension that trickled its way into their lives would dissipate soon.

A thud broke the stillness. "What was that?" asked Cara.

Alex stood up and listened again. Quiet. But, he remembered what Elle informed him of earlier. Without a word, he sprinted toward Cassie's room.

32

After shooting RJ a few text messages, Elle decided she needed to get out of the house. Calvin was working late and she knew he'd find her there if she wasn't home or with Kat. Spencer answered the door.

"Hey Dr. Elle!" To her surprise, he ran up and gave her a tight hug instead of the usual fist bump.

"Hi there, Spence, good to see you, Kiddo!" Elle kissed the top of his head and tousled his hair. "Your dad around?"

"For sure. Follow me."

Spencer led her through the entryway and back toward RJ's study. RJ sat facing double computer screens, headphones over his ears, swearing at someone for 'camping.' Upon noticing Elle in his periphery, he let out a soft laugh, lowered the head set and said, "Well, that didn't take long."

"It's a ten-minute drive, RJ."

"I suppose it is. What can I get you to drink? Oh, and before you answer, yes, we do have ice to add to hard liquor."

Elle smiled, "Scotch on the rocks."

RJ got up from the computer set up and led her into the kitchen. "Cal know where you are?"

"Texting him now. He might swing by once work lets him off the hook, if that's cool."

"Absolutely. I'll save some booze for him, too," RJ laughed, adding ice into two glasses. He set them on the counter and poured some Dewar's into each.

The two sat down in RJ's rec room. He had a couch that wrapped around a portion of the perimeter, all seats capable of viewing a fifty-seven inch plasma screen. Elle didn't notice any changes from her last visit. The coffee table still held stacks of mail that were either junk or already sifted through. The lamp shades on either side of the couch still needed dusting and the only reason Elle noticed this was because they were sapphire. The bases of the matching lamps were ivory, and the contrast looked great. *The upkeep, well...,*

"Whatcha thinking about, Ellbea?"

"You need to dust."

RJ chuckled and raised his glass to her. Finally settling, Elle curled up on the chaise portion of the couch and RJ took advantage of one the couch's recliners. The two sipped their poisons in silence. Glancing at him, Elle wondered how he stayed so damn cheery. Even in light of recent events, his daily smile and the color of his bow tie never faded.

"Elle," he interrupted her thoughts. "God, you must be drained. Why aren't you home passed out?"

"Fun story: my body's exhausted but my brain won't power down."

"Ah. Yes, I can see where that'd be an issue." The ice in his glass clinked as he swirled the whiskey-scotch blend.

Elle's eyes rested on a piece of artwork RJ had hung over one of the large speakers on the wall facing her. It was an abstract piece, but he had had it since medical school. The two of them used to spend hours trying to find familiar figures out of the multitudes of colors and shapes. She smiled and told him she was happy he held onto it all this time.

RJ raised his eyebrows. "Like I could ever part with the Clashing Colors of Chaos. Do you even remember why I bought it in the first place?"

"Didn't you get it when we took a trip to Michigan for the week? Needed a break from clinicals, so we went to one of those small, tourist towns, rented a beach house and hid from the world?"

RJ grinned, "Yea, that's the trip. I was still with Noelle at the time. Pretty sure she was there too, at least for part of it."

Elle nodded. "Yep. She was worried we'd be staying in the same room, or something."

"Ha! Yes, that's right," RJ set his glass in the cup holder and rubbed his hand over his chin. "Wow, yea and didn't she...?"

"Give you a bedtime? And lock your door so I couldn't get in?"

Both hands covered his face now. "God, that was so bad," he laughed. "And you were oblivious to it, too."

"Of course! Why the hell would I go in your room at night?"

RJ shrugged. "She never trusted anyone. It wasn't personal."

"Never took it that way, but anyways, the painting."

"Ah, right. Well, we went to that local art walk, remember? Wine & Walk, I think the name was."

Elle remembered that part, but, "Why was this one your top pick?"

RJ smiled at her. "You pointed at it and said, 'This one would be the kid in class who's weird now, but everyone knows will move to New York and become famous one day."

"Well, this isn't exactly New York."

"No, but I don't think you meant it literally. You were more hinting at the fact that it was ok to be different. You usually reminded me of that, in your own way. Remember?"

"Vaguely."

RJ sighed. "I don't want to get all mushy on you, but I felt like a total freak at that school. Surely you recall that much." When Elle nodded, RJ continued, "You told me, 'You're not a freak. You're extraordinary; an original piece of art.' You said that being unique wasn't a crime and that I shouldn't accept anything less than complete acceptance. This painting, uh, always reminds me of that."

Silence followed, except for the ice cubes jingling against their glasses. They both stared at the painting, until the doorbell rang. Both of them jumped and Elle managed to slosh some of her drink onto her chest. "Crap," she muttered.

RJ tossed her a tissue box on the end table next to him and got up to answer the door. Spencer beat him there, and RJ greeted Calvin in the entryway. They headed toward the rec room, stopping in the kitchen to get Cal a drink, then back to the couch where Elle still sat.

They sat chatting for a couple more hours. Spencer joined them for a portion of that time. He even turned on the TV and linked up his YouTube account to it, showing Elle and Calvin the latest video clips. "Just trying to keep you two hip and up to date," he explained.

When the Conways finally called it a night, RJ and Spencer walked them to the door. As Elle headed toward her car, her phone rang. She paused before getting in and answered.

"Kat? Everything ok?"

"E-Elle?"

"Yes?" Elle unlocked the car and sat behind the wheel.

"Hey. It's me."

Elle rolled her eyes. "Yea, I know. What's going on? Are you alright?"

From the street where Cal parked his car, Elle could see him motioning to her thumbs up or thumbs down. She gave him the thumbs up sign and Calvin mouthed, "See you at home," waving good-bye.

Her key hit the ignition and the engine hummed. Elle tried to hear what Kat was attempting to say. Something about something in Genie's old room, but she was talking too fast to make most of it out.

"Kat, Honey, slow down, slow down, are you--?"

"Dammit, will you just get your ass over here and help me figure this out?"

Pulling out of the driveway, Elle put the car in drive and said, "Be there in ten," hung up, and called Cal to give him a heads up that she may not be home any time soon.

33

When Alex reached Cassie's room, he saw smoke curling up from under the closed door. He yelled her name as he gave the door several shoves. No response. The door felt warm against his hand. Nevertheless, he proceeded to press his face against it, hoping to hear something, anything. But the only answer came in the form of crackling. He pounded harder on the door and yelled to Cara to get Justin out of the house. She flew by him, grabbed their son from his bedroom, and bolted outside. Alex took a step back, which wasn't far due to the narrow hallway, and jumped into the door, shoulder first. It budged a bit, but remained closed. Alex drew the pistol from his holster and aimed it at the knob. He yelled to Cassie to stand back and fired a single shot at the stubborn lock. The wooden door swung open and a blast of heat and smoke poured into the hallway.

Alex dropped to his knees and crawled into the bedroom. The coughing began within seconds. The charred bedding and furniture closest to the door appeared empty. *Where was she*?

He then remembered the window and thought that if Cassie had enough sense to escape, she would've headed there after trying the door. As he felt his way toward the back of the room, he heard the door slam behind him. He did not turn around. Pressing his palms over anything on the ground that could indicate Cassie's location, Alex finally felt an arm. He grabbed it and pulled. Cassie's limp body slid toward him. Alex gathered her into his arms and hugged her close to his chest. He stood, stumbling at first, and faced the closed door. Taking a running start, he used the last of his energy to throw himself against it. This worked. The door splintered at the force of his weight, sending Alex and Cassie tumbling into the hallway. Regaining his stance, Alex scooped Cassie back up and ran toward the living room and out the front door.

Firefighters met him in full swarm. They took Cassie and placed her on a stretcher. *Cara must've radioed for help via the squad car.*

The paramedics checked her for a heartbeat and hooked her up to an oxygen mask. After several agonizing minutes, Alex heard the greatest sound in his life; his daughter gasping for air. "She's conscious!"

yelled one of the paramedics. "Couple of burns though. Hey! Wound kit, let's go!" he shouted to the other medic in the ambulance.

Cara stood with Justin in the neighbor's yard, a safe distance from the house. The firefighters had the hose spraying gallons of water, but seconds after they started, everyone heard a rumble, followed by a fiery blast.

The explosion threw Alex back a few feet. Cara and Justin were far enough away to avoid any injury and the ambulance shielded Cassie. Some of the firefighters flew back, too. Groaning, Alex sat up. "Everyone ok?" he called out.

Several people gave the affirmative and started checking the perimeter for anyone not responding. The neighbors all gathered around the Kingman property, despite several firefighters' efforts to keep them back. As water sprayed over the last of the flames from the firehose, Alex saw a half-shattered porcelain face without a body facing them amid the rubble. The eyes were closed. He prayed that whatever this all was had come to an end.

34

"Does it ever end?" yelled Kat.

She paced across the living room and back. Walt gave up several hours ago and went to bed. Elle stood in the corner of the room, arms folded, waiting for her to finish ranting. "I mean, this place, it always comes back. Why can't it just leave us alone? For all I know, it killed her. I know it did. God, why didn't I tell her about it sooner? She might've listened!"

"Maybe, maybe not," said Elle. "She is your daughter. She'd do whatever the hell she wanted regardless of what you told her."

"This is a rhetorical rant! Audience participation not welcomed!" shrieked Kat.

Elle shrugged and headed toward the kitchen. Kat stomped after her, continuing to vent. Elle still wasn't exactly sure what happened or how Kat somehow connected The Doll House to all of this, but she clearly had and seemed a little upset about it.

"Upset doesn't even begin to describe what I'm feeling right now," hissed Kat. "Seeing that, that, thing! In my house...*my house!*

Violating, that is what it is. Invasion of my space, a disruption, no, no an attack! On my home!"

Elle nodded and brought down two wine glasses from Kat's cabinet. She went to the fridge and produced a bottle of half-consumed chardonnay and filled the glasses. Without saying a word, she handed one to Kat.

Kat took the glass from her and said, "This is that small town voodoo shit people are always so paranoid about. Well, guess what? They should be paranoid!" She drank a large gulp of the wine, paused, and then took another.

Using Kat's silence to her advantage, Elle cautiously raised her hand, accompanied with a nonthreatening head tilt.

"Oh for god's sake, speak!"

"Could we, just for a second, time out? Kat, you lost me. Truly, you have."

"At which part?"

"The screaming rage part."

"You'll have to be more specific."

Elle sighed, "What made you call me tonight?"

Kat took another sip of wine. "I went into Genie's room."

Taking a sip of wine herself, Elle nodded and waited.

"I haven't been up there since, well, you know...,"

"She died?"

"Yes, Captain Sensitive, thank you, since then."

"Sorry, this isn't my first drink," mumbled Elle, blushing.

"Anyways, first time up there. I was straightening some things out and I found a doll that looks like it was dragged straight outta the nineteenth century."

"Creepy."

"Right?" Kat set her glass on the counter and reached for the bottle to refill it. "Anyways, I thought back to everything that's ever happened in that house. The stuff you dug up about Byron Easton, our run-in, and thought of the one rule we had."

"Wait, Kat, before you go any further...,"

"We said we wouldn't take anything out or do anything to expose the house. Put it at risk of being changed or destroyed."

Elle nodded. "We did say that, but no one else concluded that was a real rule to follow. Besides, how do you know that doll came from Millerton? There are tons of antique stores, and I'm sure Genie had a lot of dolls as a kid!"

Kat downed half of her second glass. She moved to her phone, punched a few buttons, and held it to her ear.

"What...what are you doing? Kat, it's almost midnight."

Kat ignored her. "Hi, Maggie? Sorry to bug you—no, no, everything is fine. Yes, mhm. No, I couldn't sleep either."

Elle listened. *Margaret, or 'Maggie' McDowell, mother of the late Aubrey McDowell*, she recalled. *But why?*

"Would you check for me?" she heard Kat saying, "Of course, sure, talk to you soon."

Kat hung up and set the phone back on the counter. She finished off the second glass of wine and pulled another bottle from the back of her fridge. A white blend, Elle noticed. The blends always helped Kat fall asleep, Elle recalled her once saying. Without protest, Elle watched Kat refill her glass. She topped Elle's glass off, too, ignoring that she mixed two wines. Elle didn't mind.

Kat's phone rang a few minutes later and Elle heard Kat say, "Well? Dammit. No, no, no, I'm sure it's fine. Fuck. Um, just leave it where it is. I'll stop by tomorrow and take a look, ok? Elle's here. Yea, uh huh. White wine, come by if you need a night cap. K, buh-bye!"

"You know," said Elle as Kat hung up, "If you want people not to worry? Try not to use phrases such as 'dammit' and 'fuck' right before you say there's nothing to worry about."

"Shut up. I'm stressed and slightly buzzed."

"But you play it off so well."

Kat scoffed and said, "Listen Eleanor, you want in on this or not?"

"It sounds like you're not giving me much choice, but to be safe, I'll say that I'm in."

Kat grabbed Elle by the arm so hard her fingernails dug into Elle's skin. She pulled Elle to Genie's room and opened the door. She turned on the light and they stood together just a few feet from the door frame. Kat pointed to the doll sitting on the shelf in the corner and hissed, "See it?"

"Kind of hard not to."

Kat walked forward and grabbed the doll. She took hold of Elle's arm again and marched both of them back into the kitchen. She guided Elle to one of the chairs and took a seat across from her. She set the pale, blonde porcelain doll between them.

"Lucy," read Elle, caressing the collar of the doll's dress. "And this outfit is hand sewn. It'll probably disintegrate if you so much as blow on it. It's so faded."

Kat rotated the doll and pointed to the backpack. "This is hand-made as well. I'll bet even the shoes and socks were hand stitched."

Familiar with the American Girl doll line, Elle asked Kat if it were possible this was one of them. The doll matched the size, at least. Kat shook her head. "Genie was into those when she was about nine, but even the historical ones appeared new."

"Hm," mused Elle, removing the backpack from the doll. "Ever open this?"

"Until today, I didn't even know 'this' existed," Kat answered.

Undeterred, Elle unbuttoned the small pack and pulled out a small notebook and a sapphire necklace. "Well, that's unexpected," she said, checking the bag for anything else.

Kat picked up the necklace and examined it. "This is real," she said, "Or if it's a fake, it's a really good one." She moved the thin chain between her fingers, causing the dark stone to swing like a pendulum.

More focused on the notebook, Elle thumbed through the pages. It was about the size of her hand and had taken up the full length and width of the backpack. But since it was flat, the backpack too lay flat, and Elle figured this was how it went unnoticed for so long.

"Kat," murmured Elle.

"Hm?"

"This isn't just a school girl notebook."

"Then what the hell is it?"

"It's, it's a diary."

"No shit," said Kat, reaching for it.

"Careful! If that's what it actually is and this isn't some farce, it's pretty old."

Flipping to the back, they began to read the faded writing on the last few yellowing pages.

September 29, 1887

Carnival Day. The dolls were lifelike and this frightened me. Frank says not to worry, but doesn't know how much I hate it. I hate the city. I hate the nuances. I spend time on clothes and accessories for Lucy. My life succumbs to this banality. Hopefully the school year will be more fruitful.

M.J.S.

November 15, 1887

Ever since the carnival, things aren't the same. Feeling worse, actually. Hard to write about it because it makes me sad. Lucy feels different, too. She's with me when I dream. It's like always having a friend to visit. This I can live with. Frank would think me crazy if I ever told him. More later.

M.J.S.

November 23, 1887

Failing to write here more and more, but I get lost in thought and forget to jot it down. The dreams are so real, I feel as if I could talk to her when I awake. Frank still works long hours. At least I see him on weekends. I have trouble making friends in town. It's like they know I'm not from here. I miss Kansas. I miss my sisters, and I miss my home. Lucy seems to bring me back to that. More soon.

M.J.S.

December 12, 1887

Finally, the dreams are a constant in my life. Lucy is there for me in my sleep and a doll-like reminder for me to know she's there when I am awake. Frank would think I'm crazy for such a suggestion, but I know what comes to me in my sleep. Lucy is more a friend than a doll. She comes alive and night, and there we visit.

M.J.S.

December 30, 1887

Lucy and I talk often in my dreams. She's convinced me that leaving this place is my only source of happiness. I fear my existence, however, fuels hers, and would hate to rob her of it. Everything else seems so mundane. I long for sleep, I dream for dreams.

M.J.S.

January 3, 1888

I've decided to heed Lucy's advice. Soon I'll be with her as friends are with each other. Tonight, I return home.

M.J.S.

Kat glanced at Elle. "Think this is related to anything or are we just wasting time?"

Shrugging, Elle answered, "So far we are wasting time. Who knows what any of it means." She yawned. "But it's getting late. Maybe we ought to...," She flipped the page, "That's odd."

"What? What now?"

"Well, the diary ends with that last entry." Elle checked again. "I mean, it's small, so these few entries take up most of the notebook, but still, that is all she--I am guessing it was a she--wrote. Not a consistent journalist, either."

A soft series of taps on the front door interrupted Elle. Kat rose and headed to see who in their right mind would show up close to midnight. "Oh, Maggie!" Elle heard her say. Elle stayed at the kitchen table and took another swig of her wine. She heard, "No, no, not a problem. Thanks. Yes, of course, I will." Then the door closed and Elle heard a car pulling away from the driveway. Kat's phone started to buzz before she returned to the kitchen. 'Alex Kingman' flashed across the screen. Elle reached over and answered it.

"Alex?"

"Uh, Elle? Did I dial the right--?"

"No, no you did. I'm at Kat's and her phone's by me."

"She doing ok?"

"What you'd expect. Why the late night phone call?"

Alex sighed. "Would've called you too, if I thought you'd be awake at this hour."

"Turns out I am. What's going on?"

Alex explained the fire, the explosion, and seeing the face of the doll at the end of it all. Kat since returned to the kitchen and sat down. Elle had the phone set to 'speaker' so they could both hear. When he finished, Kat reported she too found a doll in Genie's room, and to raise further suspicions, she set down a second doll on the table next to Lucy.

"What the hell is that?" asked Elle.

"What's what?" Alex's voice echoed over the speakerphone.

"Kat just set another doll down on the table. Where she got it, I'm not entirely sure."

"Maggie dropped it off. Aubrey's mother," Kat explained. "She found it in the bathroom sitting on the countertop after the paramedics came and took Aubrey to the hospital. Guess she didn't notice it at first."

"Who would?" said Alex.

"Anyways. I'm not going to sleep with both of these things in my house," continued Kat.

Elle rubbed her eyes. "It's after midnight, Kat. You gonna stick em in the backyard?"

"I'll come get them," offered Alex. "I won't be sleeping worth a damn tonight anyways."

Elle and Kat both offered their homes to the Kingman family for the time being, but Alex said they'd be fine staying at Cara's mother's house for the next few days. "If homicidal thoughts occur, we'll make our way north," he assured them. "Anyways, you two hang tight. I'll make my way up and be there in a couple of hours."

After hanging up Kat's phone and handing it back to her, Elle said, "Well, if both of you are going to stay awake, then you don't need my help."

"Crash on the couch."

"I'll crash on your couch," agreed Elle.

Situated at opposite ends of the couch with their feet on the middle cushion, Elle and Kat fell asleep in minutes. They woke up a bit later to the sound of Alex's spare key unlocking the Muller's front door.

Elle sat up and brushed her hair from her face. Kat was already standing and making her way to hug Alex. "Hey, wow, you made good time," Elle heard her say.

Elle rose and greeted him too. Then, the three made their way into the kitchen. As Kat crossed the threshold, both dolls turned to face her. She jumped back, almost knocking Alex over.

"Worst Deja vu ever," muttered Elle.

Both dolls blinked, returned their heads back to the original poses and stayed motionless after that. Slightly shaken, Alex leaned against the counter, saying, "Yea, it's been awhile since I've seen them do that. Can't say I miss it."

Kat shook her head. "No, and I hope it'll be one of the last times we ever deal with it."

Elle went to put on some coffee. It was closing in on four o'clock in the morning, and she had a hunch that Kat had no plans to go back to sleep. Kat pulled some mugs from the cabinet and added them to the collection of empty wine glasses that still sat from several hours earlier. Once the coffee brewed and Elle filled up their mugs, the three sipped in silence for a few minutes.

"You think the dolls have anything to do with, well, anything over the past month?" asked Kat.

"What I do know," said Alex, "is that each teen that ran into harm's way had one of these things in their possession, whether they knew it or not."

Kat glanced up at him. "What do you mean 'if they knew it or not'?"

"Just that, well, do we think any of them tried to leave with a few dolls in hand? When I picked up Aubrey and Cassie, they were terrified, and both swore they didn't go beyond the front counter."

"The dolls aren't even visible until the mirror room," mused Elle. "Unless one found its own way out, but that isn't typical."

"Nothing is typical when it comes to that place," said Kat, taking another sip from her steaming mug.

"No," said Elle, shaking her head, "But we have to establish some known constants and work under those assumptions or anything is fair game and we'll get nowhere."

"Ok, ok, ok," Kat waved a hand at Elle, "Let's say Aubrey and Cassie did not see or take a doll. They left without much of a fight from the place, right?"

Alex nodded. "From what Cassie told me, yes."

"Alright. And what about Genie and Billy? Sounds like you've held a lot of information back, Alex, and I'm thinking now would be a great time to let me in." Kat's voice remained steady, but her body was trembling. Elle reached over and took her mug from her hands and placed it back on the counter.

Alex sighed. "Kat, listen, sorry doesn't even begin to start this off."

Kat put up a hand to cut him off. "Look, just tell me what happened. I know you didn't do anything to hurt her, so skip it and just...just tell me what the hell happened."

Alex started from the beginning and told her what he saw, what Cassie told him, and when he finished, none of them could conclude how the three dolls found their way out of the mansion.

"Billy," said Elle. "Our missing link. He went in with Genie. He knows the rest."

"Think he'll tell the truth?" asked Alex.

"Only one way to find out," said Elle, dialing his number on her phone. "He'll still be up. He isn't sleeping a whole ton either."

Billy sounded borderline delirious from sleep deprivation and grief. Fortunately, it was a great formula to extract the whole, unadulterated version of their little Doll House visit. Billy explained the whole thing as Kat and Alex leaned in to listen. Elle had Billy on speakerphone, but kept the volume low so she wouldn't wake up Walt. They didn't need another volatile temper added to the mix.

When Elle hung up her phone, a dazed Kat sat down at the kitchen table. Alex took several steps toward the stove and fridge with his hands clasped behind his head, and then turned and walked back. Elle just stared at the phone with her arms crossed over her chest.

"They kept the dolls," whispered Kat. "They took them out of the house...that's probably why they had such a hard time getting out."

Alex rubbed his face with his hands and continued pacing between where Elle stood and the stove. "It's a long shot, but, Ellbea, you wouldn't happen to have those old articles and notes from when we visited Byron Easton back in high school, would you?"

Looking up, Elle said, "Not sure. That was forever ago. If I did, it'd be in a box in our attic. I dwindled down all paperwork and folders to one box over the years."

"No," said Kat.

"No?" Elle raised her eyes to her.

"No. You don't have it," said Kat, standing.

She walked over to the hall closet, opened it, pulled out a step stool, and rummaged around the top shelf until she produced a faded shoe box covered in a layer of dust. Turning back, she blew the dust off, causing Elle and Alex to cough. "I don't know how, anymore, but I wound up keeping it with my stuff," she told them.

Returning to the kitchen, Kat dumped out the contents of the box. Before them, they found Elle's old notebook, copies of the newspaper articles about the deaths of the interns, and a bunch of faded sticky notes.

Alex picked up a few of the sticky notes. "What's this?"

Elle took them and glanced over the writing. "Oh, quotes, mainly. I couldn't hear a lot of what you guys talked about that day, but I wrote down what I did hear, and some stuff we discussed on the car ride home." She passed the notes back to Alex.

"House's revenge from plotting to expose it," Alex read. He flipped it over and read, "He the weapon equals rifle?"

Elle and Kat exchanged looks and shrugged. "Keep going," said Kat.

"Ok, uh, 'interns planned to film the house, sell for $$$." He said dollar sign, dollar sign, dollar sign as he read it. "The back says, 'Valors' involvement and knowledge of events?' Lot of question marks on these things, Elle."

Elle pushed back a strand of dark hair and reached for another sticky note. "They were to take what wasn't theirs...home and see the events unfold," she read, then said, "I think this was something Byron actually said."

"Sounds like it," said Kat. "He spoke in third person and riddles the whole time, remember?"

Elle flipped the note over and continued, "The man ran from all the red...None were saved or survived, except the protection of the house."

Kat nodded. "I remember that part. He started saying everyone saw red and red sprayed all over the house. I think he meant after he shot the interns. Think the house made him crazy enough to do it?"

Alex shook his head. "Couldn't say. Remember when we talked on our way back, Elle said something about when you guys were attacked?"

"Oh yea, I remember that, somewhat," said Kat. "Weren't you asking about something we said that might have pissed the house off? Or whatever runs the show there?"

"Mhm," Elle shifted and turned to face Kat. "I think you threatened to take...oh god, you threatened to take a doll out of the house to freak me out!"

"Fucking wonderful," muttered Kat. "So there's a chance that all this is linked to these dolls being away from their eerie domain."

Alex filled his mug up with another pour of coffee. "Assuming all of these events are related, it puts us back to the mansion." He took a sip. "I mean, literally, we should go back and see if there's anything else in that place that sheds any light on what happened."

Rubbing her temples, Elle answered, "That sounds terrible."

"It totally does, especially since our entire theory sounds completely insane," agreed Kat. "But, I'm curious. Plus, we have these two," she nodded toward the dolls, "things to return. Doubt the house will attack if we bring 'em back, ya think?"

"I honestly don't know," said Elle, "Nothing that ever happens with that place follows a predictable pattern anymore. Hence why they closed it."

Alex paced back to Elle and Kat, mug in hand. "That's just it, though," he said, "The only connections we've ever made always link back to the house preserving itself. Anything that threatens that preservation suffers some form of ramification."

Too tired to argue, Elle just nodded and took another gulp of coffee. She glanced at the digital clock on the stove that read 4:45. Kat disappeared down the hall and returned with a duffle bag and her purse. "Where do you think you're going?" Elle asked her.

"Millerton. And so are you, so run home and throw some clothes in a bag. Oh, and tell Calvin you'll be MIA for the next twenty-four to forty-eight hours."

Before Elle could use the "I have work" excuse, Kat cut her off by saying, "Monday is MLK day. Your office is closed. Nice try."

After a quick chat with Calvin and a mad collection of clothes shoved into her own tote, Elle loaded her stuff into the trunk of Kat's car, along with the two dolls. Alex took off, the women leaving only a few minutes later. Before they pulled out of the driveway, Kat shot Walt a quick text she knew he would read when he woke up: **Going to Millerton with E & A; be home in a day or so. Txt if u need me.**

She then flipped the phone off and stuffed it into her purse, threw the car in reverse, and drove south.

Cara spent a good part of her night watching reruns on her mother's television set in the living room. She fell asleep for a few hours, but woke up to Justin sitting on the other end of the couch. He pulled at the end of her blanket, but she sat up, repositioned him to lay next to her, and they drifted back to sleep for a short time. The back door leading from the garage opened with a click, and then closed, but Cara heard soft footsteps make their way into the family room. She sat up and replaced her arm with a pillow so Justin would stay asleep. Moving across the living room on her tiptoes she met Alex as he entered the dining room. They hugged and chatted about the past night. When Alex told her that Elle and Kat were on their way down too, Cara started rubbing her hands together and pacing across the room.

"W-why are they c-c-coming here, Alexander?" she whispered. She wrapped her pink bathrobe tighter around her shoulders and started rubbing her arms.

"Honey, we need to put this to rest, once and for all."

"This is crazy! And you three know it! It's some childhood witch hunt that somehow y-y-you've all held onto and dwelled on all this time." Alex tried to cut her off, but she interrupted him, saying, "And they aren't staying here! My m-m-mom is already putting herself out keeping us under her roof."

"Oh, c'mon, Cara, they can crash on the couch!"

"They can't! I've been using the couch, a-a-and, well, then there's the food situation, and the dishes-they'll use dishes, and--,"

"Cara, shhh! For god's sake," hushed Alex.

"No, no, I won't! They can't stay here. Mom's too nice to say no, and if I have to be the bad guy, I'll do it."

Alex shook his head. "You're draining me. How is this so much of a problem for you?"

"Yea, if it's this big of an issue, we can crash at the hotel in Uptown," said Elle, entering from the family room and appearing in the doorway of the dining room.

Kat peered over her shoulder, nodding. "We'll head there now. Alex, meet us for breakfast at the cafe at eight and we will go to the mansion afterwards."

Realizing Kat had no intention of including Cara, Elle added, "You're welcome to join us," and turned back to head to Kat's car.

After checking into Riverbend's only hotel and cleaning up a bit, they made their way back to Millerton. They went to the only breakfast cafe there. It popped up right before Elle and Kat left for college. They used it as their go-to meet up spot whenever they were back to visit. It was called Off the Cup, but being the only cafe in town, locals just referred to it as 'the cafe.' The two sat facing each other, wondering if Cara would allow Alex to join their caffeine session, let alone come with him. Five minutes after eight, Alex walked through the double glass doors, unaccompanied. He followed the faded blue carpeting toward their booth next to the giant picture window. Kat slid over on the cream-colored seat and patted the vacancy next to her. "Sit," she said.

Alex plopped into the empty space, caught the server that was passing and ordered a cup of coffee and a stack of pancakes. "Chocolate chip, please."

Elle and Kat stared at him. He looked at their furrowed brows and added, "With whipped cream on top."

Shaking her head and laughing, Elle said, "Can I get a bowl of oatmeal and a scrambled egg?"

"I'll have the Denver omelet, sausage links on the side," said Kat. She leaned back in the booth, rubbed her temples, and added, "And for god's sake, turn off this damn pop music. It's nauseating and frankly, I judge anyone who considers it to be music."

The server, who looked like he was barely sixteen, nodded and jogged back to the counter, flipped the radio station to classic rock, and added their order to the kitchen's ticket rack. He returned with more coffee, sounding winded from the unexpected activity. Once the food arrived, the trio ate in silence, accepting multiple refills on the coffee from their nervous server.

Halfway through her third cup of coffee, Elle raised her eyes to see Cara walking through the glass doors. She was dressed in a bright red pea-coat, yellow pumps, black tights, and wore her thick, dark hair piled on top of her head. She kept a brisk pace as she blew past the server stand. She only stopped once she arrived at their booth. Glancing up and over his shoulder, Alex smiled at her and offered, "Pancake?"

Cara shook her head. "I just came to see if you were actually going through with this, this bone-headed idea!"

"What, breakfast? Why it hardly seems irrational given the time--,"

"Not that!" she hissed, "You know gosh darn well what I'm referring to!"

Kat and Elle stared at her, then Elle said, "Gotta pee," and stood up, with Kat following suit.

"Sit, both of you!" Cara snapped.

Elle sat, but Kat remained standing on the seat of the booth. She leaned her back against the window, arms crossed over her chest. She couldn't get out of the booth without Alex moving, and she doubted that would happen.

"This ends today! All of it. I don't want you three getting killed!"

"You don't get to call the shots on this one. Sorry, Cara, it's out of your hands," said Kat.

"Maybe regarding you two," Cara nodded at Elle and Kat, "but I wanted you to at least hear to my concerns."

"Kinda hard not to," whispered Kat under her breath.

Elle suppressed a smirk, stood, and stepped out from the booth. "Message received. I'm going to use the restroom."

Kat sat on the table, swung her legs to the other side, and walked the length of the worn booth, following Elle's exit path. "Ditto," she said, making the additional effort to nudge Cara aside with her shoulder.

Once they left, Cara sat in Elle's former spot, facing Alex. She drew in a deep breath. She apologized for the outburst and pleaded with him to come home after breakfast. With a mouthful of chocolate chip pancakes and whipped cream smeared on his cheek, Alex explained it wouldn't take long. By the time Elle and Kat returned, both his pancakes and wife were gone. Alex signed the bill, stood up, and asked, "Shall we?"

***

Pinecrest Park, IL

The marshmallow dome engulfed over a third of the parking lot. It held up in all weather, which was what RJ banked on when he invited Cal to the indoor driving range with him that afternoon. The Bubble, as locals referred to it, was the only indoor facility where golfers enjoyed the benefits of the driving range without the harsh conditions of the Midwest winters. The Bubble had two levels to hit from and just over four hundred yards of AstroTurf with flags, bunkers, and slopes. A bucket of balls went for a fair price without additional bells and whistles. *Just a bag of clubs, a basket of golf balls, and an artificial fairway,* RJ smiled.

"Hey man, over here!" Cal waved as RJ made the transition out of the frigid air and into a heated lobby.

Removing the instantly fogged glasses from his face, RJ nodded and made his way over. Cal finished paying at the counter and took two "Giant Sized" green baskets from the clerk. He passed one to RJ and said, "The dispenser's inside the range. Load 'er up and let 'em fly!"

The forest green Range Servant clamored and shook with each "Giant Sized" load dispensed. Cal ran down the few stray balls that managed to bounce away. They toted their gear to the second floor and turned right. RJ took the furthest box, and Cal, the one left of that. After a few practice swings, some obligatory over-head stretches with the initial club in play, and a couple of curse words following the practice shots, the guys found their rhythm. Cal stifled a chuckle every now and again. Despite RJ's best efforts, he was an above-average golfer. His hits were clean and his aim was consistent. His stance, swing, and follow-through, however, looked like the disjointed combination of a low-seated squat and upper body pendulum interrupted by a hiccup mid-swing. Not a fluid motion, not even a synchronized movement between his torso and legs, but somehow, he made it work to his advantage.

"I like your weekends when you fly solo. Gives me an excuse to improve my golf game," RJ glanced over his shoulder at Cal with a grin.

Cal chuckled. "Well, an excuse to waste a day on golf, at least."

"Where'd your other half go again?" RJ asked.

"Millerton. Something with Alex and the kids. Kat went with her, which usually lends itself to a good story once they return."

RJ launched another ball with his driver toward the red flag. "Walt join them?"

Cal readjusted his stance and took aim at the same flag. "I doubt he knows they even left. Besides, Elle mentioned something about a mansion they used to work at as kids. Doubt Walt would have any interest, even if he was included."

"Mansion? I thought they grew up in a small, one-horse town."

"More of a museum...haunted and shit."

"I've heard Elle mention it a time or two. Aren't they all haunted?"

"This one is known to be haunted. That's the attraction, or, it was. Place got shut down in the late eighties courtesy of Kat and Elle. The activity of the place became dangerous and Kat got pretty beat up from it."

Pausing to turn and look at Cal, RJ leaned against his driver and cocked his head to the side. "You do realize how insane this sounds, don't you?"

Cal laughed and shrugged, "Yes, well, be that as it may, the place exists, was open for a period of time, and isn't anymore. And the Hardy Boys are convinced Genie's passing is linked to it somehow." He sent another ball sailing right of the target, and cursed under his breath.

RJ shook his head and turned back to his tee. "I have a feeling we are going to have to discuss this further over lunch when we are done here."

"Not much else to discuss. Elle never mentioned much more about the place. She said that the building housed a collection of dolls from the 1800's on, and while some people came for that reason, the majority came because the mansion was alive."

RJ scoffed. "Alive? Seriously, Cal?"

With a smirk, Cal replied, "I'm starting to see why she never said anything about it to ya."

They changed up their clubs and continued to launch the golf balls onto the range. Finally, RJ asked, "So you gonna leave me hanging or what?"

Studying the angle of his pitching wedge before taking another swing, Cal shrugged again and said, "Well the stuff in the house moved. On its own, of course, which is what made it a tad unique. The dolls' heads would turn, their eyes would blink, doors would open and close at their leisure, but it was all predictable. So as bizarre as the phenomena was, people didn't fear it because they expected it."

"Small towners, man," RJ shook his head.

"Right? That shit would creep me out. But not these people. Until it stopped becoming predictable, that is. Then, for a reason Elle has yet to either determine or divulge, the movements of the building became threatening. That's when Kat got beat up, they stopped working there, and the place shut down altogether."

"Still sounds absolutely crazy. And if this was that big of an ordeal, how come no one else outside of this little town has heard of it? Hell, if it weren't for you, I'd never have known! Something this strange should've made headlines!"

Cal collected his now empty basket and nodded in the direction of the stairs to refill it for another round. "You'd think. I don't have an answer for that either. Maybe it sounded too far-fetched for any news source to capitalize on it, so they left it to the local press."

RJ tossed him his empty basket as well. "I'll grab us drinks and meet ya back in five."

Cal nodded and headed toward the Range Servant. RJ, still trying to piece together the Millerton story, settled on asking Elle once she returned. For all he knew, Cal was messing with him. *But,* he smiled, *it does make for one hell of a story.*

***

Millerton, IL

They piled into Alex's squad car and drove off. As they coasted down the familiar path and approached the fork that led to either the Marionette Mansion or the Valor property, Kat suggested veering right. Alex shrugged. The Valor house was still unoccupied. The narrow drive ducked down a slope and into a wooded spot.

Emerging from the car, the three trekked up the paved drive toward The Valor's front door. "Looks the same," murmured Elle, glancing around the front porch.

Alex alerted them to a crawl-space entrance on the side of the house that afforded them access to the entire under workings of the home. Climbing, then stooping down, they fumbled through the dark space for several moments. Finally, they came to an area with a lone step ladder. Alex climbed up and pressed on the ceiling, finding a loose panel that let them in the house. With this, he shook his head. "Small town folks are so trusting," he said with a laugh, and climbed into a large closet inside the Valor home.

He helped Elle and Kat through, too. They walked out of the closet and into the kitchen. Surveying the area, Elle smiled and echoed, "Exactly the same."

It was; everything appeared as it did the few times Elle and Kat visited as teenagers.

"What exactly are we looking for?" asked Alex.

Elle shrugged. "I'm not entirely sure, but I'm guessing that the Valors did a lot of work covering up the events that took place back in 1983. If I'm correct, they'll likely have it stored somewhere in the home."

"Don't you think it would be in a safe? Or destroyed?" asked Alex again, rubbing his chin.

Elle took a few steps across the kitchen. "They might've been rich but they weren't high tech or really safety savvy. There's no alarm system, even now. They grew up in a town of generally trusting folk, and as a result, I'm guessing, well, more hoping, they went about their cover up job in the same mindset."

"That's a leap," said Kat, "But say that you're right. Where do you think they'd hide stuff?"

"Off the top of my head, attic or a bedroom closet."

They checked both locations. After a few screams from spider webs, curse words from hitting a noggin or two on the low beams of the attic, and some disturbing finds of old pieces of lingerie in the guest room closet, they ventured to the master bedroom. Kat slid the mirrored closet door open and a whiff of perfume mixed with Old Spice immediately invaded her sinuses. Coughing, she stepped back and shook her head. "Damn, that's strong!"

Combing through the clothing, she pushed back the clothes near the corner of the closet, only to reveal piles and piles of shoes.

"Doesn't look like they threw much out, huh?" commented Alex.

Kat shook her head. "Pack rats."

Glancing up, Alex noticed worn cardboard boxes with crude scribbles for labels on the sides. "What'd ya suppose they kept stored up here?"

With a shrug, Kat said, "Hopefully some damn answers."

Most of the boxes read the usual: "Photos," "Baby Clothes," "Medical," "Auto." When they got past a point where Alex could reach, Elle bumped him to the side and planted a step-stool she'd found in the hallway. She climbed up and reached as far into the corner as possible. She couldn't see anything, but her hand touched another box. With a hop, Elle grabbed a corner of it. Pulling the box toward her, she lifted it over the rest of the clutter. Checking the sides of the box, she couldn't see any type of label.

"Think this might be worth exploring?" Elle asked the other two, stepping down and setting the box on the bed.

Kat sat on the corner of the bed and began removing items from the box. Alex sat on the other side of Elle and joined in on the content exploration. Elle pulled out a folder stuffed with paperwork. Most of it contained old newspaper articles and police reports. There were some receipts and a few notes from a doctor's office.

"Dr. Earnest Karcher, PhD in Psychology and Neurostudies," read Elle.

Kat paused and looked up. "We know that name."

Alex nodded. "Why would the Valors have information from Dr. Karcher though?"

"I mean, Byron worked for them for over ten years. We don't know what the pre-existing or underlying relationship was. Maybe he was related to them. Or they were taking care of him," said Elle.

"Haven't seen one of these in ages!" exclaimed Kat, producing a black, dust-covered tape recorder from the bottom of the box.

She blew a layer of dust off, this time away from the other two. "Looks like there's a tape in there," Kat murmured.

"What are you waiting for?" asked Alex, "Play it."

Kat pushed the recorder's ON button, surprised that the batteries still worked. They all heard static and mumbling for the first few seconds, then:

"Audio log twenty-six. Dr. Earnest Karcher speaking. Patient Byron Easton. Now Byron, you are aware that we are recording. Today's session will focus on a revisit and replay of the events up to and including November fifth, 1983. It has been seventy-two hours since Mr. Easton's last dose of medication. I slowly tapered him off of his medications last week, leaving him without any sedation or stimulating enhancements in attempts to clear his mind for this session. Now, Byron, I need you to just relax, close your eyes, and take some deep breaths. Very good, very good. In, and out, in, and out."

"Doctor, I feel--,"

"Shhhh, sh, just focus on your breathing. Good, great, keep going. Now, I'm going to ask you a series of questions. While keeping your eyes closed and your body relaxed, just answer with the first thing that comes to mind. If you can't remember, that is fine, we are just going to ask some basic questions.

"Mhm."

"Now, Byron, a little over ten years ago, you worked in a small town, correct?"

"Mhm."

"Can you tell me the name of that town?"

"Millerton. Millerton, Illinois."

"Great. Deep breath. There you go. Now, while you were there, you worked for a--,"

"Man, cut the crap."

"Excuse me?"

"I said cut the crap."

"Mr. Easton, might I remind you we are doing this recording session as a court-ordered documentation and I am to follow their protocol...,"

"Crap! All of it is crap!"

"Mr. Easton?"

"You people drugged me. You fed me lies upon lies. You kept me sedated for ten goddamn years. I was in a state of shock, and you threw me in a cell. Then you loaded me up with sedatives and kept feeding me a story that everyone deemed to be true. A story I heard so many times. So much and with so much shit pumping through my veins that I believed it myself."

"Mr. Easton, you were arrested on charges of first degree manslaughter."

"You think I don't know that?"

"My point being, you were arrested. At the time of your arrest, you had a psychotic break, requiring us to intervene with medicine. You were violent toward staff and on occasion, myself. So we kept you heavily medicated for our safety, and for yours."

"But now I'm thinking clearly. Why don't you just ask me what happened?"

"I don't want to send you back into psychosis."

"Risk it. What do you want to know?"

An audible, labored sigh, then, "Alright. We'll do it your way, Mr. Easton. Tell me what happened leading up to and the night of November fifth, 1983."

"He became more and more possessive of the house. I tried to tell you this from the start. He was...obsessed. He'd find any reason to have me fix something, paint something, improve something. It was more than an attraction site; it was a shrine. His shrine."

"Who's, 'he,' Byron?"

"I did everything he asked. Mowed the lawn. Repainted the porch. Every update that rundown shack required. Then he hired those damn interns to run the place over the summer. They come in with their city styles. They're goddamn newfangled ways to make money. They were always trying to make more, even though they didn't do much for the place."

"Byron, who are we talking about? You?"

"Those interns had this plan. This asinine plan. They wanted to record the events. Record the movements. Record the house. You gotta understand, Doc, no one records anything. No photographs. No movies. And above all, nothing leaves the grounds that's meant to stay on the property."

"Why's that?"

"You know what happens when people threaten? He'd become the house's puppet...its security system...its protector. He was in charge of removing threats. That night, my last night there, I worked late. I heard screams, *god-awful screams*. Then the gun shot. Twice. Then no more screams. Silence. The house stood silent as well. I ran toward the porch, up the stairs, and pushed my way into the main entrance. That's when, that's...*that's...oh god*!"

"Byron? Deep breath. You're doing great. What did you see--,"

"*Blood!* Blood everywhere. Sprayed on the walls, on the floors. He painted the room red with their blood."

"Byron, calm down, look at me. Here, here, take some water."

"Red, everywhere was red! A sprinkler of crimson splattered over the walls."

"Here, here, drink, drink. Nurse? Can we get an injection of five milligrams of lorazepam ready?"

"No! No! Wake up! Wake. Up. You must! But they won't. Why won't they wake up? "

"Nurse, now!"

"Valor and his fucking shot gun. Took them both, and he might come back for me. Oh god, no, no, *no, no*!"

"Thank you, Nurse. Byron you're going to feel a pinch. Hold still."

"He shot them! *He shot them and I took the fall!* All I could see was red. All there was to see was red. Sprayed. Splattered. All the walls, all over the place. He did this. He did this, and he'll do it again and again, until the house is safe. *No one rests*!"

"Shhhh, shh, rest now, Mr. Easton. We will resume your medications tomorrow. Thank you for your cooperation. You've been of great help."

Static followed, then the recording stopped. Elle, Kat, and Alex stared at the tape player until they heard the ON button 'click' when the tape ran out.

"Pull the tape out," said Elle, finally.

Kat popped the recorder open and removed it. Elle took it from her and flipped it over, looking for a title or any clue as to why this tape was in the Valors' possession. "Well, what does it say?" asked Kat.

"Just, "*Easton 1993*," and then a long number."

Alex took the tape from her. "This serial number could be a case number. Either a medical case or a legal one."

Nodding, Elle said, "Sounds about right. The Valors did a great job keeping all of this under the rug. Why wouldn't they still have any piece of damning evidence locked away?"

Kat sighed. "So that night we were attacked, that asshole wasn't coming to rescue us, he was coming to finish us off, if need be."

Elle shuddered. "I hope there's more to it than that, c'mon. This is still the words of a mad man against...," she didn't bother finishing the thought.

"Against what? A murderer who kept his sanity?" said Kat.

Alex flipped through the remaining contents of the box. He then put everything back in. "Regardless, this is now evidence and if it hasn't been brought to light yet, I'll need to log it into the system. I'll get a few of my guys to help me sweep the rest of the house too, now that we have a reason."

Kat flopped back and stared at the ceiling. "Before we go all heroic and bring about justice, let's just...lie here for a bit."

Laughing, Elle stretched onto her back too. Alex placed the box of evidence on the ground and joined the lounging duo. "Just a few minutes," he said, "Then we've got stuff to take care of."

Forming a pinwheel shape with their heads toward the center on the Valor's king-sized bed, each drifted off in minutes.

Alex slept soundest; he could sleep through a nuclear explosion, Cara once informed Elle. The man had a way with ridding his mind of anything for the sake of sleep. A light snore accompanied this restful state, and possibly the notion of a dream.

Elle, being the insomniac, knew she was still partially conscious, but beyond the point of being able to snap out of it. *Plus,* she reasoned, *it felt good to relax, even if it was just a light stupor.* Even still, she started to dream.

Kat immediately slipped into a dream state. She found herself standing in a wheat field, either at sunrise or sunset, given the way the sunlight tinted the horizon with a golden hue. She turned and looked around. Miles and miles of wheat and tall grasses blew softly as she heard the wind whispering with their movements. Holding out both hands, she felt the air move between her fingers. It felt warm, she noted, no chills or shivers with each faint gust. In the corner of her eye, she noticed something. Turning, Kat saw a small wooden table with two chairs facing one another. With some curiosity, she made her way toward it. No one appeared to be there to explain its existence, so Kat sat in one of the empty chairs. No sooner did she sit down, a pale, blonde girl appeared in the seat facing hers. Kat studied her. She saw dark eyes, painted red lips, and milky white skin. The girl wore a faded patterned dress with an embroidered collar.

"Lucy," read Kat. She paused, then, "Wait, you're Lucy?"

The figure didn't appear to hear. It simply responded, "Are you here to help?"

Kat crossed her arms. "Help what? You? Who are you?"

The figure continued. "The others weren't there to help. They had personal gains."

Kat felt her face flush. A sinking sensation slammed through her stomach and Genie flooded her thoughts. "What...did...you...do?" she stammered.

The figure tilted its head to the side. As it did, two more appeared in Kat's view. On the right, one wore vibrant robes and sparkling jewelry. Kat noticed the mocha colored skin and hair to match. The second had similar skin tones and clothing, but Kat quickly noted that half of its face was removed. *No, not removed. Smashed.*

The figure on the left didn't move or speak like the others. *Deactivated?*

As the pale porcelain figure re-centered its blonde head, the vibrantly cladded one on the right began murmuring words Kat could not make out. With each word chanted, the blonde figure appeared to gain strength. It became more animated, more capable of interaction, and, *more capable of inflicting harm. But why would they be creating such a strong front?*

In her periphery, Kat saw another figure. She turned, only to see Alex wandering toward their gathering. He seemed entranced. He stood next to Kat, but remained silent. Kat tried to talk to him, but words no longer formed from her lips. Frightened by this, Kat attempted to raise her arms and alert Alex. No movement. Her arms felt like they were weighed down with cement. She tried to stand but a similar heaviness enveloped her waist and legs. All Kat felt capable of doing was keeping her eyes open and witnessing this destructive trio.

She felt a strong clap on her shoulder. Without being able to turn her head, Kat prayed the hand belonged to Alex. She felt a friendly squeeze as the movement in her periphery vanished.

Refocusing her attention on the figures in front of her, Kat realized the pale one appeared more lifelike than it had moments before. The chanting gave it this new-found vivacity. "You're a tougher one," she heard the pasty figure announce. "It takes more strength with you. Our reunion will be your demise."

Why? thought Kat, hoping maybe they could read her thoughts. *Why are you so set on getting rid of me?*

"Because," smiled the blonde, "you wanted so badly to rid the world of us."

With that it leaned forward toward Kat, ivory limbs pressing into the table, and said, "First, the lungs, they must rest."

Kat felt the air escape her world. She gasped and tried to claw at the blonde bitch, but no part of her cooperated. She felt her lungs collapsing under the suffocating command.

"Now, your heart; the blood flow must desist. I need the pump to silence."

A drop in Kat's chest let her know that whatever powers this figure possessed were fully operational. Finding her world growing darker by the second, she tried to see if Alex had returned. Unable to turn her head and without anyone in her peripheral sight, Kat's dream continued to spin into deadly chaos.

36

A sudden noise startled Elle awake. She sat straight up, but found the other two sound asleep. She brushed the tangle of dark hair from her eyes to glance at her watch that told her it was half past two o'clock in the afternoon. She shifted her weight to check on Alex and Kat. Alex seemed to be coming out of sleep. Elle reached over and shook his shoulder.

"Hmm?" Alex sat up but his eyes were still closed.

Giggling, Elle said, "Morning, Bright Eyes."

"Morning," mumbled a partially conscious Alex. Once he found his bearings, he turned to Elle and asked how long they were out.

"Couple hours, I'm guessing. Kat's still out cold."

Alex's eyes widened. "Elle, this will sound crazy, but...,"

Before he could say anything further, Kat began to gasp. Alarmed, Elle jumped to her feet and circled the bed to where Kat lay. Alex sat on his knees, staring at her and whispered, "Should we wake her?"

Elle shook her head, "She hasn't slept in weeks, I'd hate to disrupt the soundest sleep she's had in lord knows how long."

No sooner did Elle say this, that she noticed Kat's gasping became stronger and her body began to writhe and shake. The color of her skin started to change from rosy to "cyanotic," whispered Elle.

"What?" asked Alex.

"Change of plans. Wake her up, *wake her up!*"

Alex reached over and shook Kat's struggling frame, but she choked and writhed nonetheless. Elle jumped up and screamed her name, but without further progress. Pulling her into a seated position and holding her by the shoulders, Alex shook her enough to wake her, but not enough to cause harm. No response.

"It's like rescuing a drowning person without them actually drowning!" shrieked Elle.

"Drowning," repeated Alex, as a thought dawned on him. *They kept the water on.*

Eyes full of terror, Elle stared at him, then lunged forward to catch Kat when Alex dropped her body and sprinted out of the bedroom. Elle kept trying to wake Kat, unsuccessfully. Every now and then Kat appeared to be able to take a deeper breath of air with Elle's movements, but beyond that, she stayed in a deep stupor.

Kat's view of the destructive trio blurred in and out of focus. The wench on the right of Lucy kept murmuring things. Lucy stared at her, orchestrating the malfunction of each vital organ, one by one. Kat wondered what was next, since she could no longer breathe or feel her heartbeat. *Seconds, she had seconds, but she could still think, she could still...* "Your mind," *god no,* "it's been working quite a bit these days," *please no,* "It must--,"

An icy blast electrocuted Kat's body. Screaming, she shot up and gulped air into her appreciative lungs. She jumped back, curling up and frantically attempting to relocate her near-killers. Instead, she saw the tear-soaked face of Elle and panic-stricken countenance of Alex surrounding her. In Alex's hands was an empty bucket, and Kat realized, she was sitting in a puddle of cold water.

37

Elle tackled her in a hug. "God, you need to stop doing this to me," she sobbed into Kat's shoulder.

Still reeling from what happened, Kat hugged her back and murmured, "Sorry, Ellbea, but I'm afraid it isn't over just yet."

If it was one thing that Elle knew about Kat, it was that her temper trumped any other emotion when fully activated. This moment, Elle knew, was one of those moments. Elle was still putting the pieces together to what just took place. Kat, however, seemed to already know.

Rolling to the side, Elle planted a kiss on her cheek and whispered back, "Don't you dare die, you feisty bitch."

Kat smiled at her, but even her smile flashed fury. Jumping to her feet, Kat broke into a sprint. Elle and Alex tried their best to keep up. Kat unlocked the front door, ran out and leaped from the Valor's porch screaming, "Unlock the trunk, *the trunk, Alex!"*

Alex fumbled through his pocket as he ran through the entryway and out of the front door. He aimed the remote key at the car and it 'dinged' as soon as Kat reached it. She flung open the trunk and grabbed both dolls. With her two fists full of hair, Kat sustained her run. She headed down the driveway and yelled over her shoulder, "Catch me along the way!"

Panting, Elle and Alex reached the car just as Kat disappeared at the edge of the fork in the drive. Alex glanced at Elle, "Think she's lost it completely?"

"Not yet, but if we don't follow her, she might. Drive!"

Alex made a swift three-point turn and followed the narrow drive to the fork. He caught sight of a very determined Kat still sprinting with both dolls in tow toward the Marionette Mansion. "This can't end well," muttered Alex, as he caught up to her.

"Get in!" he yelled.

Kat paused and hopped into the back seat. "Go, go, go! What are you waiting for?"

Alex sped down the degraded, gravel path and pulled up to the mansion. Without further explanation, Kat jumped out of the car and again opened the trunk. Alex kept a spare canister of gasoline in there for emergencies. She took this and placed both dolls onto the gravel. Saturating them in fuel, she muttered something about a match. Alex and Elle exchanged glances. "Uh, Kat?" started Elle.

Kat turned toward them, blue eyes blazing. "Get me a mother. Fucking. Match."

With her golden hair flying around her face and eyes wild with rage, neither had the courage to argue. Elle reached into her purse and produced a book of matches. "Cigars," she explained, as she handed it to Kat.

Kat took a running start and rammed her shoulder into the front door. To Elle and Alex's amazement, the door opened. *The damn dolls really do want to go home*, thought Elle.

Stumbling forward from the door's give, Kat steadied herself in the main entrance, both dolls soaked and hanging by their hair in her fists. She lumbered past the desk and paused just before leaving the entryway. She slammed both dolls onto the formal room floor, and doused more gasoline on top of them. Ignoring them when they both sat up, she kept the canister of gasoline tilted, trailing the fuel after her as she exited the mansion. A familiar and horrifying roar echoed behind her as she did this. The main door slammed behind Kat as she stepped onto the porch, but she could still hear the groans and howls of the house. Without hesitation, Kat lit a match, bent down, and ignited the line of fuel that stopped just inches from where she stood. Turning to face Alex and Elle, who remained at the foot of the porch, mouths gaping, Kat smirked and jumped from the top step.

The three linked arms and watched as a whirling rage of orange blaze engulfed the rotting wood, producing a mass of black smoke. From inside, each of them swore they heard faint shrieks from that first-floor dining area. The flames consumed the mansion over the next few hours. A cacophony of crackling and snapping droned out any other sounds from the surrounding woods. Once the fiery beast reduced the home to a charred, smoking foundation, Kat stepped forward, and for the first time in months, sported a genuine grin. Gripping Kat's arm, Elle followed her gaze and noticed the smashed figures of Lucy and the doll from Aubrey's mom. Elle gave Kat's arm a squeeze and the two turned back to the car. Alex breathed a sigh a relief and said, "Well, Ladies, can I count on you not to stir up anymore shit for at least a decade? Cara really will kill me if it's any sooner than that."

With a weary nod, both agreed a decade was an appropriate waiting period before anything close to this could re-emerge.

38

A warm, soft breeze whispered through the leaves of the maple tree in Alex's backyard. *My new backyard,* he thought smiling, and turning to face the white brick ranch home that stood several yards away.

They moved in four months ago, but this was the first weekend of the summer Cara felt it was in acceptable condition to have visitors. Turning from the house, Alex arranged and rearrange the splintered logs in the black metal fire pit. A circle of lawn chairs surrounded him. In those chairs sat Kat, Walt, Elle, Calvin, and Justin. Cassie and Cara stood over the grill roasting veggies and hamburgers. "Kat, would you do the honors?" asked Alex, handing her a lighter and winking.

Kat smirked and took it from him. "You know, this won't be as impressive without a gallon of gasoline," and lit the crumpled newspaper at the bottom of the log pile.

The group stared, mesmerized as the small flame licked the paper, increasing in size as it crept toward the wood until a small fire engulfed the metal basin. Several pops and snaps echoed across the yard accompanied by the comforting smell of burning wood. Dusk dimmed the yard enough for a warm glow to appear on the surrounding faces. "Alex!" called Cara, "Did you spray the lawn before you put up the fire pit? You *know* it's been a dry summer. We don't want one of the sparks to catch the grass and--,"

Alex shook his head and laughed. "I watered the lawn, Dear, fear not."

Cara turned to them in a blue sundress patterned with daisies. She wobbled as she attempted to balance the food and walk in her wedges across the backyard. Cassie followed with a pitcher of lemonade that Kat and Elle added a hint of vodka to prior to joining the circle around the fire. They just had to be sure the kids didn't take refills. They ate dinner and toasted marshmallows until the fire and the moon were their only sources of lighting. Standing, Elle collected the paper plates and empty plastic cups and made her way toward the house. Kat got up to follow her, kissing the top of Walt's head before she did.

Back inside, Elle started to stuff the trash as best she could into the black garbage bag tied to the refrigerator handle. Kat hoisted herself onto the countertop next to Elle, watching her struggle with the final disposal of some plastic dishes. Without looking up, Elle said, "So, coffee and some shopping tomorrow?"

Kat shrugged. "I could go for a new pair of shoes."

"Cal and I are meeting RJ for happy hour. He said you're welcome to join that, too. Walt's presence contingent on your approval."

With a smile, Kat said, "We're doing better, you know, Walt and me. Started some counselling bullshit."

"Is it working?"

"Obviously."

Elle stood up and faced her. "I'm glad. And you're safe?"

"I bought a gun."

"Is Walt safe?"

Kat laughed. "We're both safe. Like I said, doing better. It'll be a long road, but I don't give up that easily."

"No, you definitely don't."

Elle gave a final tie to the stubborn trash bag and motioned Kat to follow her. They made their way back out to the bonfire, lemonade refills in hand. As they sat down, Walt asked what they decided to do about the burnt property in the back of the woods. Elle took a sip of lemonade and said, "We just put up a warning sign stating *No Trespassing*."

With another grin, Kat added, "Superstitious as she is, Elle also insisted we pour a ring of salt around the perimeter."

"That was an entirely logical--,"

"Five canisters of kosher salt!" interrupted Kat.

Everyone giggled. "So that's where it all went," Cal mused.

"Costco, Babe," replied Elle. She paused, and then added, "You know, I gave serious consideration to hanging onto the diary in that Lucy doll's backpack."

When a stunned silence and horrified stares followed her statement, she quickly added, "But, I didn't. It burned with the rest, don't worry."

"Why would you keep it?" asked Cassie.

Elle shrugged. "Despite everything that happened, it's still a small doorway to the past; a piece of history."

Cassie nodded. "I feel safer knowing that you destroyed it."

The rest of the party nodded and murmured in agreement.

"It's always intriguing to have a connection to another place and time we weren't a part of," said Alex. "I get the reasoning."

Kat raised her plastic cup and clicked it against Elle’s. They smiled and resumed staring into the hypnotic flames dancing over the glowing embers. As they watched, Kat touched the small, sapphire stone dangling from a delicate chain around her neck and echoed, “Some doors are meant to stay closed."

Made in the USA
San Bernardino, CA
09 June 2019